The Untamed Earl

VALERIE BOWMAN

St. Martin's Paperbacks

This is a work of fiction. All of the characters, organizations, and events portrayed in this novel are either products of the author's imagination or are used fictitiously.

THE UNTAMED EARL

Copyright © 2016 by June Third Enterprises, LLC.

All rights reserved.

For information address St. Martin's Press, 175 Fifth Avenue, New York, NY 10010.

ISBN: 978-1-250-07258-0

Our books may be purchased in bulk for promotional, educational, or business use. Please contact your local bookseller or the Macmillan Corporate and Premium Sales Department at 1-800-221-7945, ext. 5442, or by e-mail at MacmillanSpecialMarkets@macmillan.com.

Printed in the United States of America

St. Martin's Paperbacks edition / May 2016

St. Martin's Paperbacks are published by St. Martin's Press, 175 Fifth Avenue, New York, NY 10010.

10 9 8 7 6 5 4 3 2 1

For my sister, Leslie Bowman Stauffer,
one of the best people I ever met.
Your strength inspires me.

PROLOGUE

Surrey, the country estate of the Duke of Huntley,
July 1813

Being fifteen years of age and a bit plump and unconventional when one's elder sister was eighteen years of age and willowy and ethereal—if waspish—was decidedly unpleasant. Being sent to bed early and told in no uncertain terms to stop lurking at the top of the staircase leading down to the ballroom was also unpleasant. But if Alexandra Hobbs strained her ears, she could just make out the soft chords of a waltz floating up from below. It was a curse to be so young when one's elder sister was already having her come-out ball. Alexandra spun slowly, holding out the skirt of her dressing gown, pretending to curtsy to a handsome gentleman who had just asked her to dance.

The door to her room flew open and cracked against the wall. Alexandra whirled toward the sound. *Not this again.* Her thirteen-year-old brother came trotting in. His shirt was mussed, as was his dark hair, and he had a large streak of dirt across his jaw.

"Thomas." Alexandra dropped her skirts and plunked her hands on her hips. "I thought I asked you to knock."

"It's just me, Al. Why would I want to do that?" He sauntered past her toward the window. Alexandra knew precisely what her brother was about. Her bedchamber just so happened to have much better access to the roofline and a shorter jump to the terrace below than his did. Thomas faced the window, wrenched open the sash, and leaned out. He braced his hands on the wooden sill and stuck out his head and shoulders.

"You there, Will?" he called in a half whisper, half shout.

A soft whistle was the only response. Will, the stable boy, was meeting Thomas below. This was their nightly ritual while Thomas was home from Eton.

"I'm off." Thomas stretched one leg out the window.

"Be careful." Alexandra turned her face away for a moment. "You know I cannot bear to see you climb onto the roof that way. I live in fear that you'll break your neck."

Thomas looked back at her through the window and grinned. "Where's your sense of adventure, Al?"

Alexandra sighed. "You've always had more sense of adventure in your smallest toe than I do in my entire body."

"Being adventurous is an acquired skill. Give it a try sometime. You might find you like it. At any rate, I cannot stay in my bedchamber all evening and listen to that awful racket," Thomas added, then nodded toward the door.

"Racket? You mean the music?" Alexandra spun around again, a dreamy smile on her face. "I think it's beautiful."

Thomas scrunched up his nose. "I'll never understand girls as long as I live."

Alexandra perched her hands on her hips again. "I don't see why not. We're quite simple to understand. We appreciate music, and laughter, and beautiful clothing, and flowers, and—"

"*You* do, Al," Thomas interrupted. "Lavinia enjoys cutting people to shreds with her tongue and throwing fits when she doesn't get her way. That's why I like you so well. You'd never tell Mother and Father that I use your window to sneak out. Lavinia would set the guard on me."

Alexandra bit her lip. It was true; their elder sister was decidedly . . . difficult. "Be back before midnight, won't you? I dread it when Miss Hartley comes around, asking questions."

Thomas rolled his eyes at the mention of the governess. "Just pretend you're asleep."

Alexandra wrapped her dressing gown tighter around her waist. "I'm rubbish at pretending."

"I know," Thomas replied with a laugh.

Alexandra sighed and spun around again. "I want to sneak downstairs and watch all the lovely ladies in their gowns and handsome gentlemen in their formal evening attire. Instead I'm stuck up here, dancing alone."

Again, Thomas nodded toward the door. "Sneak down there, Al. You can do it."

Alexandra put her hands back to her hips for the third time, a common pose when speaking to her brother. "You are a horrible influence, Thomas Marcus Devon Peabody Hobbs."

His grin widened. "I know."

Another faint whistle indicated that Will was getting

impatient below. Thomas inserted two fingers on either side of his mouth and let out a soft whistle of his own.

"What are you two planning to do?" Alexandra asked, though half of her didn't want to know the answer. No doubt it was some boyish bit of trouble that would cause her anxiety should she be privy to the details.

"We're going to the stables to play cards," her brother said. "Will's uncle used to work in a gaming hell in London. He taught him all the tricks."

Alexandra pressed her hand to her cheek. "Don't cheat, Thomas!"

"I would never cheat," Thomas replied, a chagrined look on his boyishly handsome face. "But I must learn *how* to cheat, Al; otherwise, how'll I ever know if I'm being cheated?"

Alexandra contemplated that for a moment with a frown wrinkling her brow. "I suppose you have a point."

"I'd better go," Thomas said, "before Will's whistling attracts attention."

It was true. The terrace below could be accessed by French doors that led directly from her father's study. An enterprising guest in search of air might very well happen outside.

Alexandra watched, wincing, as her brother climbed through the window, scaled the roofline, and then jumped like a silent cat to the terrace below. She tiptoed over to the window to close it but stopped to watch her brother greet his friend. She shook her head and sighed again. Thomas, at the age of thirteen, was self-confident and carefree. Alexandra longed to be like him, daring and adventurous. She couldn't help it if she became nervous at the prospect of breaking rules and doing things she ought not. She spun around again in time to the music, but a thought struck her and she stopped abruptly. Thomas had said that being adventurous was an acquired skill. Was he right? If she tried it, would she enjoy it? Leaving the window open, she trailed over to her writing desk nearby, where she sat and opened her new leather-bound journal. At her age, it was high time to list the principal things she hoped to accomplish in life.

1. *Become brave and daring like Thomas.*
2. *Become beautiful, willowy, and poised like Lavinia. Never stain my gowns with food, et cetera.*
3. *Have a come-out during which an exceedingly eligible gentleman asks me to dance, thereby making the affair a smashing success.*
4. *Marry my true love. Must be handsome, dashing, witty, kind, true, and honorable. Name to be determined later.*

Alexandra sat back and surveyed her list. Becoming brave and daring would take a great deal of work, and she had little idea how she would accomplish such a thing. She tapped the end of the quill against her cheek. She must be on the alert for opportunities. Yes. That was the way to go about it.

As for becoming beautiful, willowy, and poised, it seemed more difficult than the first task. She was pretty at best, if dull brown hair and dull brown eyes could even be considered pretty. "Poised" was not a word that would ever be used to describe her. In fact, "clumsy" was probably more apt. And "willowy" was beyond an impossibility for her body. She'd already begun to develop hips and breasts and a little belly that her mother despaired of when they went to the modiste. Alexandra sighed yet again. Unless she became beautiful and poised and willowy, she had little chance of accomplishing a smashing success of a come-out in three years. Let alone one during which an exceedingly handsome and eligible gentleman asked her to dance. And if that didn't happen, how on earth would she have other gentlemen interested enough to find her true love out of the lot of them? It was a conundrum, no question about it.

Raised voices coming from behind the house caught her attention. Dropping the quill, Alexandra hurried back over to the window, where she pushed aside the curtains and blinked out into the dark night sky. A few scattered candles resting on a table on the terrace below illuminated the space. Two young bucks stood there, speaking to someone who was hidden under the eaves.

"Say that again!" one of the bucks shouted.

"I s-said I d-don't have no qu-quarrel with you two gents."

Alexandra froze. She recognized the stutter of Will, the stable boy.

"You d-d-don't?" the second buck teased.

Alexandra scowled and clenched her hands into fists. How dare those young men make sport of Will? The poor boy was barely thirteen, whereas these two had to be in their early twenties at least.

"N-n-no. I d-don't," Will replied. His stutter always worsened when he was anxious.

"Leave him alone!" This clearly came from her brother, who moved into her view. Thomas's fists were raised, obviously willing to defend his friend from males who were far older and taller than he.

The two bucks laughed. "Or what? You'll take a swing at us, lad?"

"Yes!" came Thomas's sure voice. She admired him for his bravery, but that didn't make her less worried. What should she do? Fetch Father?

"Try it, and we'll lay you flat in the span of two seconds," the first buck answered.

Alexandra held her breath. Thomas could easily tell these two fools that he was the future Duke of Huntley, but that was something else she admired about her brother. Even at his young age, Thomas never acted entitled to anything, nor desired special treatment.

"If you don't stop harassing my mate here, I'll lay you flat in one," Thomas retorted, his fists still held at the ready in front of him. He bounced around anxiously, brandishing his knuckles.

"I daresay you'll regret that, lad." The second buck stepped forward and raised his fist to Thomas.

That was it. Alexandra couldn't stand the injustice of the thing. How dare these two young men try to fight her brother and his friend? She'd been looking for an opportunity to be brave. Perhaps this was it.

"Why don't you pick on someone your own size?" Alexandra called out, heedless of the fact that she was standing in her bedchamber, wearing her night rail and dressing gown. She did her best to remain hidden behind the curtains.

The two bucks immediately stopped and looked up, squinting at her.

"What? Lo? A fair maiden speaks from above," the first buck said. The other laughed.

"You heard me," Alexandra replied, trying to keep her voice from shaking. "Why don't you go instigate a brawl with someone who could actually give you sport?"

"Al!" her brother cried indignantly, stamping his booted foot.

"Al?" the first buck said. "Is that your name? Are you certain you're a female?"

Anger spread through her limbs like quicksilver. She

squeezed the curtain so hard, her fingers ached. "If I were a boy, I'd climb out this window and pummel you both!" she called. "And another thing—"

"What in the devil's name is going on here?" A deep male voice sounded from somewhere below, but Alexandra couldn't see its owner.

The two bucks blanched. "My lord," they said in unison, quickly backing up toward the shadows.

"Did I hear you say that you intend to fight these two young lads?" the deep voice continued.

"They were giving us lip, my lord," one of the bucks offered in an obviously shaky voice.

The owner of the deep voice stepped into the light then, and Alexandra sucked in her breath. He looked like Adonis. Blond hair, wide shoulders, perfect black evening attire. She couldn't make out the color of his eyes, but whoever he was, the man was handsome in spades. Exactly the type of suitor she'd expect Lavinia to have. No doubt the man had just come from inside, where he'd danced with her sister to one of the lilting waltzes. Alexandra leaned forward to see better.

"I believe you are one-and-twenty, are you not, Yardnell?" Lord Handsome said.

The first buck hung his head and nodded.

"And you, Antony. You're two-and-twenty if you're a day."

The second buck kicked at the stones with his boot and also nodded reluctantly.

"Then I must not be hearing you correctly," Lord Handsome continued. "You cannot possibly be meaning to fight two *children* who aren't more than a dozen years old. Why, that would be not only unsporting, but also quite embarrassing for you, especially if the boys win."

The first buck opened his mouth to speak, but Adonis stopped him.

"Ah, ah, ah. I sincerely hope you aren't about to argue with me. I think we can both agree that a young man, a supposed *gentleman,* has no reason to fight a *boy,* does he?"

The second buck jerked his head in the semblance of a nod.

"That's what I thought," Adonis continued. "Now, run along before I decide that even at my advanced age of eight-and-twenty, I have no compunction striking either of you."

"Yes, Lord Owen," one of them said before the two bucks left nearly as quickly as they'd come, leaving Adonis with Thomas and the stable boy. Alexandra continued to watch with wide eyes from her perch at the window.

"Thank you, my lord," Thomas said, bowing formally to the older man. "I'm certain I could have handled it, but I do appreciate your assistance."

"Oh, no doubt, Huntfield," Adonis replied. "As you say, I was merely lending my assistance."

Alexandra's heart cartwheeled in her chest. He'd called Thomas by his title. How terribly endearing.

"Th-thank you, m-my lord," Will muttered.

"It is my pleasure, Mr. . . ."

"Atkins. W-Will Atkins."

And he'd called a mere stable boy "mister."

"My pleasure, Mr. Atkins. And should you have further trouble with those two chaps, I do hope you would not hesitate to inform me."

"We certainly sh-shall," Will said.

The two boys ran off and Alexandra held her breath,

waiting for Adonis to blend back into the shadows. Instead he remained there, under her window, a hint of light from the inside of the house caressing his fine cheekbone. Lord Owen? Lord Owen? She searched her memory for such a name.

His hand stole into his inside coat pocket, and Alexandra soon realized that he was lighting a cheroot. She glanced away. Oh, she should really shut the window. This was not the type of behavior a young lady should witness. She placed her fingertips on the sash and began to pull.

"I admire your method," Adonis called.

Alexandra's hands froze. Was he speaking to *her*? She jumped behind the curtain again and peeked out.

He turned then, the cheroot falling to his side, and looked up at her. "I admire it quite a lot. Threatening to climb out the window and pummel them was truly inspired."

Alexandra's cheeks heated. So, he'd heard that, had he? Not particularly ladylike of her, but then again, he didn't seem to mind.

She drew a shaky breath and projected her voice enough for him to hear. "I, er, those two had no business picking fights with children."

"Agreed," Adonis replied, inclining his head and smiling at her.

Alexandra's breath was stolen from her throat. The man had a dimple in his cheek that could make a saint swoon.

"I, uh, I thank you for helping my brother, my lord. Er, Lord . . . Owen . . ."

She let the last word hang, obviously waiting for him to provide his surname.

"Monroe," he replied smoothly, bowing at the waist. "At your service, my lady."

Alexandra sucked in her breath again, but for an entirely different reason this time. Yes, of course. She knew that name. Why, Lord Owen Monroe was one of the most famous rakehells in London. The man was known for his drinking, his gambling, his loose behavior with ladies of questionable morals, and his exceedingly high taste in fashion. The only son of the Earl of Moreland, he stood to inherit the title, but regardless, he was a scoundrel of the first order. Alexandra knew all this from the gossip she loved to listen in on when Mother and Lavinia were talking.

Alexandra shook herself and forced herself to reply to him. "My thanks, Lord Owen," she said, still peeping out from behind the curtains. "My family is in your debt."

"Absolutely not," he replied with another knee-weakening, dimple-revealing smile. No wonder so many ladies of ill repute fell victim to his charm. Who wouldn't fall victim to that smile? That dimple? "In fact," he continued, "I must insist you tell no one of this incident tonight."

Alexandra blinked. "Why not?"

"It would absolutely ruin my blackened reputation." He winked at her, and Alexandra was completely lost. She had to pinch herself to keep from sighing.

"Very well, if you insist," she replied.

"I hope you don't mind me saying that one as lovely and spirited as you shouldn't be cooped upstairs with such a delightful party going on."

Alexandra bit her lip and rubbed her bare feet together. "I'd love to dance, but I've not yet had my come-out, my lord."

"*That* is a pity." He tossed her a sly grin. "Come down here and I'll dance with you."

Alexandra's cheeks heated. She gulped. Oh, but she was sorely tempted. "I couldn't possibly do that, my lord. It would be far too scandalous."

"I happen to have a fondness for scandalous things," he replied with a second slight inclination of his handsome head. "Perhaps another time, then."

Her breathing hitched. *Yes, another time. Please.*

"I wish you well, my lady. Until your come-out." He bowed again and, with that, was gone into the night.

Alexandra held her breath now, watching the space Adonis had just occupied, hoping against hope that he might materialize again and say something equally as wonderful as what he'd just said. He thought she was lovely? A god like him? He thought she was spirited? A man who threatened antagonistic bucks and smoked cheroots under windows? Unimaginable. She wasn't spirited at all; she was just . . . well, injustice had made her furious. That's all there was to it.

After a few moments, Alexandra realized he wasn't coming back. She blinked into the darkness and finally forced herself to turn away from the window. The smell of smoke still lingered in the air, teasing her nostrils. He had been there, hadn't he? It hadn't been a dream, a figment of her imagination. He was handsome, he was kindhearted, he was witty. In short, he was everything she wanted in a husband one day. His reputation might be a bit tarnished at present, but there would be years to change it.

Alexandra hurried back over to the writing desk and pulled out the journal with her list written in it. She crossed through "Name to be determined later." Next to it, in large scrolling letters, she wrote: *Lord Owen Monroe.*

CHAPTER ONE
London, October 1816

"You heard me, Owen, and this time I'm putting my foot down." The stamp of a boot lent credence to that particular claim.

Owen tugged at his sleeve and did his best to keep from rolling his eyes. He'd been summoned to his father's study for what was likely the sixth time in as many months. Only this time, Owen had the misfortunate to be completely . . . sober. Blast, he should have stopped at the club and been even later than he already was to his father's favorite pastime, dressing down his son. At least it would be more palatable if he were half in the bottle.

"I understand," Owen drawled, standing up from the leather-upholstered chair that sat in front of his father's large mahogany desk. Owen inched toward the door. He had learned over years of such meetings that it was best to get out quickly before his father had a chance to toss more empty threats at his head.

"No. I don't think you do understand," the earl said, stamping his foot against the wooden floor again.

Owen pressed his lips together to keep from saying something he'd regret. Which was usually everything he said. "I understand perfectly. You're tired of my drinking?"

"Yes!"

"My gambling?"

"Yes!"

"My fondness for light skirts?"

"Yes!"

Owen picked an imaginary bit of lint from the front of his impeccably tailored blue coat. The garment had cost a small fortune, but then again, high fashion didn't come cheap and Owen prided himself on being well dressed. Well dressed, well fed, well entertained. Well everything. He focused his gaze on his father's red face. "There, you see? I've cataloged all my faults. You want me to find a wife and 'settle down.' I understand entirely."

"No. You don't understand, Owen." His father clutched at the lapels of his own burgundy coat and tugged viciously. Owen winced. There was no need to take it out on the garment. "You don't understand at all," the earl continued. "How many times have we had this discussion?"

"Too many to count," Owen muttered under his breath. He was already thinking of the hand of cards he'd be playing tonight at his favorite gaming hell.

"What was that?" His father narrowed his eyes on him.

Oh, devil take it. His father had heard his mutter. "Quite a few," Owen answered in a clearer voice.

"And how many times have you left here and done absolutely nothing to comply with my wishes?" his father replied, still tugging on his lapels.

"Too many to count," Owen muttered again, glancing

down at the tabletop so he wouldn't have to witness the assault on the garment.

"You've *never* complied with my wishes!" The Earl of Moreland banged his large fist against the desk. The ink-pot bounced. "Damn it, Owen, you're to inherit the title one day. You're to be an earl, for heaven's sake. You're to take your seat in Parliament and be a productive member of Society. You cannot continue to comport yourself as if you're nothing more than a gadabout."

"But I *am* nothing more than a gadabout." Owen sighed and scratched at the underside of his chin. "Haven't you told me that ever since my days at Eton?"

"We're not going to talk about *that* again," the earl replied, a thunderous expression hovering across his brow.

That's right. His father had never even asked him what happened. Just assumed the worst about his son. And Owen had set about proving him right ever since.

"And you're not a gadabout," the earl continued. "Or you won't be." He banged his fist on the desk again. At least he'd surrendered the poor, blameless lapels. "I'm tired of having this conversation with you to no avail. I'm tired of seeing you while away your days drinking and gambling. I'm tired of hearing stories about your exploits all over town."

Owen rubbed a knuckle against his forehead. "Oh, come now. They aren't *all* over town, are they?"

His father's jowls shook as he clutched his lapels even more tightly again. "Don't be impertinent."

"I've long since passed impertinent. And *please* have a care for your jacket, Father." Owen smoothed a hand over the thigh of his coffee-colored breeches. Also not cheap. Living the lifestyle to which he'd grown accustomed was, in fact, quite expensive, and his monthly allowance from his father was the means by which he maintained his lifestyle. Hence Owen's willingness to come here regularly and receive his dressing-down. It was a means to an end. He kept his father happy, and a large bank draft was deposited into his account each month. Of course, he sent a sizable portion of his allowance each month to an orphanage near one of the gaming hells he frequented, but he'd never tell his father that. Why spoil the man's bad opinion of him? Besides, Owen wasn't in the business of untarnishing his reputation. In fact, he'd been doing the exact opposite for years. It was a sport for him, really, much like training his beloved horses.

"Damn it, Owen. You must care about *something*."

Owen did care about something. He adored his younger sister, Cassandra, and his horses. In that order. Neither had ever let him down. Neither had ever believed the worst of him. "I care about the damage you're wreaking on your lapels," he drawled.

The earl lifted his chin. "That's it. I've given you plenty of opportunities. I'm officially finished putting up with your behavior. You will return here one month from today with an affianced bride or else!"

Owen's gaze flicked over his father. Was that spittle on his chin? The old blighter really had his back up this time, didn't he? But Owen couldn't help himself. "Or else what?"

"Or else . . . or else I will cut off your allowance. Yes. That's it. I should have done it long before now. I am not giving you another pound until you are properly engaged."

Owen arched a brow and picked another invisible piece of lint, this time from his coat sleeve. "That's a bit dramatic, don't you think?"

His father's face turned even redder, if that were possible. "No. I don't."

Owen studied his father's countenance. By God, the old man was actually *serious*. Or at least seemed to believe he was serious. His face was a mottled purplish color and his neck was bulging beneath his neckcloth. Yes, Father was serious, indeed. Owen groaned. He'd always known this day would come. The day when his father insisted he take a wife. He supposed he couldn't escape the parson's noose forever. He'd had a good run, actually.

Owen shrugged. "Fine. If I must choose a wife, I'll pick one out. Someone biddable, willing, quiet. One who'll look the other way. Someone passably pretty and exceedingly meek."

His father shook his head. "You don't understand, Owen."

Owen flicked at his cheek. "Understand what?"

"I'm not asking you to choose a wife. I'm telling you whom you'll marry."

Owen's head snapped up. "You mean to say you've already got a candidate in mind?"

His father nodded, his jowls shaking vigorously once more. "Yes. Her father and I have already been discussing the contract."

Owen leaned back into his seat, the wind knocked from his lungs. Well, he hadn't seen *this* coming. Not at all. And he was rarely caught by surprise. He leaned far back in his chair, stretched out his long legs in front of him, and crossed his feet at the ankles. Perhaps this was even more serious than he'd guessed. "Discussing the contract? Good God. Who is it?"

His father cleared his throat, released his beleaguered jacket, and calmly folded his hands on the desk in front of him. "Lady Lavinia Hobbs. The Duke of Huntley's eldest daughter."

Owen scanned his memory. Hobbs? Lavinia Hobbs? The name was familiar, but he couldn't recall a face. Blast. There were far too many pretty little daughters of overly entitled aristocrats to remember them all. And they were certainly not the sort of company Owen preferred to keep. The Duke of Huntley owned land adjacent to Father's in the country. He knew that much. He'd been to parties at the duke's country estate countless times. But none of that mattered to him at present. What did Lavinia Hobbs look like? More important, what did she *act* like? Was she biddable? Was she meek?

He couldn't recall and he wasn't about to ask his obviously enraged father. No matter. One eligible innocent was as good as another, Owen supposed. What did it matter whom he married? He'd stop his merrymaking long enough to participate in a wedding, get an heir or two off her, and then resume his style of living. It was more the norm than the exception among his set. It signified little. This was nothing to worry about.

"I'm certain she's fine, Father. Whatever you say." Again, Owen stood to make his way to the door. He'd simply go to the club and get a good drunk going, and then he would continue to live his life exactly the way he had been doing for the last thirty-one years. A sennight or so before his next visit to his father, he would track down this Lavinia Hobbs, toss around a bit of charm, smile at her, kiss the back of her hand, and finally ask her to marry him. She'd jump at the chance, of course, because despite his sullied reputation, he was still one of the most eligible bachelors in the *ton*. Inheriting an earldom tended to whitewash even the most tattered reputation. Then, he'd return here in a month's time, announce his success to his father, secure his allowance, and go about his routine, while Lady Lavinia planned a wedding worthy of a future earl and the daughter of a duke. After the wedding, he'd install the chit in one of their homes in the country, and that would be that until it was time to beget an heir. Not so difficult, really. He shrugged.

"You agree so easily?" His father's bushy eyebrows flew to the top of his forehead.

Owen grinned at his father. "Yes. Lavinia Hobbs it is. I'll see you in a month, Father." He made his way toward the door.

"Not so fast."

Owen paused, his fingers resting on the door handle. He turned slowly and arched a questioning brow in the earl's direction. "Yes?"

The earl cleared his throat. "There is a catch."

"A catch?" Owen echoed. He didn't quite like the sound of that. "What catch?"

"Her father insists that she should choose you."

Owen's hand fell away from the door. He turned to fully face his father. "*Choose* me? What do you mean?"

"Apparently, the girl's got it in her head that she will marry only for love."

Owen scowled and rubbed a hand across his forehead again. "Love? What nonsense is that?"

"Her parents value her highly and are quite indulgent of her. They've promised her she can marry for love. Until she fancies herself in love with some chap, she won't accept his suit."

Owen did roll his eyes this time. "How droll. Good God, Father, why this girl of all girls?"

"Because she comes from impeccable lineage. And once the match is made, the combination of our lands will secure the future of the title for centuries. She's the perfect mate for you. But *you* are going to have to be the biddable, willing one. *You* are going to have to be the meek one. *You* are going to have to court this girl. Make her see your, ahem, assets, however questionable they may be."

Owen snorted. "Your faith in me is truly astounding, Father."

"Be that as it may, you're going to have to convince her not only to marry you but fall in love with you as well."

Owen's grin widened. "I doubt it will be as difficult as you believe. I do possess a modicum of charm, you know?"

His father's face adequately reflected his skepticism. "There's one other thing."

Owen groaned. "Dare I ask?"

"You cannot tell her that we are already planning a contract."

Owen rubbed his temples. He wished he hadn't had quite so many brandies last night at the club or quite so few earlier this afternoon. "Seems the whole thing could be put to rights with just coming out and telling her we're to marry."

"Absolutely not. Her father will stop the proceedings if she is made aware. She's a bit, er, excitable, it seems."

Owen scowled. "Excitable?"

"Gets her back up about certain things if she's not happy."

"Fine. Whatever you say. I'll think of something. I'll manage it." Owen turned again, wrenched open the door, and took a step into the corridor.

"You have a month to get her to agree to your proposal, Owen," his father called.

Owen turned his head and grinned at his father. "That

should be plenty of time." He strolled off down the corridor, whistling to himself. A month to get a Society miss to fancy herself in love with him? How difficult could it be?

CHAPTER TWO

Alexandra peered around the wall and waved at her maid to stay back. It was a delicate business, leaving the house without her mother seeing. Fortunately, Alexandra had had three years of practice.

"My lady—," Hannah began.

"Shh." Alexandra turned, still crouched, with her finger pressed to her lips. Hannah was clutching one small basket full of embroidery, and Alexandra was clutching another. "Mother will hear you," Alexandra warned.

"But, my lady," the maid continued in a softer whisper. "I intended to say that I believe your mother is in the study."

Alexandra bolted upright, nearly dropping her basket. "The study? But Mother is never in Father's study." Alexandra turned her back to the corridor she'd been stalking and directed her attention toward the study instead.

Hannah nodded and shifted the basket in her arms. "I heard the duchess say earlier that she intended to speak with the duke."

Confound it. What was Mother about? Alexandra peered down the corridor that led to the study. Hmm. This was unexpected and, as a result, interesting. Quite interesting, indeed. Normally, she would be pleased to find Mother preoccupied during Alexandra's twice-monthly visits to the poorhouse; she gave her embroidery to the people there to sell in the streets for whatever they could make from it. She might as well make something useful out of the odiously dull pastime. Of course, Mother would have a fit if she knew her daughter was doing such a thing, but what Mother didn't know didn't hurt her. Or so Alexandra had decided years ago. It was no easy feat to pretend she was taking a nap, sneak out, convince Hannah, and bribe the coachman to take her to a less-than-savory part of town. It certainly didn't hurt that Alexandra suspected the coachman was sweet on Hannah. That, and keeping Alexandra's reputation intact, made Hannah's presence an absolute necessity to the mission. Yes, normally she'd welcome Mother's preoccupation. Breathe a sigh of relief, actually. But today—today Alexandra was intrigued by the idea of her parents speaking to one another in the study in the middle of the afternoon. Unprecedented!

Instead of hurrying through the back corridor and out into the mews, Alexandra plunked one fist on her hip. "What do you think Mother wants with Father?"

Hannah shrugged and shifted the basket in her arms again. "I'm certain I don't know, my lady."

Alexandra cocked her head to the side and stared toward the study. Her parents lived in the same home, but they could always be counted upon to keep to their own worlds. Her mother managed the household, the shopping, and the social affairs. Her father managed his property, his seat in Parliament, and his outings to the club. Theirs was quite an efficient marriage, actually. Alexandra rarely saw them in the same room together. Such a spotting would be a novelty.

"It cannot be good," Alexandra breathed. No. If Mother was going into the study in the middle of the day, something was wrong, and Alexandra had a sinking feeling that that something might very well have to do with her. "You don't suppose it's because of my failure in Society, do you, Hannah?"

There were few secrets Hannah wasn't privy to. The maid was Alexandra's closest confidante, outside of Thomas. It wasn't as if she could talk to her sister. All Lavinia ever wanted to talk about was herself. "Oh, no, my lady," Hannah hastened to assure her. "Your mother cannot fault you for your . . . your . . ."

Alexandra sighed. "You might as well say it."

Hannah winced. "Your late blooming," she finished magnanimously.

Alexandra shook her head slowly, biting her lip. "It's more than late blooming, Hannah. I'm a wallflower. A complete failure." It was true. Despite her list, despite her wishes and dreams, Alexandra's debut last spring had been a dismal failure. No handsome gentleman had asked her to dance. No other gentlemen had asked her either. Not even the unhandsome, ineligible sorts. It had dampened her spirits, to be sure, but it hadn't crushed her dreams. No, those were still impossibly intact.

Hannah continued to whisper. "It's not your fault that Lady Sarah Highgate has captured the attention of all the eligible gentlemen this Season. She's a diamond of the first water."

"Yes, and I'm a rock in the brackish bit." Alexandra laughed.

"Now, that's not true, my lady," Hannah replied loyally. "But your mother has already told you that you cannot marry until Lady Lavinia does. So I'm certain the duchess is not concerned with your marital prospects. Besides, Lady Sarah will no doubt be engaged before the Season's end, and the rest of the gentlemen will come to their senses. They say the Marquess of Branford intends to offer for her."

The Marquess of Branford was the most eligible of all the Season's bachelors. Well, he was the one with the most prestigious title, at least. Which practically made him the most eligible. The fact that he'd declared himself to be in the market for a wife also didn't hurt. He was handsome and titled and rich, but Alexandra hadn't given him a second look. He wasn't Lord Owen Monroe, after all.

She took a tentative step toward the study. "Be that as it may, I don't think it could hurt to have a quick listen."

"My lady!" Hannah gasped.

Alexandra turned around and gave her maid a pleading look. "You know I cannot help myself. Please don't judge me, Hannah. I need you."

"Very well, my lady." Hannah nodded.

"Let's leave the baskets here." Alexandra pointed to a spot behind a table in the corridor. The two women stooped and pushed their baskets behind the table to hide them. Then they sneaked down the marble-floored hallway and around the corner and tiptoed toward the door of the duke's study.

Alexandra held her breath. Eavesdropping was detestable, of course, but sometimes necessary. What if something truly awful were happening? What if, God forbid, Mama had picked out a suitor for her? Alexandra would be forced to stop it. Only one man would do for her. Granted, a man who had been noticeably absent from events of the Season to date, a man who had never declared himself ready or willing to take a bride, a man who preferred drinking and gambling to all other decent pursuits. But that didn't concern Alexandra overly much. She would find a way for their paths to cross now that she'd officially made her debut. Besides, it was true that she had been merely fifteen when she wrote that list and chose Lord Owen Monroe. She should get to know him better before she made a final decision, but there would be time for that. She had to ensure that Mama didn't have other plans first. And to that end, a bit of properly timed eavesdropping seemed to be in order.

Alexandra and Hannah sneaked up to the study door. Thankfully, it was cracked. Mother's high-pitched breathless voice was floating about inside the room. Alexandra leaned forward and pressed her ear near the opening.

"I'm telling you, Martin, I don't like it. Not one bit." Her mother's voice rang out.

"I don't see why not." Her father's voice was strong and calm in comparison.

"What can you possibly mean?" Mother replied. "He's completely inappropriate for her."

"His family is one of the most esteemed in the country."

"He's a ne'er-do-well."

"His father is one of my oldest and closest friends," Father replied.

"He's a rakehell."

"So was I once."

Alexandra couldn't see inside the room, but she pictured her mother waving her handkerchief and turning red. "I cannot believe you would allow our darling girl to be carted off by the likes of *him,* of all people."

"I daresay she could use a good carting off, Lillian."

"Don't be indecent."

"It's an excellent match. We'd be lucky to have him. A man's actions speak louder than his words. I believe he's got quite a lot of good in him."

Alexandra held her breath. It was worse than she'd thought. Whoever the chap was, he must be particularly odious for Mother to be arguing with Father about it. Mother never argued with Father. She would gainsay him nothing.

"But we don't even know how she feels about him. She may not even *like* him," Mother pleaded. "And if actions do indeed speak louder than words, then he's a drunken lout."

"Nonsense. He merely hasn't decided to settle down yet. My money's on the lad. That devil can be downright charming when he wants to be. And as for her feelings, that's why I insisted that he court her. She must choose him."

"You admit he's a devil?" Mother replied, her voice reaching such a pitch that Alexandra worried for the glassware in the study.

"He needs to settle down, Lillian. A wife and children will make him grow up. I've no doubt."

"What if you're wrong? What if his egregious behavior doesn't change? I don't think we should be taking that gamble on our daughter, for heaven's sake."

Alexandra slowly let out her breath. They must be talking about a suitor for Lavinia, mustn't they? Lavinia was the one who must marry first. Lavinia was the one whose marital prospects were forefront in her mother's mind. But what if they were talking about Alexandra? An icy sweat broke out on her brow. What if they'd received an offer? Alexandra didn't think she'd had any offers, and no one had shown any particular interest in her, of course, but neither had they shown interest in Lavinia. And hadn't Mother mentioned just last week that she despaired of Lavinia ever making a match with her "difficult" behavior? Given that, her parents might well be speaking about Alexandra after all.

She was just about to push through the door and insist that her mother was right. She couldn't possibly marry a man she didn't know and didn't love. Though she was certain they'd fall over in dead swoons if she announced she intended to marry the infamous Lord Owen Monroe.

"I'm telling you, Martin," Mother continued. "I think it's all wrong."

Her father's voice grew cajoling. "Let's just see how they get on at the ball we're planning for them."

Her mother sighed. "Yes. And now I must plan a ball. As if this match weren't bad enough."

"We want them to have every opportunity to enjoy each other's company, don't we?" Father replied.

"Fine, but I daresay I know my own daughter well enough to guess her mind."

Alexandra nodded firmly.

Mother's voice held an edge of anxiety. "There's simply no way Lavinia will willingly accept the suit of that rogue, Lord Owen Monroe."

Alexandra gasped.

CHAPTER THREE

Owen had been sitting in his favorite seat at the club for the better part of an hour, and he'd yet to hear any good news. In fact, his friends seemed to be reveling in telling him the exact opposite of good news. It was bad. All bad. Exceedingly bad. And it centered around Lady Lavinia Hobbs.

Normally, Owen kept company with a group of like-minded aristocrats. All of them bored, all of them drinking to excess, all of them gambling a bit too much. But today he hadn't been looking for sport. He'd come to Brooks's seeking some good advice, and while he might hate to admit it, his sister's husband and his closest friend were two of the wisest people Owen knew. Both of them were war heroes who'd fought at Waterloo. The third man present, Captain Rafferty Cavendish, was a military officer recently turned viscount. He was engaged to marry Swifdon's younger sister, Daphne. Those in their close set knew that Daphne and Rafe were actually already married. They'd legally married more than a year ago, before they completed a mission for the Crown together, but for the sake of propriety and to ward off the hint of a scandal, they were planning a large Society wedding.

Swifdon, Claringdon, and Cavendish. They were all good, to a man. They tolerated Owen's debauched company because of Cassandra.

"Why so glum, Monroe?" Derek Hunt, the Duke of Claringdon, asked soon after the cards had been passed round and the brandies ordered.

"My father is on the warpath." Owen assessed the looks in the other men's eyes and quickly cleared his throat. These were three men who had seen *actual* war. "My apologies. I meant . . . he's giving me hell."

"What seems to be the problem?" asked his brother-in-law, Julian Swift, the Earl of Swifdon.

Owen rolled his neck. "He insists I marry."

"As fathers will do. Don't you think it's time you settled down?" Claringdon replied.

"Yes, Monroe, marriage has a way of catching up to the best of us," Cavendish said with a unrepentant grin.

"It's not that," Owen replied. "I'd actually resigned myself to the marriage part. It's the prospective bride to whom I object."

Swifdon whistled. "Who, may I ask, is the lucky lady?"

"Lavinia Hobbs."

All three men winced simultaneously. And thus, the bad news had begun.

"You know her?" Owen asked, sitting up straighter in his chair and searching their faces.

"Can't say we've ever met," Cavendish replied.

"But her reputation precedes her," Claringdon added.

"She's known to be a bit . . . difficult, I believe," Swifdon finished.

"Yes, I've noted that 'difficult' seems to be the preferred adjective used when describing her," Owen replied with a snort.

"Why in the devil's name would your father choose her?" Claringdon asked as the footman returned with their drinks.

"To torture me?" Owen replied, knocking back half his drink.

"Now there, slow down," Swifdon said. "This isn't one of your gaming hells. It's the middle of the afternoon, for God's sake."

Owen grunted at his brother-in-law.

"If Monroe here has to marry Lady Lavinia Hobbs, I daresay he might need something stiffer than brandy." Cavendish shook his head.

"Your father's reasoning cannot truly be to torture you. Why is he insisting upon the match?" Claringdon wanted to know.

Owen leaned back in his chair and blew out a deep breath. "Seems her father and mine have got it into their heads that a match between our families is an excellent idea. Joining estates and all of that."

"Ah," one of them muttered, and they all three nodded as if the joining of estates explained it all.

"Daphne mentioned Lady Lavinia is excitable," Swifdon offered.

Now Cavendish whistled. " 'Excitable'? That's one way to put it."

"What's that supposed to mean?" Owen asked, shifting uncomfortably in his chair.

"I once went to the duke's town house on some business for the Home Office," Cavendish replied. "There was a god-awful racket coming from upstairs. Seems Lady Lavinia was in a temper. The duke himself apologized to me for the bother and the noise."

Owen winced. "A temper? What happened?"

Cavendish tossed a card onto the table. "When I was leaving, I heard two of the footmen talking. Apparently, the feather in one of milady's hats had wilted and she was none too pleased. They mentioned she'd smashed a vase and slapped her maid."

"The duke should take care to keep his footmen from talking so much," Claringdon said, tossing his own card onto the table.

"I believe you're missing the point, Claringdon," Cavendish replied. "She was in the devil's own temper over a *feather.*"

"I heard you," Claringdon replied, still surveying his cards. "I was trying not to focus on that part."

"Thank you for that," Owen said, sarcasm dripping from his voice.

"You're welcome." Claringdon inclined his head with a smile.

"I hesitate to admit that I've heard similar stories about the girl," said Swifdon.

"Blast. What have you heard?" Owen eyed Swifdon warily.

Swifdon shuffled his cards in his hands. "Daphne mentioned she's a bit of a shrew."

"You're not *a bit* of a shrew," Cavendish replied. "You're either a shrew or not a shrew. There's no 'bit' about it."

"What did Daphne say?" Owen asked.

Swifdon's nose wrinkled. "She said that she'd heard that Lady Lavinia threw a screaming fit in the ladies' retiring room at the Houghtons' ball last spring."

"A screaming fit? Good God. What for?" Owen ventured. "Or do I want to know?"

"I believe Daphne said that Lady Houghton had failed to serve the salmon puffs that Lady Lavinia preferred after Lady Lavinia had clearly expressed her desire for them when she'd met Lady Houghton on Bond Street not two days before the ball."

Owen braced his elbow on the table and let his forehead drop to his hand. "You *must* be joking."

Swifdon shook his head. "I wish I were."

Claringdon plucked another card from his hand. "She sounds charming."

"She sounds half mad!" Owen barked.

"No wonder she's on the shelf," Cavendish offered with a snort, poking out his cheek with his tongue.

Owen tossed his cards to the table, no longer interested in the game. Instead, he picked up his brandy and took another fortifying gulp. "Yes, but apparently, my father has decided that I must be the martyr who marries the chit."

"She does have impeccable lineage," Claringdon said.

Owen arched a brow at him. "So does my horse. I don't want to marry it."

"Her lineage may be impeccable, but it seems her temper is quite pecked." Cavendish tossed another card on the table.

"Ah, there you are."

The four men looked up to see Garrett Upton striding toward them. Upton was Claringdon's cousin by marriage, and Upton's wife, Jane, was a close friend of the other men's wives.

"Upton, have a seat." Swifdon stood and clapped his friend on the shoulder as he approached.

Upton quickly settled in and ordered a drink. "I was

visiting my friend Berkeley today but couldn't convince him to come to the club. He's a sort of solitary chap, Berkeley. Not to mention he's not much for drinking . . . or gambling."

"Pity, that," Owen mumbled, cradling his brandy glass in his hand.

"What have you lot been up to?" Upton asked as the footman returned and handed him his brandy.

Cavendish elbowed Upton. "We've been lamenting Monroe's upcoming nuptials."

Garrett Upton's glass nearly slid through his fingers. He fumbled to catch it. "Monroe? Don't tell me you're engaged. Why, I'd never believe it."

"Not engaged. Not yet," Owen replied, handing his empty glass to the footman and promptly ordering another.

"No, not yet," Swifdon echoed. "But told in no uncertain terms by his father that he must be engaged before the month is out. And to a particular lady. In fact, it turns out she's quite particular."

"Is that so?" Upton said, lifting his brandy glass in salute. "Sounds as if congratulations are in order, then. Who is the fortunate bride?"

"Lady Lavinia Hobbs," Claringdon told him.

Upton's face fell and his glass sank back to the table.

"What? Don't tell me you've another horrid story to tell about her," Owen said.

"Well, I . . ." Upton glanced away.

"You might as well say it," Cavendish said. "He's already learned a bit about her temperament."

"Yes, go ahead. Tell your worst. It cannot be more awful than the stories I've already heard," Owen said.

Upton cleared his throat. "I was at the Kendalls' dinner party last year when Lady Lavinia became so enraged by the attentions of a certain gentleman that she tossed a glass of red wine in his face and then ripped a tapestry from the wall and stormed from the room."

Swifdon's eyes widened. "Was the chap offensive in some way? Did he say something indecent?"

"No," Upton replied. "He later told Kendall that all he'd said was that he thought their hostess was looking very fine and in good spirits that evening. Seemed Lady Lavinia doesn't appreciate other ladies' looks to be praised in her presence. Lord Mertle had been sitting on the other side of her and confirmed that that indeed had been what set her off."

Owen gulped and tugged at his cravat. Seemed the thing was smothering him today. "I take that back. It was worse. I wish you hadn't told me."

"It's a wonder she continues to be invited to Society events given her behavior," Swifdon added.

"Being the daughter of a duke probably explains it to some degree," Claringdon added. "Though I daresay I'd think twice before inviting her to *my* home."

Upton gave Owen a sympathetic smile. "Sorry, old chap. I'd no idea your father would pick her of all the ladies in Society. The good news is that she's quite beautiful."

Owen pinched the bridge of his nose. "I don't even remember what she looks like."

"She is beautiful," Cavendish agreed. "Or would be, if she didn't have such a sour expression all the time."

"Perfect." Owen called for the footman. He needed that glass of brandy immediately.

CHAPTER FOUR

Alexandra stood outside her sister's bedchamber and steeled her resolve. She took a deep breath. Then another one. Speaking with Lavinia was never pleasant, but Alexandra had to get answers to her questions before she decided upon the appropriate tactic. Namely, did Lavinia have any sort of regard for Lord Owen Monroe? If she did, Alexandra couldn't possibly interfere with their courtship, as disappointed as she might be. But if she didn't—and Alexandra highly suspected she didn't—then she would be free to use whatever means at her disposal to thwart their parents' plan.

Please, please don't have a regard for him.

Alexandra clutched her sweaty palms together to still their trembling and forced herself to knock.

"Come in," came her sister's short, cranky voice.

Alexandra slowly turned the handle and pushed open the door to Lavinia's opulent bedchamber. It was decorated in a variety of shades of pink silks and satins with large white bows, fluffy down pillows, pink striped wallpaper, and paintings of pink flowers on the walls. Lavinia sat at her silver-mirrored dressing table in front of the looking glass, preening like a peacock.

For the thousandth time, Alexandra thought how beautiful her sister was. Lavinia's complexion was white as milk. Her hair was dark brown with a slight curl. Her nose was patrician, her eyes crystal blue. She looked like a perfect doll. A tall, willowy, thin, gorgeous doll. The exact opposite of Alexandra's middling height and curviness, with plump cheeks and brown hair and eyes. Alexandra sighed. Life was simply not fair.

Lavinia wasn't all bad, of course. She'd been a sweet little girl. Or so a vague memory told Alexandra. But then she'd taken ill, and all that had changed. It wasn't her sister's fault, exactly, that she could be so unpleasant to be around. She adored her horses in the country and she was quite well read. Mostly books about knights and damsels, but still, someone who loved to read as much as Lavinia did must have *some* redeeming qualities as far as Alexandra was concerned.

Lavinia's beleaguered maid, Martha, was painstakingly rubbing cold cream onto her mistress's small hands. Alexandra rarely administered cream to her hands, and she certainly never asked her maid to do it. She'd never subject poor Hannah to such ministrations. Lavinia, however, rarely lifted as much as a finger for her own care unless she was forced to. And that on a very rare occasion indeed.

Alexandra made her way into the room with a smile on her face. She'd learned long ago that it was always best to approach Lavinia casually until one determined what sort of mood she was in. Alexandra hoped for the best today. At least Lavinia hadn't raised her voice or thrown anything yet. That was a success.

"What are you doing?" Alexandra asked in as cheery a voice as she could muster.

Lavinia closed her eyes and relaxed into her seat, wiggling her shoulders back and forth. "What does it look like I'm doing, you dolt? Having my hands creamed, obviously."

The smile temporarily dropped from Alexandra's face. Despite her calm façade, it seemed her sister was already in a fine temper. Too bad. Alexandra studied her stone-like face in the looking glass. Poor Lavinia. She'd always been given precisely what she wanted precisely when she wanted it, but still she wasn't happy. Alexandra doubted anything could make her sister happy. Though she desperately hoped it wasn't Lord Owen Monroe.

"Oh, yes. I see," Alexandra replied, redoubling her efforts to be cheerful and replacing the smile on her face.

Lavinia cracked open one ice-blue eye and stared at her. "What do you want? You never come into my bedchamber."

Not if I can help it. "I came to tell you something," Alexandra replied in a conspiratorial voice, hoping to intrigue her sister. Lavinia liked nothing so much as gossip.

Lavinia's second eye opened. She narrowed both of them on Alexandra through the looking glass. Aha. There was unmistakable interest there.

"Tell me what?" Lavinia's voice curled through the air like smoke.

Alexandra sauntered over and took a seat on a tufted cushion near the wardrobe not far from her sister. "Just something I overheard . . . about Lord Owen Monroe."

Lavinia's eyes snapped shut again. "Ugh. I couldn't care any less if I tried. Lord Owen is a complete scoundrel. I can't imagine what Mother was thinking, inviting him to the ball tomorrow night."

So Mother had already told her he'd be coming to the ball. "But he is extremely handsome, don't you think?" Alexandra ventured, trying not to get too excited over her sister's declaration that she couldn't care any less about Lord Owen. That was a good start, but Alexandra had to be certain.

Lavinia sighed. "I suppose he's passably good-looking if you like the arrogant, overly confident sort—which I decidedly do not." Lavinia flipped over her hands to allow poor Martha better access to her palms.

Alexandra had to bite her tongue to keep from snapping out a reply. Passably good-looking? Was her sister blind?

"He does seem confident," Alexandra replied calmly instead.

Lavinia sniffed. "Yes, well, he's been far too indulged by his parents for far too long."

Alexandra nearly choked. She pressed her hand to her throat. Oh, the irony. But pointing out such a thing to her sister would not only be useless but would also most likely end in a tirade from Lavinia and a severe scolding from their mother for upsetting the delicate flower that was her sister. Instead, Alexandra changed tactics.

"Speaking of liking a certain sort, if you don't fancy Lord Owen, whom do you fancy?"

Lavinia opened her eyes and then rolled them. "No one. The entire *ton* is full of ne'er-do-wells and ignoramuses. I cannot possibly imagine whom I'm to marry if the selection is no better than it is at present."

"You don't truly believe that," Alexandra replied, then winced. She couldn't afford to anger her sister this early in the conversation.

Alexandra glanced at Martha. Alexandra had to credit the maid with a straight face and the patience of a saint. Martha calmly rubbed cream into every inch of her mistress's hands without so much as blinking an eye. Lavinia preferred a long, leisurely hand massage. Alexandra hoped Father was paying the young woman well. Alexandra made a mental note to slip her some of her own pin money next time she saw her.

"Of course I believe that," Lavinia replied with a half snort, pursing her lips. "And don't think I don't know what you're about, coming in here and asking questions. You merely want me to choose a husband so that *you* will be free to marry."

There was no use denying that. "Do you intend to become a spinster, then?" Alexandra asked.

"Certainly not. But I fully intend to wait until I find the perfect gentleman, though I daresay that task will be easier said than done. I refuse to settle for the first chap or even the fiftieth who comes along, hoping to win my hand. I deserve the best of the lot, do I not?"

Alexandra and Martha exchanged skeptical glances. Alexandra decided to keep her reply to herself. However, her sister had just given her the perfect opening.

"Why don't you tell me what you're looking for, and I shall endeavor to help you look."

Lavinia pushed her perfect nose into the air and seemed to contemplate the question for a moment. "Hmm. I suppose it cannot hurt. You and I do have the same interest in mind."

Yes. Getting you married off.

"Very well," Lavinia said. "First of all, I severely dislike any man who drinks. Especially if he drinks to excess. It's vulgar."

Alexandra kept her face completely still. Of course her

sister disliked drinking. Lavinia hated all fun. "I see," Alexandra replied simply.

"And he cannot be overbearing. I detest an overbearing sort."

Takes one to know one.

Lavinia flipped her hands back over, indicating for Martha to proceed with the second coat. "Gambling of any sort is completely out of the question. It's an absolute abomination."

"Of course." Alexandra nodded. That was not news to her; she'd had her own unfortunate incident in which her sister had discovered her gambling—or more precisely, encouraging others to gamble—and raised holy hell. Again, Lavinia was the opposite of fun.

"Cursing and a bad temper are also entirely unacceptable," Lavinia continued.

Ah yes, only one of them could curse and have a bad temper in Lavinia's marriage. Alexandra had to smother her smile at that thought.

"I detest dancing," Lavinia added thoughtfully. "I cannot abide a gentleman who is forever endeavoring to ask me to dance."

It's one of my favorite things, Alexandra thought wistfully. "What, specifically, do you object to when it comes to dancing?" Alexandra couldn't help but ask.

Lavinia flared her nostrils and glared at her. "There are much better things to do with one's time than dance."

"Such as?"

"Such as anything!" Lavinia's voice rose sharply, and Alexandra quickly decided to abandon that line of questioning.

"Very well, what else do you require in a gentleman?" Alexandra said.

Lavinia pressed her lips together. "I adore poetry. The

man who wins my heart must write me not only poetry but ballads as well."

"Ballads?" Alexandra wrinkled her nose. The maid gave her mistress a questioning sideways glance.

"Yes, love ballads. I adore them," Lavinia said. "And he must bring me flowers every time he comes to see me. Scads and scads of flowers. Not those sad little offerings from the park, but large, lovely ones he has carted in from his conservatory in the country."

Alexandra shook her head. Of course, his conservatory. Because any man worthy of Lavinia would be the proud owner of a conservatory filled with large, gorgeous flowers with which to woo her.

"And he must be a fine horseman," Lavinia continued. "You know how much I adore my dear Bonnie in the country."

It was true. The only living thing her sister seemed to cherish was her horse. "Is there anything else?"

"All the normal things, of course. He must be handsome, titled, honorable. He cannot live too far away. I shouldn't like to travel a great distance to visit Mother and Father. That would be terribly inconvenient."

Mustn't inconvenience her.

"And he shouldn't be of such a strong mind that he won't allow me to redecorate our country house as I see fit."

Never think it.

"He shouldn't be too terribly interested in politics. I shouldn't like to have to discuss such boring subjects at every dinner party."

The horror.

"What about wit?" Alexandra offered.

Lavinia bared her teeth. "Wit? Why would I want that? Wit is overrated."

No, it's not. "Anything else?"

"I prefer a man with an artist's heart who can speak to me about horses and poetry with equal verve. Someone with soft hands who might play me a love ballad on a mandolin." She sighed and stared dreamily off toward her pink wallpaper.

An artist's heart? What did that mean? And a mandolin? Really? Alexandra and Martha exchanged another skeptical glance. Her sister's perfect groom didn't sound appealing to Alexandra in the least. Though, thankfully, he also sounded completely opposite of Lord Owen Monroe. As she had suspected, her sister and Lord Owen were not suited at all.

"You're quite certain Lord Owen doesn't tempt you?" Alexandra asked.

Lavinia raised a brow and wrinkled her nose. "Not in the least. Why, I'm looking for the perfect romantic gentleman. Can you imagine Lord Owen being a romantic? Or a gentleman?"

A *romantic* gentleman? No, indeed, Alexandra could not imagine it. She breathed a sigh of relief. "Very well, if you're certain."

"Entirely. I suppose I'll eventually have to go to the Continent to find such a man," Lavinia finished with a sniff. "I daresay I've yet to meet a suitable candidate in three years of attending those monotonous *ton* parties."

"I have a much better idea of what you're seeking," Alexandra said, her cheery tone returning. She stood, smoothed her light green skirts, and headed for the door. "That's exactly whom I shall look for. I'm certain such a man exists." *Somewhere.* Though Alexandra doubted it. He sounded like a medieval knight straight out of a tale worthy of King Arthur, only without the manliness.

Lavinia contemplated her creamy hands. "I doubt *you'll* have luck when Mother's failed all these years."

"I'll certainly do my best," Alexandra replied, smiling optimistically at her sister. Why did Lavinia never respond to a genuine smile? Alexandra began to turn toward the door.

"Wait," Lavinia said, pulling her hand away from the maid sharply with a loud, "That's enough!" Martha backed away quickly, most likely in fear of being slapped.

"What?" Alexandra stopped and stared at Lavinia.

"You never said what you heard about Lord Owen. About *me*."

Of course her sister couldn't resist discussing her favorite topic. Herself.

Alexandra cleared her throat. "I heard he's taken with you and intends to court you."

Lavinia smiled a catlike smile and settled back into her seat. "Oh, of course he does. Too bad for him, he doesn't stand a chance."

CHAPTER FIVE

Owen set his horse, Apollo, to a gallop. He'd ridden out to the countryside just past town today in order to see a bit of horseflesh he was considering buying. Of course, the horse had been no Apollo, but the sleek Arabian was an incomparable. He stroked the horse's dark silky mane. The new animal would be for training. Training and selling. Owen's favorite and only decent pastime and one with which he augmented his monthly allowance. He'd decided to purchase the stallion. He had only to make arrangements with his father's stable master first.

As Owen rode back toward the tollhouse just before the road that led into London, he cursed his latest bit of misfortune. Namely his obligation to marry Lavinia Hobbs. Damn it. He wasn't even left to handle it how he saw fit. He should have known that not only would his father meddle in his affairs with Lady Lavinia, but his mother would, too. To the tune of planning a ball with Lavinia's mother, the duchess, for the express purpose of inviting Owen and giving him a chance to court the duke's daughter. His parents should bloody well know he didn't need their help courting anyone, let alone some boring little drip of a duke's daughter, no matter how "difficult" she might be. But hadn't that always been his parents' attitude when it came to Owen? He never made the right decisions himself, did he? Never quite measured up to his father's expectations. No. His father had made up his mind about Owen a long time ago. Well, he bloody well would measure up this time. Whether Lavinia Hobbs liked it or not.

So the lady wanted to fancy herself in love? Very well. Owen was more than confident in his own charm. He'd had ladies declare their undying love for him after just one night in his bed. Certainly, he couldn't take an innocent to bed, but that wouldn't keep him from being charming. In fact, the lady he'd spent the last two nights with assured him of his appeal when he left her bed this morning, reminding her that he never spent more than two evenings with the same female companion. There were far too many others to meet and choose from. But she'd seemed pleased with his performance, too. They all were. How much different could the chaste courting of a "difficult" young lady be?

As he neared the tollhouse, Owen drew up the reins to signal Apollo to stop. The horse tossed his head and slowed accordingly. There was a small queue at the tollhouse and Owen waited impatiently behind a rickety cart filled with vegetables and occupied by a poor farmer.

When the farmer finally was next in line, the sounds of raised voices caught Owen's attention. Apparently, the farmer and the gatekeeper were having a disagreement about something. Owen maneuvered Apollo closer to hear the conversation.

"But I can't afford it," the farmer said. "Last time we came through, it weren't so much."

"I don't set the prices," the gatekeeper replied. "Parliament's decided to raise taxes. That's all I can tell ye."

"But I won't have any more money till I can get me goods ta the market in London."

"Ain't me problem," the gatekeeper replied. "And ye're keeping this fine gent behind ye from passing. Out of the way if you can't make the toll."

The farmer glanced at Owen. Shame marked his haggard features. "I'm sorry for the trouble, me lord, but me daughter's sick and me wife wanted me ta take her to the surgeon what lives near St. Paul's."

Owen glanced into the back of the man's rickety cart to see a thin child lying on an even thinner bed of hay, amongst the vegetables. She was wrapped in a dirty old blanket and coughing as if her lungs might explode.

Owen swallowed the lump in his throat. He pulled his purse from his inside coat pocket, loosened the string, fished inside, and tossed the farmer a sovereign.

"This is far too generous of ye, me lord," the man said with tears in his bleary eyes.

Owen nodded at him. "Think nothing of it, sir. Just see to it that your daughter receives the care she needs."

"I surely will, me lord. Me wife thanks ye and I thank ye."

Owen glanced back into the cart in time to see the little girl close her eyes and drift back to sleep.

Owen paid his own toll and kicked Apollo's flanks to set the horse in a gallop toward town. He needed to get back immediately to prepare for the ball. But as he rode, he knew for certain that child's image would haunt him.

CHAPTER SIX

That evening, Owen stood in the Duke of Huntley's town house at a bloody ball planned in anticipation of him wooing the duke's daughter, and Owen had yet to see the lady in question.

And he was bloody well getting impatient. Owen was used to being the one making ladies wait for his arrival, not the other way around. As a result, he was becoming increasingly surly. He glanced around the large, crowded ballroom. Where was a footman with some brandy when one needed it?

"Where is this blasted girl?" he whispered to his sister, Cassandra, who had just arrived with her husband, Swifdon, at her side. Cassandra had floated in looking fresh and pretty in lavender silk, her blond hair piled atop her head and a stunning row of diamonds around her neck. Cassandra had never been a disappointment to their parents. Quite the opposite, actually, she'd been their favorite child. Right until she'd tried to marry a mere captain in the army, regardless of the fact that he was the second son of an earl. Until, that is, Julian's older brother was murdered in France and the captain conveniently turned into an earl overnight. Cassandra and Julian had been devastated, but that unfortunate turn of events had recaptured the Monroes' interest and approval. Funny, that. But despite the difference in their sex and circumstance, Owen had always loved his younger sister, even if they hadn't been particularly close as children. He would do anything for Cass and she, him. He didn't doubt it.

"I don't see her. You do remember what she looks like, don't you, Owen?" Cass asked with hint of humor in her voice.

Owen tapped a finger against his temple. "She's blond, isn't she?" He couldn't remember. And he'd been testing his memory all week over it. His regular set of friends had proved no help, of course. They didn't remember the look of one particular little Society miss any more than he did. Instead, at the hells, they'd done nothing but unmercifully tease him about being caught by the parson's noose and offered him another drink and another hand of cards. Both of which he'd readily accepted. As usual.

"No. She's not blond at all. Her hair is dark brown," Cass said. "And you've been introduced before, so it would be odd for me to attempt to introduce you again. Do try to search your memory."

Swifdon snorted. "Excellent start, Monroe."

Owen rolled his eyes. "Fine. Just point her out when you see her, won't you? I need to get this over with." He was still searching for a footman. A duke, of all people, should bloody well have more footmen at hand.

Cass shook her head. "What a romantic."

"If you don't like my methods, why have you come?" Owen scowled at his sister.

Cass shrugged. "You're in a fine mood tonight. But if

you must know, Mother asked me to. She insisted that we have a good showing. I fear she's worried for the Monroe reputation."

Swifdon laughed aloud at that.

Owen glanced around for a footman again. A drink was long overdue. "Of course they wanted to emphasize that *I'm* not the only family member. What a disgrace *that* would be."

Cass frowned. "I only meant—"

Poor Cass. His sweet sister. She always believed the best of him despite every bit of evidence to the contrary. "No. I understand," Owen replied. "No need to explain. Besides, I'm hardly worried. If the duke and duchess didn't approve of me, they wouldn't be discussing the marriage contract with our estimable father already, now, would they?"

Cass inclined her head toward Owen. "True, but I don't believe it's the duke and duchess whom you need to impress. It's Lady Lavinia herself."

Owen gave his sister his most infamous grin. "I've never had a bit of trouble charming ladies."

Cass's blond brow arched. "I fear you may have met your match with Lavinia. She has a reputation for being a bit . . . difficult."

Owen eyed his brother-in-law. Swifdon coughed into his hand, but Owen strongly suspected it was done in an effort to cover his laughter.

"Yes, I've heard as much," Owen replied to Cass. "Difficult, eh?"

"Just a bit . . . prickly," Cass replied.

"No matter." Owen's grin widened. "I've found few ladies who can resist my charms. When I *choose* to be charming, that is."

"So modest, dear brother," Cass said, rolling her eyes.

"Though I must admit, I'm looking forward to your interactions with Lady Lavinia. I cannot wait to see if she can, ahem, resist your charms. I think it's high time you settled down, you know."

"Ah, the refrain of the married. They always think everyone else should marry as well," Owen replied.

"It isn't half bad, Monroe. You really should try it. Though it makes all the difference when it's done with the correct partner." Swifdon pulled his wife's gloved hand to his lips and kissed it, his eyes shining with what Owen could only assume was love.

Owen pressed a hand to his flat abdomen. "Blast. I had too much to drink last night, Swifdon. Don't induce my nausea."

A footman walked past just then, carrying a silver tray filled with champagne glasses. "Ah, there you are, my good man," Owen called out.

Swifdon snorted. "I thought you said you had too much to drink last night."

Owen grabbed one glass for himself and one for Cass. Swifdon followed suit. "I did have too much to drink last night, which is why I'm sorely in need of *another* drink at present," Owen said with a grin, downing the contents of his glass quickly.

Cass frowned at her brother and slapped him on the shoulder with her fan. "Don't be so—" She stopped short, staring at something beyond Owen's shoulder. Owen turned to look.

"There she is," Cass breathed.

"Who?" Owen saw only a room full of ladies and gentlemen in a dazzling array of colorful evening attire. No one in particular stood out.

"Lady Lavinia, of course," Cass replied, rolling her eyes again.

Owen's gaze scanned the room "Where?"

"She's over by the potted palm. I believe she's talking to her sister." Cass nodded toward the far end of the room.

Owen glanced over to the potted palm that rested in a corner where two dark-haired young ladies were speaking. He squinted but could not see either's face. Blast. "Which one is she?"

"Really?" Cass's face wore an exasperated expression, and her free hand rested on her hip.

"I cannot see their faces," Owen protested.

Cass sighed and nodded toward the two. "The one in peach."

Owen wrinkled his nose. "Do you mean orange?"

Cass snapped shut her fan and expelled a deep breath. "I mean peach."

Owen turned back to look. Fine. The other girl was wearing light blue, at any rate. He handed his empty champagne glass to another footman. "I'll be back."

"Best of luck, old chap." Swifdon clapped him on the back.

"I don't need luck," Owen replied with yet another grin. He straightened his shoulders, lifted his chin, and took off toward the potted palm. If he could get this over with quickly enough, he might be able to salvage this evening and get in a rousing game of cards at one of the hell clubs on the other end of town.

He casually strolled over to where the ladies were speaking. The one in orange quickly turned and made a funny little squeaking sound.

The one in blue turned to look at him. She was a beauty, tall and thin with dark hair and blue eyes that seemed to contain . . . hostility. In fact, she looked entirely unimpressed. It was not a look he was used to seeing from a lady. Thank heavens it was the one in orange he was after. He turned his gaze toward her. She was shorter with an eye-catching bosom, and curves that made his hand itch to caress them. Moreover, she had a twinkle in her eye that said she found their meeting . . . amusing. Why?

"Ladies," he said, bowing at the waist and giving them his most persuasive smile, the same one that had been known to charm the stays off many a lady of the *ton*. He'd been told more than once that his dimple could be practically irresistible.

"My lord?" the one in orange said amiably. The twinkle remained in her eye.

"And you are?" the blue lady said, arching a dark brow and curling her lip.

He straightened back to his full height. "It wounds me that you don't remember me, my lady."

She did not present her hand. "Be that as it may, I don't," she responded. Owen fought the urge to shudder. He glanced back and forth between the two again. The lady in orange couldn't possibly be Lady Lavinia. The one in blue certainly seemed the more *difficult* of the two. *That* one seemed like a viper. He'd do well to steer clear of her. She might be his future sister-in-law, but that didn't mean they needed to spend much time in each other's company. He turned his attention to the orange.

"I am Lord Owen Monroe," he announced. After all, it seemed fair that they didn't remember him either. Until Cass had pointed her out, he hadn't remembered Lavinia himself. No bother.

"I know who you are," the lady in orange said, smiling up at him with a dreamlike expression on her round face. Upon second look, she *was* a beautiful little thing.

Smaller than her sister but infinitely more appealing, with wavy dark hair and the most warm, appealing brown eyes framed by thick black lashes.

He smiled at her. Why had his father thought this might prove difficult? Why, the girl was already practically eating from his palm. "That makes it infinitely easier for me to ask you to take a turn around the room with me."

She blushed beautifully. "You want to walk?" She pointed at herself. "With me?"

He chuckled. "Yes, my lady. If you would do me the honor." He bowed again and then held out his arm.

The lady in blue gave him a strained pinched look and addressed her sister. "Go on, then. I'll be at the refreshment table."

"Very well." The orange beauty put her hand on his arm. Marriage to her wouldn't be so bad. She was not only lush but she seemed biddable, too. The perfect combination.

He covered her hand with his larger one. She was a bit too stiff, too anxious. He could tell by the rigid way in which she held her arm, the slight shaking of her palm on his sleeve. Owen was used to ladies who danced effortlessly, who flirted effortlessly, who laughed at his bawdy jests, and drank a bit too much wine. These balls for innocents were quite a different affair altogether. They were full of nervous would-be wives who shook as if they might break.

"Are you frightened?" he ventured.

"No. Why?" But the alacrity with which she'd said those two words belied their truth.

He shrugged casually. "I don't know. You seem a bit . . . anxious."

"Anxious? Me? No!" Again, the words were uttered far

too quickly, and her chest was rising and falling rapidly, indicating that her breathing was increasing. Though he had to admit he was enjoying the view of her décolletage, which was on full display. He could see it well, since he was a full head taller than she.

"Not anxious?" he asked, slowing their pace a bit, hoping to put her at ease.

"N-n-not at all." She pushed up her chin, and Owen had to give her a mental point for her bravery. She was clearly filled with nerves but didn't want to admit it. Well played, Lady Lavinia. Courting her in the span of a month was going to be a simple task indeed. He had to wonder, however, if she knew he was her intended after all. Why else was she so full of nerves? He sighed and decided not to give it another thought. Perhaps it was merely her disposition. Father had sworn the lady knew nothing about their intended courtship.

"So, tell me, my lady. How are you enjoying the ball?" he asked, staring deeply into her eyes. He'd yet to find a lady who wasn't enthralled with his dark blue gaze.

She glanced away first. He'd won.

"I like it very well," she said with the twinge of a tremor in her voice. "Though I don't think my sister is enjoying herself much."

"It's kind of you to have such regard for your sister."

"It's rather a pastime in our family," she replied.

Owen narrowed his eyes on her. Now, *that* was an interesting thing to say. Perhaps Lady Lavinia wasn't so vapid as he'd expected her to be. She certainly hadn't proved difficult. Not yet, at least. Obviously, everyone had been exaggerating her temper.

He put his hand on her elbow and pulled her a bit closer to see how she would react. Surely she wouldn't slap him or throw a fit here in a crowded ballroom.

Instead, she sucked in her breath sharply but otherwise remained as stiff as a board. Nothing difficult about her. He resumed their walk.

"Your sister is younger, is she not?" Owen ventured. "Just made her come-out recently? Perhaps she's yet to develop a taste for this type of amusement."

The lady in orange shook her head. "Oh no, Lavinia is my older sister."

First, Owen nearly tripped. Then he froze. Very bad form. He composed himself before leaning toward her. He *must* have heard her incorrectly. "What did you say?" He leaned even closer to ensure he'd hear correctly this time.

"I said Lavinia is older. By three years. Why, I've only just made *my* come-out this past spring myself."

Owen pressed his lips together. The diminutive brunette at his side continued to walk and he matched her steps as if in a trance. Now, *this* was a pickle. How in heaven's name would he extract himself from this error? "Do you mean to say that you're *not* Lady Lavinia Hobbs?"

"No, of course not. I'm Lady Alexandra Hobbs." She laughed. "And I must say I don't think you've done quite a good enough job of impressing Lavinia so far. Mother tells me you mean to marry her."

CHAPTER SEVEN

As soon as their turn about the room came to an end and Lord Owen had thanked her charmingly, Alexandra hurried back over to hide behind the potted palm near Lavinia. He hadn't known it, but Lord Owen Monroe had saved her from an exceedingly unpleasant conversation with her sister earlier. One in which Lavinia had been denigrating the looks and clothing choices of every lady at the ball, in addition to her usual rant against bluestockings and any females who chose to better their minds. She'd just launched into a similar rant against gentlemen with strong political views when Lord Owen arrived and clearly mistook Alexandra for Lavinia.

For a moment, an awful, wonderful moment, Alexandra actually believed that he'd meant to ask *her* to walk with him, that he knew who she was and had actually chosen her. But it became clear soon enough that that wasn't the case, and while her heart plummeted into her slippers, she was still fond enough of a good jest that she looked forward to the outcome of the little debacle.

The look on Lord Owen's face when he discovered he'd asked the wrong sister to walk with him had been ever so amusing. Even more amusing? Lavinia's anticipated reaction to Owen reappearing to correct his error. If Alexandra didn't miss her guess, that was precisely what he meant to do.

She watched as he grabbed two glasses of champagne from the tray of a passing footman and downed them both in quick succession. Alexandra smiled to herself. Drinking to excess? Check.

With a determined look in his eye that Alexandra could see even from her vantage point, Owen scanned the ballroom, spotted Lavinia, and stalked toward her. Alexandra's smile widened. Overbearing? Certainly. If Alexandra didn't miss her second guess, Owen was about to be exceedingly overbearing.

She held her breath and pushed her back against the wall as he approached, hoping he would not see her behind the tree. Lavinia was standing with Lady Sarah Highgate. The two were politely talking. Though from what Alexandra could overhear, Lady Sarah wasn't any fonder of her sister's negative words than she had been. Their conversation ended abruptly when Owen marched up. The click of his shoes against the parquet floor stopped, indicating his arrival. Alexandra forced herself to lean forward just a bit and peered through the fronds.

"My lady," he said to Lavinia, bowing.

Lavinia regarded the future earl down the length of her nose, her lips pressed tightly together. "My lord?" she intoned haughtily. "Back so soon? I haven't seen Alexandra, if you're looking for her."

"I am not," he said in a voice Alexandra could tell was designed to flatter.

Lavinia sighed, then flourished a hand toward Lady Sarah. "May I introduce Lady Sarah Highgate?"

"My pleasure, my lady." Owen's voice remained polite as he exchanged niceties with Lady Sarah, bowing over her hand.

"Lady Sarah is unattached," Lavinia continued, pointing her nose in the air. "Perhaps *she* would like to take a turn about the room with you." She gave him a tight smile. "Though you might have a bit of competition. The Marquess of Branford is rumored to be making an appearance here tonight, and he is extremely enamored of Lady Sarah already."

Alexandra cringed. Oh, Lavinia had really got her back up this time.

Poor Lady Sarah, who was absolutely gorgeous with black hair and light green eyes, blushed to her roots. Alexandra wanted to reach out and squeeze Sarah's arm in sympathy. Let it never be said that Lavinia didn't have a penchant for embarrassing others.

"Oh, no. No, he's not. I'm—," Lady Sarah stammered.

"Pish-posh," Lavinia replied, plucking at the overly ornate blue reticule that dangled from her wrist. The one she'd insisted have bangles, lace, *and* embellished embroidery. "Everyone knows you're the belle of the Season, Sarah. Admit it." There was an undeniable undercurrent of jealousy in Lavinia's voice.

Lady Sarah shook her head vigorously, so vigorously that one of her dark curls popped out of her coiffure and bounced along her forehead. "Oh, no, not at all. I—I must go, actually. I'm afraid my next dance is spoken for."

"I'm sorry to hear that," Lord Owen replied, smiling benevolently at the harried Lady Sarah. "But indeed, I did come to ask *you* to dance, Lady Lavinia." Uh-oh. Lavinia hated dancing, but how could poor Lord Owen know that? He gave Lavinia a charming smile that made Alexandra mentally sigh.

"Me?" Lavinia pointed to herself, a look of pure surprise on her pinched face.

"Yes," Lord Owen replied.

"Excuse me, won't you?" Lady Sarah hastened to add. "I look forward to speaking to you again sometime, Lady Lavinia. Good evening, Lord Owen, it's been a pleasure."

Good for Lady Sarah for escaping. Alexandra could only feel empathy for the poor young lady.

"Well?" Lord Owen asked Lavinia as soon as Lady Sarah hastened off.

Lavinia crinkled up her nose in that way of hers that made it seem as if she'd just smelled something exceedingly disagreeable. "Are you *certain* you wish to dance with *me,* Lord Owen?"

He bowed. "Of course. Why would you question my sincerity?"

Lavinia's voice took on a rigid, condescending tone, one that Alexandra was only too familiar with. "I don't know. Perhaps it's because earlier I got the distinct impression that you had forgotten my name." Her smile tightened further. Alexandra wrung her hands. Lavinia looked a bit like an angry skeleton when she smiled.

Lord Owen's voice rose a bit. "Of course not, my lady. How could I forget one as radiant as you?"

"Radiant? Did you actually say 'radiant'?" Lavinia's laugh was a derisive snort.

Alexandra winced again. Lavinia could be ruthless when she was annoyed by someone. Which was quite a long list of people, actually.

Lord Owen's voice took on an edge of impatience. "Will you make me repeat my request, my lady?"

"What was your request again?" Lavinia said, studying her slippers.

"Will you do me the honor of dancing with me?" His voice was definitely tight now, but still he smiled his most charming smile—the one that made Alexandra's knees decidedly weak. Oh, how could her sister say no to that? And him with that distracting dimple in his cheek? Alexandra wanted to burst through the palm and say yes herself. Instead, she bit the inside of her lip and leaned closer in order to hear more efficiently.

"I find it interesting, Lord Owen, that you seem so keen upon dancing this evening," Lavinia continued, crossing her arms over her chest.

Alexandra nearly groaned. This was it. Lavinia was going to deliver a crushing setdown. She was famous for delivering crushing setdowns, usually directly after she crossed her arms over her chest.

"Why's that?" came Owen's innocent reply.

"I've never known you to be much of one for dancing with young ladies at balls."

There was that knee-weakening smile again. "If I have not been keen upon dancing, my lady, perhaps it is because until now I had no hope that *you* would consent to be my partner." He bowed. Alexandra nearly swooned.

Lavinia laughed. Out loud. Long and overly loud. When she finished laughing, she said, "I don't know what gave you the hope that I might consent." She lifted her chin. "You're known for your charm, Lord Owen, or so I've heard, but I must ask you, do silly statements such as your last one ever truly work on the other members of my sex?"

Lord Owen's face paled for just a moment. He looked as if he'd swallowed a bug. But as quickly as it had dimmed, his grin returned. "I take it you don't find me charming, Lady Lavinia?" He eyed her warily now.

"Not in the least." Lavinia stuck out her elbow, and it nearly poked Alexandra through the palm. "Though you might charm my sister. She's easily impressed."

Alexandra had to clap her hand over her mouth to keep from squeaking in indignation at that statement.

Lord Owen slid his other hand into his pocket. "My pride is wounded."

Lavinia snorted. "I doubt it. I'm not entirely certain you're capable of wounded pride."

"I assure you, I am." He straightened his broad shoulders. "Now, must I ask you to dance a third time?"

"Save your breath, my lord," Lavinia replied, tugging at her long white glove. "The answer is no."

"No?" he repeated. "I don't understand."

"Not familiar with the word, my lord? Why does that not surprise me? It's the opposite of yes. However, let me tell you what *I* understand."

He still looked wary, but he nodded jerkily. "By all means."

"I understand that your sudden interest in me has more to do with your pocket than with any of *my* charms, considerable though they may be. I understand that until you took a turn about the room with Alexandra earlier, who no doubt set you straight, you'd in fact forgotten my name. I understand that our misguided parents are much more interested in our match than you and I could ever be, evidenced by my mother's inviting you here and recently informing me that you were considered quite a good catch when heretofore she'd often referred to you as a drunken lout, and finally, Lord Owen, I understand that I intend to leave you now. Perhaps you can locate a lady who finds you infinitely more charming than I do. No doubt it won't

be an easy task, but I wish you luck." And with that, Lavinia turned on her heel and flounced away like an
angry, flushed bluebird.

Lord Owen stood there, blinking, a completely confused look marring his fine features as if he had no idea
what had just happened.

"Blast and damnation," he muttered to the potted
palm. "Difficult? She's the bloody Spanish Inquisition."

Alexandra's smile was back. Cursing? Check.

Alexandra had seen enough. If she'd had any indication that Lavinia might actually welcome Owen's suit, Alexandra had intended to give him up, or at least to refrain
from interfering with their courtship. But not only had the
last several moments proved to her that her sister was entirely uninterested in the match, it was also obvious to
Alexandra that Lavinia and Owen did not suit. *She* and
Owen, however . . . Alexandra didn't mind cursing, bold-
ness, or dancing, and she welcomed drinks. Especially
champagne. Now that she thought on it, where *was* a
glass of champagne?

Oh yes, she would feel no guilt whatsoever in pursuing Lord Owen despite her parents' intentions. Besides,
hadn't she spent years attempting to be more daring and
adventurous? The plan that was quickly forming in her
head was both daring *and* adventurous and would give
her the opportunity to spend time with Lord Owen Monroe. A great deal of time, perhaps.

Lord Owen turned to walk away, and the words flew
from Alexandra's throat before she had a chance to examine them.

"Wait," she called. "I can help you."

CHAPTER EIGHT

Owen blinked and turned back around at the sound of the female voice. It seemed to be coming from the large green palm. The plant was speaking to him? He hadn't had *that* much to drink tonight. He squinted and ducked, peering through the fronds. "Who's there?"

A small female form waved to him from behind the botanical mass. She was beckoning him to join her behind the tree. "It's me, Alexandra." Lady Lavinia's younger sister stood there, blinking up at him with an adorable little half smile. "Er, Lady Alexandra," she corrected with the hint of a blush staining her pale cheeks.

Owen moved behind the palm to join her. Apparently, the young lady didn't want the others in the ballroom to see them speaking to one another. Or was it just her waspish sister whom she didn't want to see? He couldn't blame her there, having just been stung by the wasp herself.

"Lady Alexandra," he repeated once he'd joined her behind the palm. "It's a pleasure to see you again. I regret to think that you overheard my unfortunate conversation with your sister just now."

"Yes, I heard it all." She sighed. "I have an awful habit of eavesdropping, to be honest with you. But I can help you."

Owen couldn't repress his smile. He liked that she admitted so readily to her crime. That was refreshing. He'd been around far too many women who prevaricated and demurred. Not to mention, her offer intrigued him. How did this little scrap of a female think *she* could help *him*? He narrowed his eyes on her. "Help me what?"

Her look was entirely matter-of-fact. "Help you court Lavinia."

Despite their location, he glanced back and forth over both shoulders to ensure that no one could overhear them. He eyed her cautiously. "What do you mean?"

"You got off to a poor start with her. Lavinia doesn't like it when men challenge her. She especially doesn't like it when a man fails to notice her first."

"Notice her first?" Owen echoed.

"You asked me to walk with you," she replied.

That's because you're infinitely more appealing than your shrew of a sister.

"You've begun on entirely the wrong foot with her," Alexandra continued, shaking her head at him sadly as if she felt sorry for him. How many times had this lovely girl had to apologize for her sister's rude behavior?

"So it seems," Owen allowed, noting that Lady Alexandra smelled like strawberries and sunshine and she was distracting him with the little tug of a smile that never seemed to be far from her lips.

"I can tell you what she does like, make it easier for you to win back her good graces."

Owen arched both brows. Well, this was fortunate. Not

only was Lady Lavinia's sister pretty and friendly, it seemed she was helpful as well. He severely doubted that Lady Lavinia *had* any good graces to win. But he did enjoy a challenge, and Lady Lavinia was proving that if nothing else. Not to mention she held the future of his allowance in her irascible grasp.

"Excellent," he replied to her sister. "What does she like?"

A determined look came into Lady Alexandra's dark sparkling eyes. "I'll tell you . . . for a price."

Owen regarded the brunette down the length of his nose. Now, *this* was interesting. What could an innocent like Lady Alexandra Hobbs possibly want from *him*? But again, he couldn't help his smile. A bargain? It was exactly the type of thing he might offer, given the right circumstances. He rarely did anything unless he had something to gain or perhaps had lost a bet. He regarded her with increasing interest. At the very least, she'd managed to capture his attention. That was rare for an innocent. "A price, eh? What price?"

She swallowed hard before she responded to him, her throat working up and down. "I want you to come to the next large *ton* ball . . . and dance with me."

Owen's brows flew together. "Come to—? And dance with—? My dear girl, whyever for?"

She pressed her hands together and began to wring them in a charming manner. She, too, glanced over both shoulders to ensure they would not be overheard despite their location behind the palm. "I've been a complete failure this Season. Mother is beside herself. I was forced to cross a smashing debut off my list, but that's neither here nor there." She fluttered her hand in the air also charmingly, and Owen got another whiff of strawberry. Was she hiding the fruit in her reticule? Somehow she seemed like the airy sort who might. "I, er, have my eye on a particular gentleman, you could say," she continued in a rushed whisper. "Though he has failed to notice me."

Owen straightened his already perfectly straight cravat. "What do you think I can do to help *that*?"

She lifted her chin, and his admiration for her grew. She had pluck. He liked that. He could tell she wasn't about to give up. On the contrary, she was preparing to plead her case. "I'm perfectly aware of your reputation, Lord Owen. You're the biggest rakehell in London. But you're also immensely popular. A bit of interest from you could entirely make my reputation."

"Yes, and not necessarily for the better." Was she serious? She seemed to know a lot about him. Surprising for an innocent, but still . . . inappropriate. This young woman had absolutely no idea what she was asking for.

She leveled her dark gaze on him and Owen found it a bit off-putting. She certainly had an intriguing way about her. It was as if she already had everything planned weeks, if not years, in advance. She was like a general executing a strategy. For Owen, who usually didn't have the evening planned, let alone the next morning, she was compelling indeed.

"I disagree," she stated frankly. More frank than he'd ever known an innocent to be, that was certain. "At present, I'm a no one. A wallflower. No gentleman looks twice at me. If you were to show me a bit of interest, I've no doubt my stock in the marriage mart would increase tenfold."

He regarded her down the length of his nose. Well, well, well. What did he have here? An innocent with a spine of steel? How *very* interesting. And the girl did have a point. For all that he was considered fast, he was also extremely eligible . . . and popular. And he *never* paid attention to innocents. Any interest shown in Lady Alexandra would be sure to increase her cachet. No doubt the entire ballroom was already abuzz about the time they'd spent walking together earlier. He couldn't argue with her, really, and he had to admire not only her forethought but also her tenacity. Why, most silly young things would have run off by now. Where was the nervousness she'd shown when they were walking earlier? It seemed to have entirely disappeared. He liked her all the better for it.

But how serious was she? Could the girl be dissuaded? Was this nothing more than a burst of false bravado on her part? He had to find out. He brushed at his sleeve. "What if I told you I'm not in the business of dancing with innocents?"

"You didn't seem to mind my company earlier," she pointed out, crossing her arms over her distracting bosom.

Well done, Lady Alexandra. "That was different. I was trying to—" He stopped himself, chagrined. There was no gentlemanly way to say it.

"Court my sister, who you thought was me?" Lady Alexandra finished prettily, batting her dark, silky eyelashes at him.

He bit the inside of his cheek to keep from smiling. By God, the girl was not only intelligent, but bold besides. He couldn't help but like that about her, too. He'd always preferred honesty and forthrightness himself.

"Yes," he replied, marveling over the most frank conversation he'd had at a social event in some time. "So you see, as I said, I'm not in the business of dancing with innocents."

Lady Alexandra shrugged and tapped her fingertips along the sides of her crossed arms. "I'm not in the business of taming rogues. I suppose we'll both have to try something new."

Owen had to struggle to keep his jaw from dropping. Taming rogues? The girl was bold, indeed. He'd never had someone call him a rogue. Not to his face, at least. But she had to be reasoned with. She didn't fully comprehend what she was proposing. He inclined his head toward her. "If I do what you're asking, there will be gossip."

Another slight shrug from her. "From what I hear of your reputation, you've never let gossip stop you before."

He couldn't help his bark of laughter. In addition to being bold, she was entertaining. "My reputation precedes me even with someone so young?"

"Yes, and I'm not that young. I'm nearly nineteen."

Oh, God. She *was* young. And completely out of her depth.

"How do you think your sister will like it if she sees me with you again?" he asked. There. She had to see the logic in *that*.

"Don't worry. I'll manage Lavinia."

"You will, will you?" He eyed her up and down. She was a determined little baggage.

"Yes. I'll tell her that all you talked about the entire time you were with me was her."

Owen frowned. "That will work?"

"Of course. Lavinia already thinks everyone would rather be talking about her than anyone else."

Owen rubbed his temple, where a headache was beginning to form. "She sounds delightful."

Lady Alexandra sighed. "She really can't help it, you know? Mother and Father have treated her like a royal princess for most of her life."

"And how did they treat you?" He tried to read the emotions that played across her expressive face.

Lady Alexandra glanced away. She shook her head. "Will you accept my proposal or not?"

Owen made a mental note to explore that topic with her again sometime. "If I did accept your proposal, how do you suggest we manage it?"

She blinked at him. "Manage what?"

He narrowed his eyes on her. She couldn't be *that* innocent. Could she? "Our meetings, of course."

Lady Alexandra coughed. She pressed her palm against her throat. "Our meetings?" she finally managed.

"Yes. You have a great deal to tell me, I've no doubt, and I have a great deal to teach you."

Her pretty brown eyes looked as if they might bug from her head. "Teach me?"

He slid his hands down his impeccably tailored coat. "That's right."

Her breathing increased again. She was nervous after all. And her décolletage was still distracting. Strawberries were suddenly making his mouth water.

"What do you have to teach me?" she asked.

That was *too* leading a question. He discarded half a dozen inappropriate replies. No. He'd keep this entirely respectable. He might be a rogue, but he wasn't about to be indecent with an innocent. He arched a brow. "How to dance properly, for one thing."

Alexandra sputtered. "How to dance properly? I wasn't aware that I dance improperly. Besides, when have you ever seen me dance?"

"I haven't. I've no doubt the dancing itself is adequate at present, but if we're going to turn you into the belle of the Season, you must learn to dance with me and make me feel as if I'm the only man in the room."

Her eyes widened. "I never said I desired to be the belle of the Season. Lady Sarah Highgate—"

"Ah, ah, ah. Where's that pluck of yours I saw earlier? Don't set your sights too low. Aim to become the belle of the Season. Besides, if you're seen with me, you'll *be* the belle of the Season, trust me."

"You're arrogant," she said, but her lips were definitely curved in the hint of a smile.

He shrugged. "You need me to be."

She stared back at him. "I was going to say I liked it about you."

He eyed her carefully. "You're nothing like your sister."

"Good thing for you."

He snorted a laugh at that. "Does that mean you'll allow me to teach you how to dance properly? Make me feel as if I'm the only man in the room?"

"How do you suggest I do that?"

He met her gaze. "There are many subtleties to it. You must look into my eyes. You must laugh at my jests, but not all of them. You must . . . tempt me."

Alexandra went hot and cold. Owen Monroe had obviously never seen her dancing. If he had, he could probably tell she spent her time on the dance floor merely trying not to step upon her partner's feet. If she were dancing with Owen, looking into his eyes would be far too much to ask of her. And *tempt* him? What did that mean? It sounded scandalous. She liked the sound of it.

"You must seem vaguely bored by my attentions," he continued.

Vaguely bored? Good heavens, she wasn't an actress. How would she ever manage even to *pretend* that she was vaguely bored by him?

She bit her lip. "I'm not certain about—"

"Of course you're not," he replied. "That's why you need my help. The reason you've failed to launch properly—and forgive me, but most likely the reason this chap you're interested in has yet to come up to scratch— is because you're too eager, too interested, too . . . available."

Alexandra gasped. "That sounds positively indecent."

"Not at all." His grin was wicked. "But if we have any hope of convincing the *ton* that I have an interest in you, let alone convincing anyone else, you must become much more intriguing and mysterious quite quickly, and that begins with dancing properly."

"You'll be—" She swallowed the lump in her throat. "—teaching me how to dance?"

He eyed her up and down, and Alexandra had the mortifying thought that he was picturing her without her gown. "Among other things. So, tell me. How will we manage to meet?"

Alexandra pressed her clammy palms against her skirts. "I'm able to slip away from home once in a while in the afternoons, but I'm not certain where we would meet."

"You sneak out of your house?" He stared at her as if she were some sort of a mythical creature, like a faun.

"Yes," she replied.

"Where do you go?"

"That is none of your business, my lord."

Lord Owen chuckled. "Indeed, it is not." He contemplated the matter for a moment, rubbing his chin. He finally snapped his fingers. "I've got it. Do you know my sister—Cassandra, Lady Swifdon?"

"Yes. Not well, of course, but we've met."

"Excellent. Pay a call on her tomorrow afternoon at two o'clock."

Alexandra frowned. "I don't understand."

"I'll be there. Bring your maid with you. It will all seem perfectly suitable."

"But won't your sister find it odd that—?"

"If you'd known some of the antics my sister and her friends got up to before she married Julian—er, the Earl of Swifdon—you wouldn't ask that question." Lord Owen grinned at Alexandra again, and she couldn't look away from that fetching dimple. "Suffice it to say that Cass will understand."

Alexandra nodded. It was a risk and her stomach was tied in knots just contemplating it, but she was the one who had started this game and she would see it through. Besides, what better opportunity would there be for the two of them to spend time together? Owen needed the chance to learn that she was, in fact, the most compatible match for him, and she needed the opportunity to confirm that he was indeed the man she wanted to marry. Not to mention this was all very dashing and adventurous of her. Thomas would be proud. She couldn't resist Lord Owen's offer. She smiled up at him hesitantly. "Very well. I'll meet you tomorrow afternoon."

"Perfect." His white teeth flashed in his grin.

"I shall tell you everything you need to know about Lavinia, and you will . . . teach me how to dance."

His grin was wicked again. "Among other things."

CHAPTER NINE

Owen couldn't sleep. He rolled onto his back in his over-sized bed. The dark blue satin sheets slid beneath him and he punched at the down pillow under his head. Perhaps his difficulty in finding rest was because he was in his own bed for the first time in half a dozen nights. His bachelor's quarters in St. James's were adequate, but he much preferred to be in the company of the lady of his choice. Spending his time at a debut ball this evening had severely limited his options, and by the time his discussion with Alexandra Hobbs had ended, he'd decided that he no longer had a desire to go to one of the gaming hells. Odd but true.

The night's events played through his mind. Cass needed spectacles. She had told him Lavinia was the one in the peach gown. She was clearly wrong, and as a result, he'd completely bungled his first attempt at wooing Lady Lavinia. Given her demeanor, it didn't appear that it would be particularly easy to win back her good graces. The lady seemed like a shrew, honestly. Everyone said she was *difficult*. They'd obviously been *under-estimating* the woman. Owen disliked shrews. He much preferred a lady who was open, happy, smiling, dancing, flirting. One like . . . Lady Alexandra. Minus the flirting, of course. She was a strawberry-scented breath of fresh air, compared to her sister. Not only that, but he also found himself more attracted to her physically than he was to her sister. Not that it mattered, but Lady Alexandra had the lush look that had always appealed to him. It had been only good fortune that she'd seemed so ready to help him. In exchange for *his* help, of course, but that only interested him more. Lady Alexandra was obviously someone who'd learned early in life that negotiation was a necessary skill that one must use to one's full advantage. Astute of her.

He had no compunction about making a deal with Lavinia's sister. They'd both be getting something they wanted out of it. He would receive the necessary information he needed to properly court Lavinia and hopefully bypass additional encounters with her prickly personality. Lady Alexandra would be gaining instant social standing due to his interest in her. A few dances at a few balls, and the collective tongue of the *ton* would be wagging.

He had only one concern: What if the plan backfired and Lavinia didn't appreciate him paying court to her sister, however innocently? Ladies tended to be quite sensitive to such things. Especially given the story Upton had told about the dinner party and the tapestry ripping. But if Lady Alexandra thought she could explain it adequately enough, he would have to trust her. Not that trust came easily to him. It did not. But frankly, he had little choice in the matter. His first attempt at wooing Lady Lavinia had been a dismal failure. Owen was not used to dismal failures. Not where women were concerned. Besides, he could tell Lady Lavinia himself that he was paying attention to her sister in order to get closer to her. That should feed her obviously large opinion of herself.

He groaned and rolled back to his stomach. This "finding a wife" business was already turning out to be more trouble than he'd bargained for. If only his father had chosen Lady Alexandra. She, at least, seemed reasonable. Though she apparently was enamored of some other chap. Owen yawned. No matter. He'd taken Lady Alexandra up on her proposal. By the end of the month, he had no doubts that he'd be successfully, if not happily, betrothed to Lady Lavinia Hobbs.

Alexandra wrapped her dressing gown tightly around her waist and made her way over to the window that looked down upon the square. Her father's town house was in the most highly sought-after corner of Mayfair, directly across from the park. She sighed. She'd grown up in a house of privilege, a house with money and servants and fine clothing and the best food. But loneliness still plagued her. If only she'd had her sister to play with—but Lavinia had been treated like a delicate doll, unable to soil her clothing or have a hair out of place. It had been the way of things in their household for nearly as long as Alexandra could remember. Alexandra understood why. When Lavinia was eight years old, she'd taken ill with a lung disease and nearly died. Alexandra recalled little about it other than how dark and quiet the house had been, how it had smelled like medicine, with doctors coming and going. Her parents had been pale and somber and alternated their days at Lavinia's bedside. The doctors had been so sure the little girl wouldn't make it, Father had commissioned the making of a small coffin. It was painted white and lined with pink satin with a silken pillow resting inside. It frightened five-year-old Alexandra terribly. After Lavinia pulled through, Father had had the coffin burned, and a great celebration ensued. Ever since, Lavinia had been indulged in every way possible. Alexandra had a vague memory of a sister who played with her and treated her well, but for years after her illness, Lavinia hadn't been allowed outdoors or anywhere that might make her ill, and she'd been catered to as if she were a tiny queen.

The duke and duchess mostly ignored their other two healthy children, as if they were afterthoughts. If it weren't for Thomas, Alexandra would have been entirely alone. Lavinia was the eldest and the most beautiful, the more highly valued daughter. Thomas was the only boy and heir to the dukedom, a marquess in his own right, which left Alexandra in her own set of circumstances. Less wanted, less desired, less special. She had learned to live with that. She had been fine with it, if not pleased, until her parents decided that Lavinia would marry Owen Monroe. Why? Of all men in London, why did it have to be him? There were plenty of other titled gentlemen who would rush to marry the eldest daughter of a duke if asked. Men to whom Lavinia might even be more welcoming.

Alexandra sank to the tufted ice-blue window seat and stared out into the darkness of the London night sky. It wasn't as if she could tell her parents her feelings. Not only would they dismiss them, but they would probably laugh at her as well. Imagine, little Alexandra thinking she should have the beau meant for Lavinia? Preposterous. To make things worse, her parents both insisted upon Lavinia's marrying first. She would find it unacceptable to be left on the shelf while her little sister took a groom. That hadn't been much of a problem until now, because with Alexandra's lackluster come-out, she was hardly in danger of receiving marriage proposals. But now, now when she wanted to woo Owen Monroe, not only would she not be allowed to, but even if it worked, Lavinia would have to find some other gentleman to marry first. *That* seemed unlikely because given her description and demands, Lavinia apparently wanted a man who didn't exist. One who loved to write poetry and sing ballads about her. One who was only courtly and courteous to her. One who would worship her and be equally interested in shopping for her fripperies on Bond Street as he was painting a portrait of her in her honor. Lavinia wanted a knight from a bygone era. At any rate, if that man did exist, he certainly wasn't Owen Monroe. It made Alexandra laugh even to consider Owen writing poetry or singing a ballad, and shopping for fripperies was entirely out of the question.

Regardless, if such a paragon did exist, where would Alexandra find him? Because now she was convinced that she would have to deliver Lavinia's perfect beau to her before she herself would be allowed to marry Owen, and that was if she could convince Owen that they were in fact perfect for each other. And were they?

Oh, it was all quite complicated and she'd made it more so by proposing that she be the one to teach Owen how best to court her sister. Perhaps someday, when they were happily married, he'd forgive her for her duplicity. Only one thing assuaged her guilt, and that was the fact that Owen and Lavinia were obviously not suited. How could Father not see that?

Alexandra mentally answered her own question. Her father cared only about social connections. As did her mother. Her parents may have told Lord Moreland that Owen needed to court Lavinia properly and gain her consent, but in the end, they would force the marriage if they had to. Alexandra knew it.

Alexandra traced her finger along the windowpane. Lord Owen Monroe. He'd seemed a bit surprised by some of the things she'd said to him tonight. Alexandra didn't blame him. It had to be a bit off-putting to have one's potential future sister-in-law offer to help you court her sister in exchange for a dance or three. Alexandra was nothing if not practical. She did want Owen to help her become sought after in Society. The ridiculous part was that she wanted to be sought after to gain *his* attention. What better way than to spend more time in his company? He'd invited her to his sister's house, and Alexandra was so excited and nervous about it, she couldn't sleep. Would Lady Swifdon think she was too forward? She hoped not. Cassandra Swift seemed quite kind and beautiful.

Her brother, Owen Monroe, however, might be thought to be a scoundrel, a rake, and a drunken lout, but he was exceedingly popular, the perfect person to assist Alexandra in leveraging her standing in Society. However, the truth was that he wasn't a scoundrel at all. He was a gentleman. A true gentleman. One who looked out for weaker people, like a twelve-year-old stable boy being harassed by two bucks.

Alexandra squeezed her arms around her middle. Tomorrow Owen would teach her to dance and she would teach him, what? Something Lavinia liked? Er, well, actually something that Lavinia didn't like. Something Lavinia detested. Alexandra said a brief prayer to the heavens to forgive her for her deceit. Oh, she'd tell him *some* truth. Some of it would actually help her case. The romantic gentleman part, for instance. The rest she would just have to extemporize. She would ask for his forgiveness later. In the meantime, let the teaching begin.

CHAPTER TEN

The knock on Swifdon's door sounded at precisely two o'clock the next afternoon. Owen had only just arrived himself minutes before. He was not an early riser. Never had been. He'd barely had time to bathe, dress, and find a meal before dashing over to his sister's house to meet Lady Alexandra for their first lesson. Somehow he'd known she would be prompt, exactly the way he was usually late. But today, for her, he'd made an effort.

Owen paced about Swifdon's foyer while the butler answered the door and ushered Lady Alexandra into the house. The smell of strawberries swirled into the foyer. She stood there, prim and proper in a bright yellow gown and matching bonnet, looking a bit uncertain but quite pretty with the afternoon sunlight touching one fair cheek. Her diminutive red-haired maid stood behind her, peeking around her mistress, a wary look on her face.

"Welcome," Owen said, grinning.

Lady Alexandra's throat worked and her dark eyes assessed him from head to toe.

Had the lady liked what she'd seen? Owen glanced down at his shining black top boots, biscuit-colored buckskin breeches, white shirt, emerald waistcoat, and dark gray overcoat. His snowy white cravat was expertly tied. He'd done it himself, waving off his valet and taking special care today. He'd always been known around town to have flawless style, and he'd certainly never had any reason to question it. But today, looking through Lady Alexandra's eyes, he found himself wondering if she would approve. Did she find him handsome or charming or dashing at all or was he just a means to an end for her to marry off her sister so she might marry, too?

He shook his head. Why did it matter? Why was he even questioning it? When had he ever given a toss what anyone else thought of him? Especially an innocent?

She took a few tentative steps farther into the foyer. Her maid dutifully followed.

Swifdon's butler cleared his throat then and offered to take the ladies' hats.

"I'm here to pay a call on Lady Swifdon," Lady Alexandra said in a quiet voice, presenting her card and removing her bonnet.

"Yes. I'll show you to her," Owen intoned. He waited until she and the maid had both handed their bonnets to the butler; then Owen took Lady Alexandra's hand and placed it atop his sleeve.

"Wait here, Hannah." Lady Alexandra glanced back at her maid and gave the woman a quick good-bye wave before allowing Owen to escort her down the corridor.

Of course, once beyond the prying eye of the butler, Owen took her to the ballroom instead of the drawing room.

"Wh-where's Lady Swifdon?" Lady Alexandra asked as soon as the door closed behind them and they were alone in the cavernous room. The enormous space was dimly lit and smelled like lemon polish and candlewax.

"I expect she's in the drawing room, receiving visitors," Owen replied with a laugh.

"Oh, I . . . I thought—"

"Don't worry. I told her you were coming. She'll say you were here with her if there is any gossip."

Lady Alexandra's shoulders relaxed and she expelled her breath.

"Are you nervous?" he asked. "There's no need to be."

"No." She snatched her hand away from his arm and moved several paces away from him. "I mean yes. I'm only sneaking away from my home to clandestinely meet with one of the *ton*'s most infamous rogues. There's no reason to be nervous."

She was funny. He liked that. "Surely, I'm the *most* infamous, not merely *one* of the most."

He could tell Lady Alexandra was suppressing a smile. He suddenly wanted to make her smile more, laugh even.

"For all that I admire my brother, Thomas, for being daring and adventurous, I cannot seem to help my nerves," she admitted.

"You mentioned yesterday that you've been known to sneak off in the afternoons. That sounds daring and adventurous to me."

"Oh, that—I—No. It's neither daring nor adventurous, I assure you."

Owen inclined his head toward her. "Very well, what can we do to calm your nerves, my lady?"

"Do you have any port wine? I always seem to enjoy it when I sneak a bit from Father's stash."

Owen nearly guffawed at that. "You sneak port?"

"Yes." She nodded matter-of-factly.

She was positively adorable. "Good God. I daresay you

could find something more tasty than port in your father's house."

Lady Alexandra wiggled her nose. "I picked it because I like the decanter it's in the best."

He tipped his head to the side and contemplated her. "A noble reason to be sure."

"And it smelled the least like poison."

"Another noble reason." Owen grinned at her. "You say you're not daring or adventurous, but that sounds like both to me."

"Please don't make fun of me," she said softly in a voice that told Owen she was not actually displeased with him. She appeared to take things in stride, this Lady Alexandra. No doubt an effect from having to live under the same roof with her "difficult" sister. "If you have no port wine," she continued, "I suppose I'll have to make do and calm my nerves some other way."

Owen bowed to her. "Perhaps you'll be more comfortable if we begin."

"Begin?"

"Yes, but first, what shall I call you?"

"Call me?"

"If we're to be friends, cohorts, you might even say, I find it quite formal to continue to refer to you as Lady Alexandra. You may call me Owen."

Her eyes widened. "Oh, that's quite informal."

"My dear, if I'm going to teach you to behave like the most sought-after lady in London, you'll need to get over a mere formality with a name."

Lady Alexandra cleared her throat. "Of course," she murmured. "You may call me Alexandra."

"Alexandra?" He posted his hands on both hips. "That still sounds awfully formal to me. Don't you have a nickname?"

"No, I don't. I—Well, Thomas calls me Al."

"Al," Owen repeated the word and then frowned. "Too short. Not nearly so lovely as you are. How about Alex?"

A blush stained her cheeks. "Alex?"

"Alex," he echoed, rolling the word around on his tongue. "Yes, it suits you perfectly. It has pluck. I shall call you Alex, if you have no objections."

She pushed a dark curl behind her ear. "Very well. It seems quite improper, but then again, you're not particularly known for being proper."

"I'm glad you agree." He grinned, leaning back against a large table near the wall and crossing his booted feet at the ankles. "Now, that's settled. You'll call me Owen and I'll call you Alex. I'm already feeling a kindred connection to you."

She blushed more deeply, gorgeously, and Owen had to glance away. It was not going to help things to become attracted to his business partner. Though it was a singularly unique experience for Owen to be in business with a female. Normally, the only business he conducted with the members of the opposite sex was that which was performed in bed. Alex was blinking up at him, her pretty face full of trust and innocence and—

Owen shook his head. It was time to change the subject. Perhaps they'd both feel more comfortable. "Why don't you tell me something about Lady Lavinia and I'll give you your first lesson in dancing properly."

"Very well." Alex paced in front of him, her hands folded tightly together. "As I said yesterday, to win Lavinia's heart, you must learn to comport yourself as a gentleman. A *romantic* gentleman."

"My dear girl, I don't even know what a '*romantic* gentleman' is."

Alex smoothed her hands down her skirts and blinked

at him. "He's the type who writes love ballads and sings them to his ladylove."

"His ladylove?" Owen's voice rose sharply, as did his eyebrow. "I'm honorable. Isn't that enough?"

Alex smiled and shook her head. "I'm afraid not. Not for Lavinia."

He rubbed his chin. "A gentleman, eh?"

"Yes, a gentleman. A romantic one. I'm certain you have it in you."

He laughed out loud. "I'm not certain I do. Not at all."

Again, Alex smiled at him—a smile that was entirely disarming. "I have faith in you."

The words Owen had been about to say caught in his throat. There was something poignant in the fact that this young woman, this stranger, had said something to him that his own father could not.

Owen pushed away the thought and moved from the table, turning in a circle. "Very well. What would a *romantic* gentleman do to properly court a lady?"

Alex patted her coiffure. "He would bring her gifts."

He gave a mock groan. "Must I?"

Alex crossed her arms over her chest and paced away from him. "Perhaps write her a sonnet."

Owen shook his head. "Not a chance."

Alex waved one hand in the air in a flourish. "Tell her that her eyes are the blue of heaven."

"Seriously, not a chance."

Alex stopped pacing, turned, and regarded him head-on. "At the very least, he should begin by asking *her* to take a turn about the room with him instead of her sister."

Owen tugged at his cuff. "Very funny. That was an honest mistake. By the by, does she enjoy a turn about the room?"

"Not particularly."

"Alex, is there anything that your sister actually *does* enjoy?"

"She quite enjoys gazing at herself in the mirror."

Owen groaned.

Alex fought her blush. No one called her Alex. Ever. Why did she like it when he did? And why was she already taking to the name herself? She shook her head. She had to concentrate on his questions about Lavinia and not on how good he looked in his skintight buckskin breeches or the fact that he smelled like a delicious combination of faint woodsmoke and soap. But this was why she'd come here, and she had to execute her plan. The threat of sonnets and poetry might not be enough. She tried to banish her guilt over the lie she was about to tell. She took a deep breath and crossed her fingers, which were hidden in her skirts. "Lavinia likes it when gentlemen are forceful, forthright."

Owen's eyebrows shot up. "Excellent. I am both. And?"

"And what?" How many things was he expecting her to tell him right away?

He came to stand near her, and Alex gulped as she realized how much taller he was than she. She hadn't been quite this close last night. Standing at his full height, he had to be at least three inches over six feet tall to her five feet five inches. Not to mention his broad shoulders distracted her.

"What else does she like?" he asked, jarring her from her thoughts.

Very well. He expected more than just one thing. She could do this. Alex sucked in a deep breath once more and searched her memory for her conversation with Lavinia. She kept her fingers crossed in her skirts so he couldn't see. "She greatly admires a man who can . . . handle his liquor."

His eyebrows hitched higher. "What in God's name is *that* supposed to mean?"

Alex shrugged. "It means the more drinking, the better."

He narrowed his eyes on her. "Well, *that* has never proved a problem for me, but are you quite serious?"

"Oh yes, quite." Alex tightened her crossed fingers until they ached. "Lavinia has mentioned it to me on more than one occasion how much she admires a man who enjoys liquor. We once encountered a gentleman who refused to so much as touch a drink. Religious reasons, you know? Lavinia was positively aghast."

Owen's brow was furrowed now. "I'm not certain which sort of religious reasons—"

"It was something quite rare," Alex hastened to add. Confound it. This was already more difficult than she'd thought. Owen was intelligent. Quite intelligent. He wasn't going to believe some of this, and she was a rubbish liar. She felt it best to remain adamant.

"I've heard of moderation—never practiced it, mind you," he added with a devilish grin. "But I've *heard* of it. I've never known anyone who entirely abstained, however."

Alex shook her head vigorously. "Oh, no. No moderation. Not for Lavinia. In fact, she once challenged two dinner guests to a drinking match." Alex said a silent prayer that she would not be struck dead by lightning for her flagrant lies.

Owen whistled. "Lady Lavinia drank, too?"

Now who was aghast? Alex managed a small but

effective laugh. "No. Of course not. But she did place a pound wager from her pin money on one of the chaps and won."

Alex's crossed fingers were getting sweaty. She was relatively certain her forehead was breaking out in a sweat, too. Guilt was not attractive. The truth was that *she* had been the one to challenge the two knights at the dinner party to the drink-off and had doubled her pin money. She'd also been scolded unmercifully by both her mother and Lavinia for her outrageous behavior. It had not been one of her finest moments, and her mother had insisted she would never find a proper husband if she continued to act like such a hoyden. Her mother was right. It was a good thing she didn't want a proper husband. She wanted Owen Monroe. She glanced at him to gauge whether he believed her story.

Owen stroked his chin with his thumb and forefinger. "I must say this news about her intrigues me. I wouldn't have expected Lady Lavinia to be fun-loving. In the least."

Alex swallowed the lump of guilt she feared would be permanently lodged in her throat. "Oh yes, Lavinia is ever so fun-loving." She'd nearly choked on that part. She glanced away, hoping the lie wasn't visible on her face.

"Surprising, to be sure," Owen said.

"My sister is full of surprises," she assured him with a firm nod. She tugged at the collar of her butter yellow gown. It was decidedly hot in the ballroom this afternoon.

Owen cocked his head to the side. "I suppose I can find a way to use that information to my advantage. Very well." He held out his arms. "Shall we dance?"

CHAPTER ELEVEN

Alex had thought she knew how to dance. That was until Owen Monroe took her into his arms and spun her around and around his sister's empty ballroom to a tune he hummed. Not only could the man dance, but he could also hum, keep time, and make her feel as if she were the only person in the room all simultaneously. It didn't matter that she *was* the only other person in the room. That was entirely beside the point.

She stepped on his foot only three times. In the first dance. He stopped humming and the dance came to an end. Alex backed away but kept a watchful eye on him, certain she'd see disapproval lurking in his cornflower blue eyes.

"I'm sorry," she murmured, pushing the tip of one slipper against the parquet floor. "I'm usually quite proficient at dancing. I don't know why I'm so clumsy today." *Yes, I do. I'm clumsy because you're gorgeous and I'm distracted by the thought of sticking my nose in your cravat and sniffing you.*

Owen chuckled. "You're still nervous, if I don't miss my guess."

"I suppose I am. A bit." She dropped her gaze to her slippers. *Nervous because you're so dastardly handsome, which is hardly my fault.*

He contemplated her for a moment. "You say your sister is fond of alcohol. How do you feel about the stuff? Besides port, I mean. Say, champagne?"

"I adore it!" She clapped her hand over her mouth. That had been far too emphatic and completely unladylike. Another reason her mother informed her regularly that she would be hard-pressed to find a decent suitor. "A true lady drinks only one glass, Alexandra," her mother liked to say. Wouldn't her mother have a fit if she knew Alex liked to sneak into the study and tipple the port?

Instead of giving her a reproachful look or arching a brow, Owen threw back his head and laughed. "I'm glad to hear it. You're a lady after my own heart. Wait here." He jogged across the floor and was gone out the door in an instant.

Alex waited with bated breath. She repeated "A lady after my own heart" in a rushed whisper—while trying to keep from squealing—so many times that the words began to lose their meaning and became a happy jumbled ball in her mouth.

When Owen returned minutes later, he was holding two champagne flutes. He crossed back over the wide parquet floor and handed one to Alex with both a flourish and a gallant bow. "My lady," he said. "It's not port, but I've always found that a bit of alcohol loosens the inhibitions, makes for less nervousness in dancing . . . and other things."

Alex felt her cheeks heat again. That sounded positively wicked. She liked it. A lot. If she were going to continue spending any amount of time in Owen's company, she really must learn to stop blushing. Why, her face might remain a permanent shade of pink, and then she'd look like Lavinia's bedchamber. An unhappy comparison to be sure. Alex readily brought the glass Owen had handed her to her lips and downed half of it while Owen watched with eyes both wide and approving.

"That's the spirit," he said with a laugh. He took a healthy sip from his own flute before plucking the glass from Alex's fingers and setting both on the nearby table. "Now, how do you feel?"

"Fine. No different, I—"

But she did feel different. The bubbly warmth of the champagne was already making its delicious fuzzy way to her belly . . . and her head. "Oh, I . . . I feel quite good."

"Excellent," he replied with his most appealing grin, his dimple making a welcome appearance in his cheek. "Care to try again?" He held out his hands and she stepped into the circle of his arms.

"Yes, please," she said with a vigorous nod.

He spun her around and around, humming again, and Alex's head felt positively light. Light and delightful. She slowly blinked. Oh, this was quite fun. Dancing around a deserted ballroom with the man of her dreams, an extremely pleasant way to spend the afternoon. Much better than paying calls to Mama's friends, practicing embroidery for the thousandth time, or hoping that Lavinia's temper stayed in check so that she might take a nap without shrill screeches waking her.

"Does Lavinia like to dance?" Owen asked as they spun around the room.

Oh, why did he have to go and ruin the moment by mentioning Lavinia? *I love to dance.* "Yes, she enjoys it immensely." *When it's over.* "You must be certain to ask her . . . often," Alex added for good measure.

"I'm pleased to hear she enjoys it. I've always been quite fond of it myself. Though admittedly not usually at *ton* balls."

It was on the tip of Alex's tongue to ask where he liked to dance, but the answer might be far too shocking and far too disappointing for her. Instead she closed her eyes and enjoyed the lightness of her head and the feel of the man beneath her fingertips. How shocking would it be if she rubbed his shoulder a bit? Just to outline his muscles and—

"Not nervous?" he asked.

She nearly tripped but caught herself in time to smile up at him dreamily. "Not a bit."

Minutes later, she realized she was actually doing quite well at dancing. It was as if her feet were moving of their own accord and she floated across the room. But then again, she'd never had such a debonair partner. Perhaps Owen was the reason the dancing was good. It was entirely unfair of him to be so handsome *and* good at dancing. She hummed along with him to the beautiful waltz. It took a few moments before she realized that it was the same one that had been playing the night she'd seen him beneath her window. She giggled to herself.

"What's so funny?" he asked, studying her face.

"I like champagne," she replied, not about to tell him the truth.

"So do I." He winked at her, and an unexpected warmth spread through her limbs. She was suddenly quite aware of the feel of his hand on hers and of his broad shoulder beneath her fingertips. The weight of his other hand along her waist was positively burning.

"You're learning quickly," he said, spinning her again.

"I wasn't aware that I'd learned anything yet."

"You should keep smiling, laugh at my jests. It's quite alluring, I assure you. But if I go too far, you should slap my shoulder and look at me out of the corners of your eyes with a mixture of warning and challenge."

"Oh?" Had she been *alluring*? How? She wanted to do it again. And the bit about slapping his shoulder and looking out of the corners of her eyes . . . it all seemed far too complicated to keep straight. Who knew there was an entirely different set of things to learn that had nothing to do with the steps of the dance? Her mother had certainly never mentioned such things.

"You should seem perfectly at ease with every partner," Owen continued. "Look around now and then at the other dancers. You mustn't seem too taken with the gentleman you're with."

Alex swallowed. If he only knew *how* taken she was with the gentleman she was with. She forced herself to glance around at the other invisible dancers.

"That's good. Keep the smile pinned to your face," he prodded.

She widened the smile that had begun to droop a bit when she'd looked away from him, until she began to feel like a grinning fool.

"What else?" she asked, wishing the dance, the entire afternoon, actually, would not have to come to an end.

Owen finished humming the song and drew their dance to an end. He took one step back, and his arms fell away from her, breaking their contact. "Would you be my partner again?" he asked.

"Of course." She held out her arms and stepped forward, quite willing to resume their dancing.

"No," he said, stepping back again. "That was a test."

Alex frowned. "A test?"

"You must never agree to two dances in a row with the same gentleman. It makes you seem far too interested, not to mention the potential gossip. Always keep your partner wanting more."

"So I can't dance with you again?" Surely, the look on her face surely was crestfallen.

"You can," he replied with a grin. "But not right away. You should always keep a gentleman guessing as to whether you'll say yes again."

"Then what should I say if I'm asked?"

"Say, 'perhaps,'" he replied. "And say it while walking away and glancing back over your shoulder like this." Owen turned and did an impression of a female batting her eyelashes and walking away that made Alex giggle so hard, she worried about ripping the seams of her gown.

She tried unsuccessfully to stifle her laughter at that bit of advice. The champagne was making her giggle. Not good. She must concentrate on the lesson. A master was teaching her, after all. This was priceless information. Not to mention the delicious irony that he was teaching her what to do to snare *his* attention. She practiced by turning sharply away from him and turning back, her chin tucked to her shoulder, batting her eyelashes coquettishly. A dark curl flew over her shoulder.

"Please, Lady Alexandra," Owen said. "Promise me you'll dance with me again tonight." He held out his hand in supplication.

Alex wanted to fall at his feet and shout, "Yes! Please!" But instead she batted her eyelashes some more and waved an imaginary fan in her gloved hand. "I cannot possibly commit to such a promise, my lord. I must consult my dancing card. I fear it is too full, as my dances are greatly in demand." She pressed her lips together hard to keep from laughing more. "My dancing card has never been full, by the by," she added.

"Never admit it, dear girl," he said with a wicked grin that made Alex feel like she'd been kissed by the sun. She sighed heavily and stared up at him.

"How was that for a first lesson?" she asked.

"Quite good," he replied. "A bit too good, perhaps."

Alex wasn't certain what he meant by that, but it sounded promising.

"Do you think you have the right of it?" he asked.

Alex bit her lip. How many opportunities would she have to dance with him so closely in a secluded ballroom? Only an imbecile would cut short such good fortune. "Not quite," she managed to reply with a straight face, also deciding to completely ignore the fact that she had the pressing need to use the convenience after drinking the champagne. She held out her arms to him and did her best to seem businesslike. "I'd like for you to show me again, please."

CHAPTER TWELVE

"Today I'm going to teach you how to be flirtatious," Owen announced the next afternoon as soon as Alex had entered Cass's ballroom. Alex was wearing a bright pink gown and looked fresh and pretty as a poppy.

"Flirtatious?" Alex echoed. "I don't think my mother would appreciate that. But at least I remembered to bring my fan today."

He cocked his head to the side. She was a funny little thing. She was full of contrasts but never ceased to make him laugh. He had dressed himself with special care again—black top boots, buckskin breeches, blue waistcoat, perfectly starched white cravat—and had ensured that he arrived on time for the second day in a row. Quite a habit he was making, this "being prompt" business. It seemed Alex was bringing out the best in him.

"Of course your mother wouldn't appreciate it," he replied. "But it will draw the eye of many a gentleman. If done correctly, that is."

"I see," Alex said. "How exactly is it done correctly?

I thought that was what yesterday's eyelash batting was accomplishing."

Owen laughed aloud at that. "Partly, yes, but there is a bit more to it. Flirtation is both a skill and an art."

"An art?" Alexandra echoed, stepping closer to him. "I quite like the sound of that." Her hair was swept up in a fetching chignon, and her strawberry scent was ever present. Coupled with her pink gown, she reminded him of a ripe little fruit.

"It's a trick, really." Owen walked around her, assessing her from head to toe. "You are an innocent, so obviously you cannot be as flirtatious as, say, some of the ladies with whom I've been known to keep company."

Alex snorted. "I'm excessively glad to hear that."

His lips cracked into a grin. "Do I sense judgment in that answer, my lady?"

She shook her head, and one large, dark curl flew over her shoulder. "Oh. No. Not at all, my lord." But the way she drew out the words and overemphasized them indicated her sarcasm. That, along with a bit of overly fluttery eyelash batting.

He eyed her up and down again. My, but she was appealing. He wished for the dozenth time that it was her and not her sister whom his father insisted he marry. Marriage to Alex might not be entirely . . . unpleasant. He shook his head to clear it of such unhelpful thoughts.

"Very well," Alex replied. "Teach me how to be flirtatious, then. What do I need to know?"

Owen circled her, his hands folded behind his back. "It's about wordplay, coy looks, the hint of a smile on your lips."

"I'm sorry to hear that," Alex said with a self-deprecating laugh. "I usually say all the wrong things and I'm not certain I'd know a coy look if it bit me upon the ankle. I suppose I could try the 'hint of a smile' part. That doesn't sound terribly difficult."

God, she was honest. It was completely refreshing. But also completely a detriment if she meant to be sought after on the marriage mart.

"I think you'll see what I mean if we try it," Owen said. "Dance with me, and let's put it into action."

Before she had a chance to respond, he pulled her into his arms. "You look ravishing tonight, Lady Alexandra."

She looked up at him with wide eyes. " 'Ravishing' is a strong word, my lord."

"It's apt."

"Flattery will get you nowhere." She slapped him on the shoulder with her fan.

"Will it get you to agree to have a drink with me?" he asked, leaning down closer to her lips.

"Certainly not." She gave him a stern stare.

"Well done," he breathed, not wanting to pull away. "Now, let's see how you react when a suitor is a bit too forward."

He pulled her up against his chest and moved his face even closer to hers. His hands were at her waist. Alex's head tipped back and her eyes were hooded and for the moment, a split second, Owen actually had the desire to . . . kiss her. She gazed up at him with those dark orbs. "Yes," she breathed.

He pushed her away to arm's length again, hoping against hope that she hadn't felt the stark evidence of his body's reaction to her lush form pressed against his belly.

Her face clouded with confusion. "Did I—? Was that right? Was that flirtatious?"

He cleared his throat. "You were supposed to deliver a crushing setdown."

Even more confusion crowded her face. "A setdown?"

"Yes, a crushing one."

She glanced up at him from beneath her dark lashes. "I suppose you'll just have to try again, then."

Try again? He already needed to cool off from his last attempt. But he could hardly tell her that. He was supposed to be teaching the girl a thing or two. Some tutor he made.

He gritted his teeth and pulled her into his arms again. She melted against him, her arms twining about his neck.

As he held his breath, every inch of his body longed to kiss her, to wrap his arms around her and—"Well?"

"Well what?" she breathed against his neck.

"I'm waiting for my crushing setdown."

"Oh, oh yes. That." She promptly pulled her arms from around his neck and took a sharp step back. "Unhand me, sir."

He arched a brow. "That may have been a bit too dramatic."

"It seems to me that a crushing setdown is by definition dramatic. What other sort of crushing setdown do you suggest?"

He shook his head. "When a gentleman is too forward, you must be forceful and direct."

"Such as?"

"If, for example, I were to say, 'Lady Alexandra, meet me in the conservatory.' What would you reply?"

"It depends."

"On what?"

"On who is doing the asking?"

He had to bite his cheek to keep from laughing aloud at that. "Let's pretend it's someone you don't want to meet in the conservatory."

"Oh, that's simple, then. I would say no."

"And if it were someone you *did* want to meet?" he asked, partially afraid of the answer.

"I might say what time."

"You can't be serious."

"I told you, there is a man I fancy. If *he* were to ask me, I cannot honestly say I wouldn't agree."

Owen pressed his lips together. Her honesty continued to amaze him. "You must at least *pretend* to be indignant. Pretend you may not be interested. Let's try again. Pretend I'm the man you fancy."

Alex glanced at her slippers and cleared her throat.

"Lady Alexandra," he said, pulling her into his arms and whispering into her ear. "Will you meet me in the conservatory?"

"Perhaps," she breathed.

He pulled away from her and gave her a condemning glare. "Perhaps?" he said in an exasperated tone.

"Too much?"

"Yes. It's too much. At the very least, you should scold me for being too forward. And far too presumptuous."

She nodded. "Very well. Let's try once more."

He pulled her into his arms again. "Meet me in the conservatory?"

She promptly slapped his shoulder with her fan. "How terribly indecent of you. I'll do no such thing." She glanced up at him. "How was that?"

"Better. But I must admit I'll still worry about you." He dropped his arms from her and stepped back. "I suppose that's enough for today." He scrubbed his hand across the back of his neck. "Let's talk about Lavinia. What else can you tell me about her likes and dislikes?"

Alex frowned and tapped a finger to her jaw. "Let's see."

"You mentioned gifts. Should I get her some flowers?" he offered.

"Flowers are . . . fine . . . or . . ." Alex glanced away.

He eyed her cautiously. "Or what?"

"Well, flowers are perfectly lovely, of course, but they're a bit . . . predictable, don't you think?"

He shoved one hand in his pocket. "Predictable? I thought all ladies liked flowers."

"I suppose some of us do. But Lavinia much prefers something unique, something interesting. Something none of the other suitors are giving the ladies whom they fancy."

He scratched the back of his head with his free hand. "Like what?"

Alexandra bit her lip. "Oh, you know, something like perhaps a . . . a . . . rock."

His eyes widened incredulously. "A rock?"

"Er, oh, you know, a nice smooth one that you found when you were out on a walk or something that, er, caught your eye." She fluttered her hands in the air.

He pinched the bridge of his nose. "I can't say that a rock has caught my eye since I was a lad of seven. Are you *quite* certain that Lady Lavinia would actually appreciate such a thing?"

Alex didn't meet his eyes, but she nodded emphatically. "Yes. Oh yes. She adores unique items."

Owen scrunched up his nose in a scowl. "She does seem a bit unconventional, I suppose."

Alex didn't stop nodding. "Oh, she is. She is. I assure you."

Owen shook his head again. Lady Lavinia sounded

mad, if you asked him. But who would know better than her sister what she liked and disliked? "Very well. I'll think of something . . . like a rock."

"She will be so pleased."

"Frankly, I'd rather give her nothing and simply talk to her."

"I would like that ever so much—I mean, Lavinia would."

Owen's grin widened. "To date, she has not struck me as the talking sort. *You* actually strike me as that sort." He shook his head once more and turned back to face Alex. "What else do you have to teach me? About being a gentleman, that is?"

Alex bit her lip. It was quite fetching. Owen had to look away.

"Have you heard the tales of King Arthur's court?"

"Yes, but—"

"Lavinia is quite interested in that sort of a hero. One who will pay her courtly love."

"Courtly love?" Owen looked as if he'd just swallowed a poisonous mushroom. "Correct me if I'm wrong, but isn't courtly love predicated on the notion of a medieval knight and a *married* lady?"

"Yes," Alex allowed. "That is true. But, of course, Lavinia isn't married—not yet."

"But she wants her husband to treat her as though he were a knight of the realm, and perhaps not consummate the relationship?"

Alex's face heated briskly.

"Forgive me if I went too far," Owen replied, responding to her blush. "But it sounds absolutely daft to me. I don't think your sister is terribly realistic."

I don't think so either.

"She's read a great deal of medieval literature," Alex offered.

"Yes, well, I'm no Lancelot. And good thing, by the way—the chap made his king a cuckold."

"I can't argue with that," Alex replied. "Nor can I explain Lavinia's preferences, but—"

Owen grabbed his head between his hands. "Enough about Lavinia for now. I shudder to hear any more. The next thing, you'll be telling me she wants me to join a troupe of troubadours and sing for my supper."

"I don't think she'd look askance upon it," Alex responded before bursting out laughing at the thought. "Do you happen to own a mandolin?"

"You find that funny, do you?" Owen said, advancing on her.

"No." Alex shook her head vigorously. "Not at all." A smile cracked her lips apart. "Very well. Perhaps a little. A very little. It's exceedingly funny to picture you playing a mandolin."

Owen crossed his arms over his chest and regarded her down the length of his nose. "The other day you mentioned a list."

"Wha-what?" Alex coughed. She pounded her fist to her chest to clear her throat. "Did I?"

"You said something about how you'd been forced to cross a smashing debut off your list."

Alex pressed her hand to her chest. "I did?"

"Yes. Tell me more about that."

Alex turned and walked over to the window that looked down upon the street, one of the most fashionable in Mayfair. "When I was fifteen, I wrote a list."

"What sort of list?"

"A list of the things I hoped to accomplish in life."

Owen slid both hands into his pockets and joined her near the window. "And?"

"And it was silly and I was young and—"

"A smashing debut was on your list?"

"Ye—yes," Alex allowed. She propped a shoulder against the window frame.

"And that didn't happen?"

Alex slowly shook her head. "No. I'm sorry to say it did not."

"What happened at your debut, Alex?" The tenderness in his voice surprised him.

Alex heaved a sigh. "I was a dismal failure. No one asked me to dance. I tripped over my hem and spilled ratafia on my gown, and then I sat along the wall the entire evening. Mother told me she was disappointed in me."

"What did Lavinia say?"

"Not much. Lavinia was interested only in the fact that it was the beginning of her fourth Season and she had yet to make a match."

"Why do you think you launched so poorly?"

Alex turned back toward the large ballroom. "I'd hoped—foolishly—that a handsome dashing gentleman would ask me to dance and launch me into Society with great fanfare."

"That's why you want me to dance with you?" Owen breathed.

"Precisely," Alex replied so softly that he could barely hear her.

"What else was on your list?"

She shook her head again and faced him with an overly bright smile. "What about you? What is on your list of accomplishments?"

He snorted. "Absolutely nothing."

"I find that difficult to believe," she replied. "There must be something you want to do. Something you're good at."

He clenched his teeth. The horses he trained flashed through his mind. Followed by the memory of the little girl coughing in the back of the farmer's wagon. "Don't confuse me with someone noble," he said. "I'm not."

"Yes, you are. Whether you know it or not."

His jaw tightened again, and he glanced away. When he looked back at her, he first ensured his typical smile was back in place. "You didn't answer me. What else was on your list?"

Alex returned his sly smile. "*That* will cost you another dance and another lesson, my lord."

He arched a brow. "I do believe you're already learning, my lady."

CHAPTER THIRTEEN

On the afternoon of her third meeting with Owen, Alex had decided to be daring and adventurous. Daring was called for because time was quickly running out. The Rutherfords' ball was to be held tomorrow evening, and she and Owen had already agreed that it was the perfect venue to put their respective plans into action. He would dance with her and thus draw the fickle attention of the *ton* in her direction, and she would put in a good word for him with her sister, thereby giving him an opening that he could then use to employ the newfound knowledge he had of Lavinia's likes and dislikes.

Alex briefly wondered if Owen would arrive bearing a rock. That might be awkward. She hoped she wouldn't bear witness to that particular bit. She mostly hoped Lavinia wouldn't fly into one of her rages at the sight of such a gift, whereby Owen might tell her where he got the idea and expose her entire charade. It was dubious, to be sure. But Alex didn't have long to contemplate it. She'd been waiting in Cassandra Swift's ballroom only five minutes before the door opened and Owen appeared, wearing chocolate-colored breeches, black top boots, white shirt-fronts and cravat, and a dark gray waistcoat. His hair was neatly slicked and the gleam in his blue eyes told her he might just be interested in being bold today, too.

"Good afternoon, my lady," he said, bowing at the waist to her.

"Good afternoon, my lord," she replied, falling into a deep curtsy.

"Are you in need of champagne for today's lesson? Or perhaps port?" He grinned at her.

"I think I can manage without spirits today, thank you."

Owen made his way across the wide expanse and came to stand near her. "If you have anything important left to tell me about Lavinia, I suggest you do it now before the Rutherfords' ball."

Alex nodded. She'd been expecting this question and she was prepared. "Yes. There is one thing."

His eyes met hers, clearly interested. Alex wished for the hundredth time they didn't have to discuss Lavinia so often. Though she supposed they wouldn't even be here together if it weren't for Lavinia. Confound it. Alex folded her hands in front of her serenely. "Lavinia, er, she doesn't like horses. Don't bring them up."

Owen's eyebrows went up. "Horses, you say?"

"Yes." Alex glanced away. "She's frightened half out of her wits by them."

"There's nothing to be frightened of in a horse."

"I know that and you know that, but for some reason, Lavinia detests the creatures." Good thing Alex wasn't standing outside, closer to the possible lightning.

Owen's voice was resigned. "Very well. I'll ensure I don't bring up horses. Or at least show no affinity toward them."

"That's probably best." Alex nodded.

"As for you, you're already a proficient flirt and a skilled dancer. I'm not certain what else to show you," he said with a laugh.

Alex took a deep breath. This next part was especially daring. But daring was the order of the day. "I have an idea."

He turned his head toward her. "What's that?"

She squeezed her hands together. "It's a question, really."

"Yes?" he prodded.

Alex chewed on her bottom lip. She couldn't even look at him when she said it. "What should I do if a gentleman becomes too forward?"

"We already went over this—"

"No," she said, her ears burning. "I mean *too* forward."

He eyed her cautiously.

"What if he attempts to kiss me?" she finally blurted.

Owen's eyes rounded. "Slap him," he said, his voice taking on a threatening, angry tone she'd never heard before.

She smoothed a curl away from her forehead. "What if that doesn't work?"

"Knee him between the legs. Then come find me. I'll handle the wretch for you." His voice was thunderous.

A thrill rushed down Alex's spine. His offer was positively tempting, but she needed to follow through with this line of questioning. She had a plan. A daring one. "What if he succeeds?" she ventured, smoothing her gloved hand down the front of her lavender gown. "In kissing me, I mean."

Owen's head snapped up. His face had hardened into a mask of stone. "Has that happened before?"

"No, of course not, but then again, I haven't been flirt-

ing before. What if I'm superbly effective? I want to ensure that I'm prepared for success."

Owen's hand clenched into a fist. "If some overly eager
blighter tries to get you alone, say no. He won't kiss you
in public."

"Are you quite sure?" Alex prodded.

"Entirely. I'll call him out myself since your brother
is still not of age."

Another thrill shot down her spine. Lord Owen Monroe calling out an overly eager suitor on her behalf? Who
would ever imagine? Well, besides her.

Alex cleared her throat. "There is one man whom I'd
quite like to kiss me, but—"

"Who?" The word shot out like a crack against the
nearest wall.

Alex stumbled over her words. Perhaps she shouldn't
have said that. "He's the—I mean to say—He's—"

"Forgive me," Owen replied. "You're speaking of the
chap from whom you're hoping for an offer, of course."

All Alex could do was nod. "Yes, but if another man,
a man I don't want to kiss me, tries to do so, I'd like to
be prepared."

His eyes narrowed on her. "Prepared how?"

"I think I should practice, if you'd be so kind." She did
her best to maintain a straight face.

Owen scowled. "Practice? What do you mean?"

Alex twined her fingers together and rocked back and
forth. "I mean that you should try to kiss me and I'll practice my reaction."

Owen's blue eyes widened once more but just as
quickly reverted to their normal size. "I'm not certain—"

She crossed her arms over her chest matter-of-factly.
The only way this would work was if she pretended it was
all merely part of the lessons. She needed to act as if it

were nothing out of the ordinary whatsoever. "Honestly, Owen. You cannot teach me how to flirt and then leave me to fend off a possibly lecherous suitor on my own with no training whatsoever." She tapped her slippered foot on the parquet floor.

He scratched his head, but she could tell by the dawning look of acceptance on his face that he was coming around to her way of thinking. *Excellent.*

"Very well." He sighed. "I'll try to kiss you and you can sidestep me and slap me with your fan. Of course, this should be done only in the most extreme set of circumstances, and again, I highly recommend you do not go anywhere alone with anyone who might make such an untoward advance."

"I understand completely," she assured him, trying to quell the nerves that had raced through her chest ever since he'd uttered the words "I'll try to kiss you."

Owen straightened his cravat and squared his shoulders. Then he faced her, puffing up his chest and waggling his eyebrows in a comical manner. "You look so ravishing this evening, Lady Alexandra. Your beauty has enchanted me, and I fear I'm overcome with my passions."

She couldn't help her laugh. "Overcome with your passions?"

He cracked a smile. "Don't make sport. I'm certain many a chap has said worse. Not me, of course. I have much more style than that, but I'm guessing at what a sop would say when he was about to make an indecent advance upon a lady of stellar reputation."

Alex gave him a skeptical once-over. "Do you mean to say you've never made an indecent advance?"

Owen's grin was unrepentant. "Certainly not. I've made more than I can count, but never on a lady whose reputation was at stake."

Her laughter continued. "Never on someone like me, you mean?"

"Precisely." He bowed.

"Very well, carry on." She fluttered her hand in the air. "What were you saying, Mr. Suitor?"

He *tsk*ed her. "Aim higher. He should at least be Lord Suitor."

She shook her head at him. "Fine. What were you saying, Lord Suitor?"

"My passions. I am overcome by them," Owen said in a louder-than-normal, overly dramatic voice that made Alex shake her head and laugh again.

"And what do you propose to do about them? Do you intend to declare yourself?" she asked.

He pulled her into his arms, and Alex abruptly stopped laughing. Her breath caught in her throat.

"No. I intend to do this." Owen's mouth swooped down toward hers. Alex knew . . . this was the moment she was supposed to sidestep him, was supposed to move away, deliver a crushing setdown, slap him with her fan, slap him with her hand. Both hand and fan were at the ready, even. But the moment his mouth moved toward hers, all she could think about was feeling his warm lips against hers. She didn't move away, not an inch, and Owen's mouth met hers in a hot, tangled kiss.

At first it was as if a tiny bolt of lightning froze them together. The shock of it caused them to root to their respective spots. But then Owen moved his lips, and Alexandra's hands slipped up his shirtfront and around his neck, anchoring him to her. His mouth shifted over hers. Her lips parted and his tongue boldly stroked inside. Alex's knees buckled.

Owen's large hands were there to catch her and instead of pushing her away, he pulled her up against his hard, muscled body, and Alex moaned. Owen's mouth slashed over hers, and his tongue slid inside her mouth again and again, owning her. He groaned, too, and Alex clung to him, afraid she would fall to a heap on the fine floor if she let go of his strong neck. He smelled like expensive cologne and a hint of smoke and wood spice. She laced her fingers together behind his neck and leaned up into the kiss even more.

When Owen finally pulled away, he was breathing heavily. So was she.

His eyes were wide with surprise. "You didn't move."

"You kissed me." She pressed a hand to her chest, hoping to correct the fact that she couldn't breathe properly. What a kiss that had been! Entirely knee-weakening. Just as she'd hoped it would be. Just as she'd dreamed it would be. Ooh, perhaps being daring *was* an acquired skill. She certainly liked it so far.

"I kissed you because I thought you were going to slap me." Owen eyed her as if she were some exotic species of animal he'd never seen before.

But the unspoken words hung in the air, too, along with the lust from their kiss. He'd kissed her far longer and with far more aplomb than he'd needed to in order to simply be staging a kiss from an overactive suitor. She wanted to ask him why he hadn't stopped, but at the same time she didn't want to know. She couldn't bear it if he told her he hadn't wanted to kiss her. No. She would just leave it alone.

"I forgot to slap you," she admitted.

They stared at each other. Attraction leaped between them. Alex looked away first. What else could she say to him?

He scrubbed his hand against the back of his neck. "I

suggest you take my original advice. Stay away from suitors who ask you to go anywhere with them alone."

All she could do was nod jerkily and press her burning lips together.

"Do you have what you need to court Lavinia?" she asked with a slightly shaking voice.

"I think so."

"The ball is tomorrow night," she breathed. That was an idiotic thing to say.

"Do you think you can employ what we've discussed?" he asked.

"Yes," she whispered.

"Is the man whom you fancy going to be there?"

"Yes," she breathed. Unexpected tears stung Alex's eyes at the thought of their meetings here in Cassandra's ballroom coming to an end. What if everything Alex had told him didn't work? What if Lavinia changed her mind and fell madly in love with him? What if her parents forced Lavinia to marry him regardless? Oh, there were so many possibilities. The more time she spent with him, the more she wanted him for herself. Why had she thought any of this was a good idea?

Because she'd wanted to spend time in his company at any price. That's why.

"Me, too," he replied. "I'll see you there." He pulled her hand up to his lips, and Alex closed her eyes to savor the feel of it. "Save the first dance for me."

CHAPTER FOURTEEN

Owen tugged off his cravat while he waited for his valet to respond to his call. It was time to dress for the Rutherfords' ball, but the thought made him vaguely uneasy. He did not look forward to spending time with Lady Lavinia. Good God. The things Alex had told him over the last few days about her sister. Why, the woman was a complete muddle. He'd been somewhat encouraged to hear that she didn't mind forcefulness, drinking, and a bit of gambling, but to hear that she expected him to write her poetry, sing love ballads, and was frightened of horses, well, that was more than disappointing. And she wanted a rock? Truly? The lady was clearly a bit mad.

But who would know her better than her sister, and a sister who was obviously motivated to assist him? For the life of him, Owen couldn't understand why Alex was the one having trouble in Society. She was beautiful, funny, intelligent, and full of pluck. Her sister might be more classically lovely, but that had never been Owen's sort. He much preferred a lady who surprised him, which Alex had continually done since he'd met her.

Owen sighed and paced across his bedchamber. It didn't matter, did it? Alex wasn't the one he was set to marry, and besides, she'd made it clear that she already had her eye on some chap. That was why she was so intent upon improving her status in Society. Not only that, but Owen's father had implied that the duke intended his daughters to marry in order of their age, and Alex was younger, which also explained why she was intent upon helping him. The sooner Lavinia was matched, the sooner Alex could set about becoming betrothed herself.

Owen couldn't help but dwell upon the references Alex had made to the man of her dreams. She'd even admitted that she'd like to kiss him. And possibly meet him in the conservatory. He smiled at the memory. That had been refreshing, too. Most young innocents would simper and affect demureness. Not Alex. Owen briefly wished he hadn't interrupted her answer when he'd asked who the man was yesterday. Whoever he was, he was one lucky bastard. Owen hoped the man knew it. Not to mention the unidentified man bloody well owed Owen a drink or three for taking Alex's shrewish elder sister off their parents' hands, clearing the way for his suit of Alex. Owen scowled. Why did that thought make him feel vaguely angry . . . and a bit jealous? He was never jealous.

No matter. No doubt he'd been contemplating Alex more than he would normally consider a young virtuous lady because their mutual goal had kept them in each other's company of late. In fact, other than his mother and Cass, he'd never spent so much time with a female outside of bed. It was a unique situation, to be sure. And one that was causing him no end of confusion.

But there were two other things that kept popping up in his mind over and over. He couldn't seem to banish them. The first was Alex asking him what he hoped to accomplish in life. It was a question his father had asked him on countless occasions. A question that usually made him want to go out and drink until he forgot it. But when Alex asked, for the first time, Owen had actually wondered at the answer himself. He'd had a thought, a time or two, about some of the things he'd like to do one day when he assumed his seat in Parliament. He'd bloody well die before he admitted it to his father, but Owen had been reading the papers and paying attention to politics for years. He just never permitted anyone to know it. Only his valet knew he scoured the papers and all the political pamphlets he could get his hands on. "Don't confuse me with someone noble," he'd said. "I'm not."

"Yes, you are," Alex had answered. "Whether you know it or not." Those words haunted him. How was it that Alex, of all people—sweet, innocent, young Alex—could see in him something he couldn't even see in himself?

The second thing Owen couldn't forget was that kiss. The one he'd shared with Alex yesterday in Cass's ballroom. The one that should never have happened. The one Alex should have slapped him for, should have pushed away from. Instead, she hadn't moved an inch . . . almost as if she'd . . . wanted it. It was ludicrous, but the thought preoccupied him. Not to mention he'd tossed and turned in bed all night, completely racked with lust over an innocent he should never have touched. It didn't help matters that he'd been without the company of a woman since—by God, since he'd met Alex. That was interesting. It seemed the little innocent was twisting him into knots.

His valet entered the room just then. "I've pressed your formal evening attire, my lord. I thought perhaps the sapphire waistcoat."

"That's fine," Owen replied, still trying to shake Alex from his thoughts.

"You'll be attending the Rutherfords' ball this evening, correct?" the valet asked.

"Yes." Owen pulled his shirttails over his head to change into the fresh ones. "That's right. I'm about to make a wallflower the most sought-after young lady in London."

CHAPTER FIFTEEN

Alex was going to cast up her accounts tonight. She was certain of it. Hannah had dressed her with painstaking care. She wore a shell pink gown of satin with tiny embroidered flowers around the high waist, capped sleeves, and embedded pearls along the bodice. Her hair was caught up in a chignon with a few tendrils curled around her cheeks. A pearl necklace and a delicate matching bracelet completed the ensemble. The young woman who stared back at her in the looking glass, however, appeared more anxious than beautiful, as far as she was concerned.

She took a deep breath. She could do this. She *could*. She could dance with Owen Monroe tonight and become the belle of the ball. They'd been practicing, hadn't they? She was prepared. So why did she feel ill?

A knock sounded at the door. Alex whirled toward it. "It's me, Thomas," her brother's voice rang out. She pressed a hand against her pounding chest. Good heavens, she needed to calm her nerves. She hurried to the door and opened it.

"Thomas?"

Her handsome brother grinned at her and bowed. "I've come to escort you to the ball."

"What are you doing here? I thought you were at school."

"I came back for a bit. With Father's permission, of course. Lord Owen wrote to me. He said tonight would be special for you. He sent the note to Windsor via private messenger."

Owen had written to her brother? Alex swallowed. How absolutely lovely of him. And private messenger? Why, that must have cost a fortune.

Alex eyed her brother up and down. He was dressed in formal black evening attire and looked altogether debonair. Her brother was already good-looking and dashing at the age of sixteen with his dark brown hair that was slicked back and bright blue eyes that sparkled with mischief.

"You look beautiful, Al."

She curtsied to him. "Thank you, my lord," she added with a giggle.

He tucked her arm under his and led her downstairs to the foyer, where she gathered her wrap. Mother and Father and Lavinia were already waiting in the coach. Thank heavens Father's coach was large enough to accommodate all five of them.

"I'm still not entirely certain why you wanted to come to the ball this evening," Mother said to Thomas as the coach took off into the night toward the Rutherfords' house.

"The lad is growing up, Lillian," Father said.

"I've come to escort my sisters. Need I explain myself any further?" Thomas replied. He turned to wink at Alex where only she could see. They both knew no good could come of it if Lavinia thought for a moment that Alex was getting preferential treatment from their brother.

"Besides, school's quite dull this time of year. It's hardly off to a start yet."

"The little Season is dull as well," Lavinia said in a huff. "I daresay it's even more dull than the spring Season, and that is a complete bore."

"Lavinia, please," their mother said.

Thankfully, the Rutherfords' house was nearby and the ride was not long. The footman helped Father and Mother out of the coach, Father assisted Lavinia, and then Thomas sprang forward to help Alex. She took his hand eagerly and alighted.

Thomas offered his arm again and escorted her through the receiving line, the corridor, and finally down the sweeping staircase to the Rutherfords' elegant ballroom.

When the butler announced them, Alex was again certain she would cast up her accounts. It felt as if all eyes in the ballroom turned to stare at her. Why?

She concentrated on looking above all the feathers in the ladies' hair and allowed her brother to lead her about the room. Alex glanced around. Why was everyone watching her?

"I should very much like a glass of champagne," she whispered to her brother.

"I'll get you one," he replied, squeezing her hand.

Thomas was off in a flash, and Alex was left alone. She scanned the ballroom for a glimpse of either Owen or Lavinia. She turned in a wide circle and caught her breath when Owen materialized from the crowd. He wore his finest black evening attire with a sapphire waistcoat and blinding white cravat and shirttails. He was so handsome, her chest felt tight.

He bowed to her. "My lady."

She offered him her hand. "My lord."

"May I have this dance?"

"Of course you may."

And then they were off. Flying about the floor as if they had invented the steps to the waltz. After their lessons together, Alex was altogether relaxed in his arms. Though she did still wish for that glass of champagne. And when she ventured a glance at the guests, she noted with no small amount of pride that they were all watching her again. She was with the notorious Lord Owen Monroe for the second time in as many balls. This time she was laughing at his jests, playfully slapping at his arm with her fan, and looking deeply into his eyes. If the assembly had been feeling a bit sorry for her having to begin the ball on the arm of her younger brother, they were no longer feeling sorry.

"Why is everyone watching us?"

Owen chuckled. "This is what you wanted, is it not?"

"Yes, but I feel as if they were staring even before we danced."

Owen tilted his head to the side. "I may have started a rumor that I was taken with you."

Alex gasped a little. "You didn't!"

"Yes, I did. Though I do hope it doesn't make its way round to Lavinia, or all our teaching sessions will have been for naught. However, I thought your reputation could use a boost."

"I doubt Lavinia would believe it even if she does hear it." She swallowed the lump in her throat. "And thank you for the . . . boost. And for writing to Thomas."

"You're welcome, my lady," Owen said with his infamous grin.

By the time the waltz ended, Alex had a bevy of

admirers lined up to ask for the next dance. Owen released her hand. "Thank you for the dance, Lady Alexandra," he said, and Alex was swept into a throng of young gentlemen, all of whom were either asking their female relatives for introductions or were asking Alex for a dance. And just like that, Owen had launched her fabulously into Society. Exactly as Alex had wished. So why did she feel a little like crying as she watched him turn away and head toward Lavinia?

Alex blinked away the tears quickly. Lord Matthew Beckett was standing at her elbow, waiting for her attention. Lord Beckett was one of the most sought-after bachelors of the Season. It wouldn't do for him to see her crying like a ninny. She pasted a bright smile on her face and turned to him. They'd already been introduced. In fact, as she glanced at the group of gentlemen vying for her attention, she realized she'd been introduced to most of them. They simply hadn't been interested in her . . . until tonight. Until Owen.

Alex didn't remember a word Lord Beckett said during their dance. Nor did she recall her conversations with Lord Sheffield, Sir Montague, or Mr. Hanson after that. All she could concentrate upon was keeping her gaze focused on Owen. First he'd spoken to Lavinia. Apparently, that hadn't gone well, because minutes later, she'd stomped off, refusing a glass of champagne he'd offered her. But now, he was back at Lavinia's side, speaking to her again. Alex desperately tried to get her latest dancing partner, Lord Gillicuttie, to move closer to where Owen and Lavinia were speaking, in the hopes that she might have the chance to overhear a bit of it. Unfortunately, not only was Lord Gillicuttie an awful dancer, but the man was a complete bore as well, and he positively refused to be led by a lady. Finally the song came to an end, and Alex hastily excused herself, dashing across the floor in the opposite direction of the steadily growing group of gentlemen who wanted to dance with her.

She glanced back at her group of admirers. Men were such silly creatures. They took no notice of a thing until one of them showed interest, and then suddenly they all had to have it. In this case, the "it" just so happened to be *her*.

Owen had apparently received another crushing setdown from Lavinia. He was far across the room, a scowl deeply etched on his face, his neck reddening. Mother had rushed over to see to Lavinia while Owen headed back toward the refreshment table with Lavinia's untouched glass of champagne clutched in one fist. Alex scurried past the crowd to hide behind a potted palm that was on his route.

"Owen," she called when he passed by.

He stopped and glanced around. "Alexandra? Is that you?" he whispered.

"Yes. Over here."

He turned around fully and must have guessed her hiding spot because the next thing she knew, he slid behind the palm with her.

His scowl transformed into a wide grin as soon as he saw her standing there. "I never noticed how deuced convenient palms are till I met you."

Alex could help but smile back. "They are convenient, aren't they?"

"Exceedingly so." He held out the glass to her. "Care for some champagne?"

"Yes, please." She grabbed the flute and downed half its contents in one gulp.

"Despite your insistence that your sister adores champagne, she just informed me in no uncertain terms that champagne makes her ill and she was aghast that I offered it to her."

Alex pressed her lips together to keep from wincing. "That's odd," she offered. A change of subject was in order. Immediately. Alex blurted out the first thing that came to mind. "Will you please take me out on the terrace? Alone."

CHAPTER SIXTEEN

Owen turned to her with wide eyes. "Pardon?" He couldn't possibly have heard her correctly. An innocent did not want to go off onto the terrace alone with *him*.

Alex waved her gloved hand in front of her face. "I've misplaced my fan and am in need of some fresh air. It's sweltering in here. I feel as if I might faint."

"Well, we can't have that." He grinned at her. "But what did I tell you about going off alone with strange gentlemen?"

She arched a brow. "Oh, so now *you're* a strange gentleman?"

Was that flirtatious? His little student learned quickly, it seemed. "A dance is one thing, but your reputation may well be shredded if you go onto the terrace alone with me."

"No, it won't. Not if we don't stay long. I think it will give my reputation just the cachet of mystery that it's currently lacking. The dance was a good start, but this may solidify my entrée into Society as an incomparable." She blinked at him innocently.

"I don't know about this, Alex," he said in a warning tone, sliding his hands into his pockets.

"Very well. I'm going out alone, then." Taking her half-empty champagne glass with her, she turned on her heel and headed toward the French doors that led out onto the terrace that in turn led down to the garden.

Owen followed her. Of course he followed her. What choice did he have? Not to mention, he found he wanted to talk to her. She was infinitely more appealing than her bad-tempered sister. And she knew how to handle her champagne, apparently, too.

They strolled outside separately, but Owen met her on the far side of the terrace. The light from twinkling candles spread throughout the gardens lit their path. The late summer air was warm and inviting. Alex turned to him and splayed her gloved hands across the balustrade behind her.

Owen tilted his head to the side and contemplated her. "Our dance was a success, it seems. Your dancing card appears to be much fuller."

"Yes. I'm suddenly quite popular. Thanks to you. I've barely had a chance to breathe, let alone have a glass of champagne, so thank you for that, too."

"You're welcome," he replied, bowing.

He watched her carefully. The moonlight touched her cheekbones, the shining crown of her head, the sparkling bodice of her gown. She smelled like strawberries, as usual. He wanted to . . . kiss her. The thought stopped him, surprised him. He wasn't in the business of wanting to kiss innocents. And he certainly wasn't in the business of wanting to kiss the young sisters of the lady he was supposed to be courting. But all he could think about was the feel of her mouth on his yesterday when she hadn't stepped away from his kiss. This was madness. The moon was doing insane things to him. That was all.

"How did you fare with Lavinia?" she asked, jolting him from his indecent thoughts.

He rubbed a knuckle against his forehead and expelled his breath. "Lavinia would barely look at me, let alone dance with me."

Alex took another tiny sip of her champagne. "Did you ask her to?"

"Yes, of course."

"Do you think she heard the rumor?"

"She said she found it crass of me to attempt to use her sister in order to make an impression on *her*."

"That sounds like Lavinia." Alex tapped a finger against her cheek. "You didn't mention horses, did you?"

"I might have."

"Did you give her a rock?"

"No. But I'm not above foraging in this garden for one if it will help my cause. Why is she such a—?"

"Shrew?"

"I was going to say 'difficult lady,' but 'shrew' is apt as well."

"She's always been given everything she wants in life."

"You're making excuses for her behavior."

Alex's hand fell to her side. "Perhaps, but she was very ill as a child, and—"

"Another excuse."

Alex glanced away.

Owen sighed. He remembered how Alex had changed the subject when he'd asked her how her parents had treated *her*. She was used to getting the castoffs of affection. His heart tugged at the thought. It was a singularly surprising experience. But he could tell that Alex didn't want to talk about it, so he turned the conversation back to Lavinia. "She's always been given everything she wants in life, and she doesn't want me."

Alex shook her head. "You're not her ideal suitor."

"Who is? Sir Lancelot?"

"Perhaps."

"She'll be waiting a long while if she's waiting for me to turn into Lancelot, for God's sake."

Alex shrugged. "That's what we've been studying, isn't it? How to make you into the perfect romantic gentleman?"

He shoved his hands into his pockets and kicked at a pebble that had somehow made it onto the terrace.

"I fear it's a lost cause. Your sister doesn't seem a bit more impressed with me tonight than she has been in the past."

"I'm sorry to hear that," Alex replied softly.

"And given her reaction to my offer of champagne, and my speech about horses, I'm beginning to wonder if everything you told me about her is correct."

Alex paled slightly. "She's . . . difficult," she repeated lamely.

Now Owen shrugged. He didn't want to talk about Lavinia. Something else was on his mind. "Did the gentleman with whom you're enamored ask you to dance tonight?" Why did Owen hope she said no?

Alex blushed beautifully and glanced away. Her gloved fingertips glanced over her collarbone.

"I didn't mean to embarrass you," he said softly.

Surprise marked her features as she turned back to look at him. "Why, Lord Owen, I do believe you're learning a bit. I don't think the man I met a few days ago would even have known he'd embarrassed me."

Owen chuckled at that. "You're learning as well. I

don't think I've ever seen you with such a fetching smile on your face, and when you touch your neck in that particular spot, I—"

She blushed more deeply, and Owen clamped his lips together. He was certainly embarrassing her now. Blast it.

He ducked his head and cleared his throat. "Well, the man's a tosser if he can't see the good in you, Alex."

Her head snapped up and her dark eyes met his. "Do you mean that?"

"Of course I do. I curse my father every day for picking your sister and not you."

Alex gasped. Her hand fell away from her throat.

Damn it. He shouldn't have said such a reckless thing. What could she possibly reply to *that*?

"My apologics. I don't mean to be so boorish," he said. "And I don't mean to seem so cavalier about it all. I know your heart belongs to someone else, but I never expected it to be this difficult to court a lady with the intention of marriage. I've never tried it before, true, but it's proved deuced difficult."

The surprised look caused by his earlier statement slowly drained from Alex's face. "I'm sorry Lavinia is so much trouble."

Owen shrugged again. "It's hardly your fault. You've done nothing but try to help me. I cannot fathom how two such different young ladies were born to the same parents."

Alex laughed. "Believe me, I ask myself that same question quite regularly."

He stepped closer and touched her hand. "Thank you, Alexandra. For helping me."

She glanced away. Those couldn't be tears in her eyes, could they?

"What do you propose to do, about Lavinia?" she asked quietly.

He tipped up her chin with his thumb. "I propose that we meet again for another lesson. Tomorrow."

CHAPTER SEVENTEEN

The next day, Owen arrived nearly a half hour early to his appointment at Cass's house with Alex. He'd never arrived half an hour early to anything in his life. Why was he so eager to see Alex again?

He was sitting in a chair in the foyer with his hands shoved in his pockets, waiting, when his sister walked by. "Come into the drawing room with me for a moment, won't you, Owen?"

Owen groaned. Cass obviously wanted to speak to him about something specific. This couldn't be good. But he was using her house as a rendezvous point with Alex, and he couldn't very well refuse his sister's request. He hefted himself from the chair and followed her into the nearest drawing room.

"Yes?" he asked brightly once the door to the room had closed behind him.

Cass turned in a swirl of white skirts. "What exactly are you doing with Alexandra Hobbs?"

Owen paced across the floor toward the fireplace. "What do you mean?"

"Don't be coy with me, Owen. I've helped you to meet her here, so I feel somewhat responsible for her. I want to know exactly what your intentions are."

Owen rubbed a knuckle against one temple. What was appropriate to tell? "We're in business together, you might say."

Cass arched a brow. "Business? Are you certain, Owen?"

He turned toward his sister and frowned. "Yes, of course. What else would we be doing?"

Cass snorted. "Do I really have to tell *you* that?"

Owen glared at his sister. "You're not implying that I'm doing something illicit with Alex, are you? Her reputation is impeccable, and she has only ever conducted herself as a complete lady in my presence."

"No. No." Cass pressed her hand to her coiffure. "I'm implying no such thing. I merely find it interesting, that's all."

Owen narrowed his eyes on her. "Interesting how?"

Cass flourished a hand in the air. "Interesting in that I've never heard you so vehemently defend a lady's reputation before, nor have I ever known you to call one by a nickname. Other than me, of course."

Owen blinked. "Don't read more into it than is there, sister dear."

"Don't be so quick to dismiss my points, Owen, darling."

The two siblings faced each other, squared off.

"She told me that she has her sights set on someone. Some chap from the *ton*."

"That's interesting." Cass tapped her finger against her cheek. "And you don't know who?"

"No. I'm helping her to become popular."

Cass's jaw dropped. "Are you serious?"

"Regardless of your disdain for my reputation, I'm still highly sought after at *ton* events. I am exceedingly eligible, Cass."

"Of course you are. I just never thought you'd use your social powers for such . . . good."

Owen shrugged. "She has something I want."

Cass shook her head. "Oh, Owen, don't be crude."

"No. Not that." He rolled his eyes at his sister. "She's teaching me Lady Lavinia's likes and dislikes."

Cass's tinkling laughter didn't stop for the next few moments. She finally had to pull out a handkerchief and wipe her eyes.

"I don't see what's so humorous," Owen said grumpily.

"I've never known you to need help with a lady before."

"Have you met Lady Lavinia?"

"You know I have."

"Then you know why I require help. You said yourself she's difficult."

"So I did and so she is. But just to be certain that I'm clear: Lady Alexandra is helping you to woo her sister, and in return you're helping her to become popular?"

"Yes. I've been teaching her how to dance and flirt, and she's been teaching me what Lady Lavinia finds acceptable in a mate."

Cass shook her head again and pressed her fingertips to her smiling lips. "Oh, Owen, does Father know what he's forced you to?"

"No. But I bloody well hope he finds out. I find it as ridiculous as you do."

Cass crossed her arms over her chest and eyed her

brother carefully. "You've never had such a difficult time impressing a lady, have you?"

"You don't know the half of it. And the worst part is . . . Lady Lavinia still seems entirely unimpressed even after everything Alex has told me. Not to mention I only have two more weeks to get her to agree to marry me."

Owen wiped a hand roughly across his face. Blast and damn. His sister had a point. He did feel something for Alex. Protectiveness? Yes. That was it. He was being protective. Just as one's future brother-in-law should be. Nothing out of the ordinary in that at all. And why shouldn't he have a nickname for a future member of the family? He called his sister Cass, didn't he? There was nothing improper about it. But he couldn't help but wonder whom Alex wanted to marry. And he couldn't help but wonder why he cared so much.

The door knocker in the foyer sounded just then, jolting Owen from his thoughts.

"That must be Lady Alexandra," Cass said.

"Yes." Owen consulted his timepiece. "She's right on time."

Cass moved over to him. He leaned down and she kissed him on the cheek. "Best of luck, dear brother, though I must admit, I'm going to have a high time watching all this unfold."

"This time we must discuss rendezvous," Owen announced as soon as Alex joined him in the empty ballroom.

"Rendezvous? Plural?"

"Yes, specifically how you should never be on time to one. Not one arranged with a gentleman."

"Like this?"

"Precisely like this. Always keep a man waiting. He'll

wonder if you've changed your mind and he'll have to work harder next time."

"But I thought you said I should never agree to go off alone with a man."

"You shouldn't." He winked at her. "But you're here with me now, aren't you? We must prepare for any possibility."

"That's why you wanted to meet me again?" Alex asked. "To tell me to be late next time?"

"Among other things."

"Such as? More questions about Lavinia?"

He strode over and leaned back against the table near the wall. "No, actually. My questions are about you today."

"Me?"

"Yes, is that so shocking?"

"What do you want to know about me?"

"What you see in the bloke you're after, for one thing."

"Wh-why does that matter?"

"I thought perhaps I might be of more assistance to you if you provided me with more details."

"Oh, I don't think—"

"Go on, tell me."

Alex took a deep breath and garnered some time by fumbling around in her reticule for her fan. She couldn't very well describe Owen to Owen. That would be preposterous. But what could she say?

"Well, he's tall, handsome, titled."

"Of course," Owen drawled, though he looked a bit disgruntled. "Go on."

"He's blond."

Owen nodded at that. "What color are his eyes?" he teased, batting his own eyelashes at her.

"Blue," she ventured.

"He sounds like quite a catch," Owen replied.

"He is. Though I daresay he doesn't realize it. He hasn't had much luck on the marriage mart to date."

"The perfect suitor for you, then, perhaps?"

"Perhaps," she replied, wondering if Owen had any clue. Of course he wouldn't guess.

"And he's not put off by your sister?"

"He doesn't seem to be. Not yet." She tugged the fan from the reticule finally, flipped it open, and rapidly fanned her face.

"Does he write poetry?"

"I seriously doubt it."

"Does he sing love ballads?"

"Not to me."

"Does he play the mandolin?"

"I sincerely hope not."

Owen expelled his breath. "Is there anything else you can tell me about him, to help bring him to heel, I mean?"

"Oh, Owen, if I knew that, he'd be mine by now."

CHAPTER EIGHTEEN

"There you are."

Alex's fork nearly toppled from her fingers. She'd been in the breakfast room, eating eggs and fruit, when her sister found her. Alex glanced around the room. No. No one else was there. Lavinia must be speaking to her.

"You're looking for *me*?" Alex asked incredulously.

"Yes, you, silly," Lavinia said with a long-suffering look on her face.

Alex laid down her fork and watched warily as her sister approached. Lavinia never ate in the breakfast room. She always had her breakfast sent up, and Mother didn't dare gainsay her. For Lavinia to be up and dressed at this hour of the morning and to make an appearance in the breakfast room . . . something was definitely not right.

Lavinia sailed around the edge of the gleaming wooden table and took a seat directly across from Alex. Then she folded her hands together in front of her and leaned across them.

"What . . . what is it?" Alex asked hesitantly, watching her sister as if she were a wildcat of some sort that might very well attack her.

"I wanted to see how your evening went last night."

"My evening?" Alex's eyes widened. She jerked her hand and knocked the lid off the delicate china sugar bowl.

"Yes." Lavinia settled her shoulders.

"What do you mean?" Alex replaced the lid.

Lavinia leaned back in her chair and shrugged. "I merely wondered how your dance with Lord Owen went."

Alex took a deep breath. Ah, this was what she'd been waiting for. Lavinia couldn't stand anyone else to receive attention meant for her.

"It was a bit of a bore, to be honest," she said, hoping her sister couldn't read the lie in her eyes.

"A bore?" Lavinia sat up straight and blinked.

"Yes." Alex nodded rapidly.

"Why so?"

Alex affected a long dramatic sigh. "Lord Owen could only talk about you all night."

"He did?" An unpleasant grin spread across her sister's face, but a kind of sparkle lit her eyes, too.

"Yes," Alex continued. "And I hope to cause no offense, but it was hardly interesting for me to answer questions about *you* all evening."

Lavinia leaned forward. "What did he want to know?"

Alex sighed again for additional dramatic effect. There was never too much dramatic effect when Lavinia was involved. "He wanted to know what you were like. Your favorite pastimes, your favorite foods, even how you take your tea."

A catlike smile unfurled across her sister's face. "He did?"

"Yes. Of course, I didn't reveal much. I know he was only fishing for information to woo you, and you've made it clear that you're wholly uninterested, haven't you?"

Lavinia tapped her fingers along the edge of the table. "Yes. Well, perhaps, but he certainly made you the belle of the ball, now, didn't he? And the rumor on everyone's lips was that he was taken with *you*."

Alex bit her lip. Confound it. Lavinia sounded jealous. That was no good. Alex had been worried that her sister might not take well to her gathering attention from gentlemen, but she couldn't very well tell Lavinia that she was courting attention from the one man Lavinia had the least interest in.

"Oh no, rest assured. If he was taken with me, it was solely for the purpose of asking about you."

Lavinia seemed pleased with that answer. "Tell me, have you had any luck finding a suitable suitor for me?"

Alex froze. She hadn't expected Lavinia to ask so soon. "No. Not yet. But I haven't given up."

Lavinia frowned at that answer, but fortunately, Alex was spared additional discussion on the matter when their mother strode into the room. She was wearing an overly formal taffeta confection of an olive hue with a matching turban. Mother loved to overdress. "Oh, there you are, Alexandra. I've been looking for you."

"Me?" Alex blinked. Her mother was rarely looking for her. To be sought after by not one but *both* of the other ladies in the household today—why, it was unprecedented. Alex glanced at Lavinia. Lavinia looked surprised, too. She shrugged again.

"Yes, you," Mother continued, bracing her hands on the top of the chair next to Alex.

"Whatever for?" Alex took another tentative bite of eggs. This couldn't be good. Mother hadn't said a word about her suitors last night in the coach on the ride home from the Rutherfords'. Though that might well have had something to do with the fact that Alex pretended to promptly fall asleep as soon as they'd all settled into Father's coach. Of course, Thomas hadn't believed it for a moment and took great pleasure in elbowing her in the ribs each time the coach jostled. Something told Alex that Mother was about to make up for it.

Her mother raised her eyebrows imperiously. "I saw Lord Owen Monroe dance with you last night."

"Yes," Alex replied hesitantly.

"She said he was asking her all about *me*," Lavinia added, her nose pointed in the air and a smug smile on her thin lips.

Her mother's face bloomed with relief. "Oh, that's good to hear."

Alex clenched her fist. "Would it be so odd for Lord Owen to be interested in me?" As soon as the words were past her lips, she regretted them. And not just because both Lavinia and Mother instantly laughed, but also because she didn't want to even hint about her relationship with Owen. Not now, not yet.

But the laughter hadn't helped. Now Alex was becoming angry. Her cheeks heated. "Who am I? Cinderella?"

"No, of course not, Alexandra, but you're hardly the sort an experienced gentleman like Lord Owen would look at twice," her mother said in a tone that was meant to be sympathetic, but came out irritatingly condescending.

Alex braced both elbows on the table. "What sort *am* I, Mother?"

Lavinia waved a hand in the air. "You know . . . short, plump, too talkative, too starry-eyed."

Plump! Alex sucked in a lungful of air through her nostrils. "There's nothing wrong with being starry-eyed."

She folded her hands together on the table to keep from slapping her sister.

Her mother shook her head. "Of course not, dear. Don't be so sensitive. I only meant you two don't suit. That's hardly news."

"But you think Lord Owen and Lavinia suit?" Alex replied.

Her mother snapped her mouth shut and glared at her. Obviously, Alex had gotten too close to her secret.

"Don't be ridiculous," Lavinia interjected, taking a sip of the juice a servant had promptly delivered to her. "I wouldn't look twice at a scoundrel like him if he were the last titled lord in London."

Mother swallowed and turned to Lavinia with a pleading look on her face. "Oh, now, dear, don't be too hasty. Your father says Lord Owen has quite a future ahead of him in Parliament."

Lavinia's eyes nearly bugged from her skull. "You cannot be serious, Mother. Why, you yourself said not a month ago that he was nothing more than a drunken lout. The man actually offered me champagne and seemed put out when I refused it last night."

Mother wrung her hands. "Yes, well, your father thinks well of him, and it's made me reconsider." She didn't meet Lavinia's gaze.

Lavinia's face turned bright red. "Father's wrong! Owen Monroe would never make a proper husband!"

Oh no. Lavinia was shouting. It was certain to get worse. It always got worse. Mother glanced around frantically, as if searching about the dining table for something else to say.

"Well, he is handsome," Alex provided.

"Yes!" Mother nodded so hard, her turban nearly flew off her head. "Don't you think he's handsome, Lavinia?"

Lavinia scowled. "Who cares what he looks like? His behavior is atrocious. Do you know he actually told me last night that he doesn't care for horses? Can you imagine?"

"I haven't heard of anything awful he's done *lately,*" Alex added. "The horse comment notwithstanding."

Lavinia narrowed her eyes and glared at Alex. Among many other things, her sister had never properly appreciated sarcasm.

"That's quite a good point," Mother hastened to add, still nodding.

Lavinia's ears were practically purple. "You two have both lost your wits."

Mother pointed a finger in the air and eyed her eldest daughter carefully. "He does seem to be enamored of you, dear. Alexandra said so. Doesn't that count for something?"

Lavinia slapped her palm against the table, making the glasses bounce. "No. No. It does not! I doubt that man knows so much as a line of poetry."

Well, she couldn't argue with Lavinia there. Alex calmly smoothed the tablecloth as she met her sister's angry glare. Sometimes Providence handed you an unexpected gift. The proper reaction, of course, was to take it and use it promptly in thanksgiving. "So you're saying that no matter what he says or does, nor how much he might hope to woo you, you've absolutely *no* interest whatsoever in Lord Owen Monroe?"

Lavinia turned her head away and sniffed. "Certainly not. None!"

Next Alex turned toward her mother. "And *you're* saying that despite the fact that you haven't always been one of his most vocal supporters, you now actually believe him to be a suitable husband for your daughter?"

Mother swallowed and tugged at the throat of her gown. She turned her gaze to Lavinia. "Yes. If your father accepts him, so do I."

Lavinia opened her mouth, no doubt to protest further, but Alex stood up and plunked her juice glass down on the table. "Then I don't see how either one of you could possibly object if I try my luck with him. Good day."

And with that, Alex flounced out of the breakfast room with an enormous smile on her face.

CHAPTER NINETEEN

Alex ripped open the note written on expensive vellum, and her eyes scanned the message. She was sitting at the writing desk in her bedchamber. Hannah had brought her the missive that had been sent over via a footman.

Please call upon me at two o'clock this afternoon.
Yours, Lady Swifdon

Alex's belly remained full of knots all day, and she discarded at least three different gowns in favor of the demure lavender one she'd finally chosen. It had to be another message from Owen. He wouldn't risk sending her a missive directly. He must have asked his sister to write it for him. He wanted to see her again. Was it just that he had more questions about Lavinia?

Guilt tugged at her conscience when she remembered the way he'd thanked her so kindly at the Rutherfords'. "You've done nothing but try to help me," he'd said, referring to his trouble with Lavinia. If only he knew how very little Alex had helped.

She'd wondered, too, at the seeming ease with which he'd launched her into Society. "Your dancing card appears to be much fuller," he'd said. Yet he didn't appear to be jealous. At least not as jealous as Alex had hoped. Though he *had* asked if she'd been asked to dance by the man whom she was smitten by. The entire thing was becoming too complicated by half. She should write back and tell Lady Swifdon she had a megrim, was busy, couldn't get away. Yes. That would be best.

At precisely two o'clock, Alex's father's carriage, driven by the ever-bribed coachman, arrived at the front of Lord and Lady Swifdon's town house. Alex and Hannah alighted. Alex swallowed and straightened her shoulders before making her way up the front steps. She hadn't been able to resist after all. Her curiosity got the best of her and she'd loaded up herself and her maid and set off for Lady Swifdon's house.

The butler answered the door and showed her into the foyer. Alex glanced around anxiously. Owen was nowhere to be seen. The butler took her bonnet and then escorted her into a drawing room. The drawing room? She'd never been shown into the drawing room before. Her anxiety grew by the moment. Perhaps Owen would tell her they couldn't meet any longer. Perhaps he'd tell her he intended to stop courting Lavinia. Frankly, that notion frightened Alex more than it should, given the circumstances. Whatever he intended to tell her, she was slowly dying of curiosity, waiting.

Five entire minutes ticked by before the door opened, and in walked . . . Lady Swifdon. She wore a gown of soft yellow silk, and her matching honey blond hair was pulled up atop her head; a silver necklace and delicate yellow slippers completed her ensemble.

"Good afternoon, Lady Alexandra." Lady Swifdon swept across the room with a bright smile on her pretty face. "We've met, but it's been a while."

Alex jumped to her feet. "Of course I remember you, Lady Swifdon."

"Please call me Cass," Lady Swifdon continued with a conspiratorial grin on her lovely face.

Well, that was exceedingly kind of her. "Very well, Cass."

Lady Swifdon must have read Alex's mind because the next thing Cass said was, "Owen's not here today."

Alex shook her head. "He's not? I don't understand."

Cass glided over to the door and opened it. Two other beautiful women came sailing through. One was diminutive and wearing deep emerald and had curly black hair. The other was a bit more plump, with dark hair and eyes, and wore a sky blue gown and silver spectacles.

"Please meet my friends," Cass continued, gesturing to the ladies. "The Duchess of Claringdon and Mrs. Upton."

Alex watched them both with awe, especially the duchess, whom she'd heard about but never met. The diminutive curly-haired woman's husband was a famous war hero who had been made a duke by the Prince Regent after his bravery at Waterloo. The duchess approached her with a wide, easy smile. When she got close enough, Alex realized that one of her eyes was blue while the other was green. Intriguing, to be sure.

"It's a pleasure to meet you," the duchess said with an ever-expanding smile. "I've heard so much about you."

"You've heard so much . . . about *me*?" Alex pointed at herself.

"Yes, from Cass, dear."

"This is Mrs. Upton," Cass said, presenting the dark-haired, spectacle-wearing lady.

"A pleasure," Mrs. Upton said, sliding a book she'd been carrying into her reticule.

Alex searched her memory. She believed that Mrs. Upton had recently married Garrett Upton, the earl presumptive of Upbridge.

"Mrs. Upton is married to my cousin," the duchess clarified.

Alex nodded. She'd heard rumors that these three ladies of the *ton* were thick as thieves. They certainly were all quite beautiful and seemed intelligent as well.

"Please sit," Cass offered, and all four of them took seats on the settee and surrounding chairs. Alex watched Cass with growing interest. She was ethereal and had the same coloring as her gorgeous brother, honey blond hair and cornflower blue eyes. Only Lady Swifdon had no dimple in her cheek. A pity, that.

"I asked you to come today to meet with us, not Owen." Cass gestured to the duchess and Mrs. Upton.

Alex frowned. "I'm afraid I still don't understand."

"I'll explain," Cass replied. "First, allow me to ring for tea."

A quarter of an hour later, the four ladies were quietly sipping their tea when the duchess blurted out, "For goodness' sake, Cass, tell the poor girl why she's here. She looks half frightened out of her wits."

"Yes, Cass, do tell," Mrs. Upton added while enthusiastically consuming a tea cake.

"Very well." Cass set her teacup aside and turned to face Alex, smoothing her skirts.

Alex tried to keep her hand that held the teacup from shaking. "Yes . . . my lady? I mean, Cass."

"I asked you here today, Alex—do you mind if I call you Alex?" Cass began.

"Not at all," Alex said with a relieved smile. "I much prefer it, actually."

The duchess clapped her hands. "Famous. You will call me Lucy and call Jane, Jane as well."

"Very well," Alex agreed after receiving a friendly nod of approval from Mrs. Upton. She turned back to Cass. "What did you want to ask me?"

Cass straightened her shoulders and met Alex's eyes. "My brother tells me you two are in business of a sort together."

Alex's hands shook so badly, a bit of tea splashed over the side of the cup and plopped on the delicate white china saucer. "Something like that," she answered. How much did the countess know? How much would Owen want her to know?

"He said you are both working toward the same goal, to ensure the match between him and your sister, Lavinia."

Alex breathed a sigh of relief. Apparently, Owen had already shared details with his sister. Alex had nothing to worry about. "That's right," she replied happily, picking up her teacup again and taking a sip.

"He said you're interested in helping to marry off your sister because you want to become betrothed yourself."

"That's correct." Alex nodded again and took another sip.

"He said you are in love with someone."

Alex's hand froze halfway to her lips for the third sip. "Ye-yes. That's true."

"And I don't want to pry, dear, but . . ." The countess bit her lip.

"But?" Alex echoed.

Several seconds of silence passed while all four ladies stared at each other.

"Oh, for heaven's sake," Lucy blurted out. "What Cass means to ask is, it's Owen you're in love with, isn't it?"

Alex's teacup clattered to the carpet.

CHAPTER TWENTY

"Oh, my goodness. I'm so clumsy. Forgive me." Alex immediately jumped up from her seat and fell to the floor, using the linen napkin from her lap to blot the tea from the countess's rug.

"Don't worry about that, dear," Cass said, meeting Alex on the carpet to tug the napkin from her hand. "One of the servants will tend to it later. My apologies for Lucy's startling you." She gave Lucy a condemning glare. Lucy merely shrugged.

Denied her napkin, Alex reluctantly moved back into her seat and bit her lip. "Lucy didn't startle me. It's just that . . ."

"It's true," Lucy said, a triumphant grin on her face. "Isn't it?"

Jane shook her head. "Lucy, leave the poor girl alone. Let her speak."

Lucy crossed her arms over her chest. "Very well, but I already know I'm right."

Alex pressed a hand against her belly to calm her

rioting nerves. She met Cass's kind gaze. "Did . . . did Owen say that? That I'm in love with him?"

"Of course not, dear. That was entirely my guess. Call it female instinct. I don't think Owen has a clue, though I daresay he's a bit jealous of your beau." Cass gave Alex a conspiratorial smile.

Alex hung her head. "I don't have a beau." At least the sick feeling had left her stomach as soon as Cass assured her that Owen had no idea.

"Aha!" Lucy pointed a finger in the air. "I'm right, then, aren't I?"

"Is Lucy right, Alexandra?" Jane asked with a sigh. "And let me assure you that I hope she's not. Not for Owen's sake, mind you, but so that she won't be so smug in the future."

Lucy rolled her eyes at her friend. Alex glanced at Lucy, who did, indeed, look smug. "First of all, please call me Alex. I've quite grown used to it of late."

"Owen calls her Alex," Cass announced to her friends. The three exchanged knowing nods.

"And secondly, it is true." Alex leaned over her lap and buried her head in her hands.

"I'm so glad!" Cass exclaimed, clapping her hands.

Alex glanced up. Had she heard the countess correctly? "You're glad?"

"Yes, ever so glad." Cass's pretty face was wreathed with a bright smile.

"May I ask why?" Alex replied, blinking.

"Because I am convinced my brother has feelings for you. Strong ones."

Alex's eyes widened. Strong feelings? For *her*? Were they speaking of the same man? "But you must know that my father and your father have already been discussing the marriage contract between Owen and my sister."

"Yes. I know." Cass's smile didn't falter.

"Then may I ask how you think this is a *good* thing?" Alex continued.

Lucy laughed. "Oh, you're adorable, Alex. You must not know the stories of how the three of us met our husbands."

Alex shook her head. "No. I don't."

Lucy patted her coiffure. "Suffice it to say, they were unconventional and unexpected, all three. Well, mine was unexpected. Cass's was accidental. And I'd say Janie's was downright . . . unlikely. Wouldn't you agree, Jane?"

Jane pursed her lips as if considering it for a moment. She pushed her spectacles up her nose. "Yes. Yes. I think that's an apt word, 'unlikely.'"

"What happened?" Alex couldn't help her answering smile. The duchess's joy was contagious.

"The tales are far too long to tell you now, dear," Lucy replied. "But the fact is that they all happened entirely without our parents' involvement or consent. We are unimpressed with the plans of parents. They are so very often wrong in matters of the heart. Don't you agree?"

Alex sighed. "Try telling that to my father. He can be quite stubborn."

"I don't think you understand, dear," Lucy replied. "We're talking about the type of to-dos that include giving prompts while hiding behind a hedge, pretending to be a fictitious person, and hiring a nonexistent chaperone."

Alex blinked. "Pardon?"

Jane nodded again. "It's all true. A stubborn father doesn't so much as give us pause."

Alex had the distinct feeling that not much gave them pause. "Lavinia's convinced Owen is a scoundrel, but I think he's much more than that."

"Oh, he is, dear. He is," Cass agreed. "Our father has never given him his approval, you see, and it's greatly affected him."

"He doesn't seem as if he gives a toss about anyone's approval to me," Alex replied.

"He doesn't." Cass glanced away with tears in her eyes. "Not anymore."

"You must tell her the Eton story," Lucy prompted.

"Don't tell her the Eton story," Jane said in between bites of tea cake.

"What's the Eton story?" Alex asked, blinking.

"Well, now you must tell her," Lucy said to Cass.

"I shall, but only because it's clear how much regard she has for Owen," Cass replied.

Alex leaned forward to hear better.

"Well," Cass began, smoothing her skirts. "Owen attended Eton, of course, but not many people know that while there, he was close with Julian and Garrett. Among others in their group."

Alex nodded.

"One day when they were around twelve, they all decided it would be a good prank to take the headmaster's horse out for a ride."

"Oh no," Alex whispered.

"Yes," Cass replied. "They spent the afternoon riding about and causing havoc in the town before the headmaster came looking for them. By that time, they'd brought the horse back to the stables."

Alex gasped. "Did he find them?"

"He found only one of them," Cass replied. "Owen."

"Where were the others?" Alex asked.

"Owen told them to hide. Apparently, he insisted. The others had recently been disciplined for their part in another prank. Owen had been visiting home at the time, probably the only reason he wasn't in on that one, too. He thought it would be better for them if he took the entire blame himself."

"What happened?" Alex breathed. But she almost didn't want to know.

"In their haste to retreat, one of the other boys knocked over a lantern. The entire stable went up in flames."

"No," Alex whispered.

"None of the people or horses were hurt, but the building was an entire loss."

"Who knocked over the lantern?" Alex asked.

"No one knows for sure. Till this day, they've all maintained their silence. It's the honor code at such schools."

"In the end, it doesn't matter," Lucy replied. "Owen took the entire blame. He refused to admit anyone else was with him, even when the headmaster pressed him."

"What happened to him?" Alex asked, this time truly dreading the answer.

"Owen was expelled. The headmaster was not in a forgiving mood. Father had to travel to the school and plead Owen's case. He agreed to pay for the cost of a new stable."

"And they still didn't allow him to stay?"

"No. He ended up at Harrow and fell in with an unruly set of boys who were interested only in drinking and causing trouble."

"And your father?" Alex asked.

"Afterwards, apparently Owen tried to tell Father what really happened, but Father wouldn't listen. He never forgave Owen. Every Earl of Moreland in the history of the title was an Eton graduate. Father told Owen he'd brought shame upon the family. He told him he was no good and would never amount to anything."

"And Owen set about proving him right?" Alex finished.

"Precisely," Cass said. "And he has far too much honor and pride to tell Father the truth now."

"It's so sad. All that lost time over something so insignificant," Alex said.

"It wasn't insignificant to Father or Owen," Cass replied.

"No, of course not," Alex agreed. "But in the end, it was just a stable. And it's not as if Harrow is a bad school."

Lucy shook her head. "Of course not. But now you perhaps might understand a bit more about him. We adore Owen, you see, and we think you are perfectly suited to him."

Alex glanced among all three ladies, not at all certain how the story she'd just heard had anything to do with her suitability for Owen. "What are you saying?"

Cass leaned forward and patted her hand. "We know you care for him, Alex, and we're saying we want to help you. But first we must warn you that our methods can often be . . . unpredictable." Cass stared at Lucy when she uttered that last word.

Lucy raised her chin in the air. "Unpredictable, perhaps, but effective."

"Granted," Jane replied, "but ever so troublesome at times."

Troublesome? Alex didn't like the sound of that. "I don't understand. What do you want to help me with?"

"Why, to bring Owen to heel, of course," Cass replied. "I'd all but despaired of him finding a love match."

Alex's eyes nearly popped from her skull. "A love match?"

Cass laughed. "Yes, of course. The way he's been

speaking about you, why, he's half in love with you already. I'm quite convinced."

Alex's face fell. "Only half?"

Cass patted her hand again. "Men can be a bit thick sometimes. But don't worry. We'll help."

"Yes," Lucy said, settling into her chair and clearly warming to her subject. "We have a plan."

"A plan?" Alex echoed, her eyes widening again.

"Oh no, not a plan." Jane groaned and put the back of her wrist to her forehead.

"Ignore her, Alex," Lucy said with a sniff.

"What exactly is your plan?" Alex ventured.

The duchess's smile lit her different-colored eyes. "Well, Cass and I have been talking, and we think Owen needs a bit of *real* competition."

CHAPTER TWENTY-ONE

The next evening, Owen steeled his resolve and forced himself to attend the Heathcliffs' ball. He'd spent far too much time trying to court Lavinia Hobbs in the way she preferred. He was done with niceties. Now he was going to court her on his terms. Whether she liked it or not.

Owen searched the crowd. Lavinia was near the refreshment table, her usual group of friends—or perhaps they were the ladies too frightened of her temper to cut her—by her side. Her nose was turned up in its usual fashion. Owen blew out a deep breath. He couldn't make his legs walk over to her. He continued his search of the room. He looked twice. There, on the dance floor, was Alex. She looked bright and fresh and pretty as usual in a light green gown with a smile on her face and a twinkle in her eye and she was dancing with . . . Viscount Berkeley. She was laughing, smiling, and batting at the viscount's shoulder with her fan. In short, she was doing all the things that *Owen* had taught her to do, and she was doing them as if she were born to the role of consummate flirt.

The two most unexpected feelings twisted in Owen's gut. Jealousy. Envy. Both so foreign to him, he nearly didn't recognize them at first. But the more he watched the viscount spin Alex around on the floor, the more he wanted to crush the man's throat in his hands and take his place. Yes. That *had* to be jealousy.

Owen watched like a scorned suitor from the sidelines with increasing envy as the dance ended and Berkeley escorted Alex over to the refreshment table, where he plucked a glass of champagne from one of the silver trays and handed it to her with a gallant bow. Owen hated gallants. He squeezed his fist as if he were squeezing it around Berkeley's neck. Berkeley was not only eligible and handsome but young and tall, too, and he had an impeccable reputation. No drinking too much or gambling too much or too much anything. In fact, if the viscount were known for anything, it was rarely coming to town and spending far too much time by himself in the North of England at his estate. *That* was whom Alex preferred? Lord Saintly?

He searched his memory for what Alex had said about the man whom she fancied. Tall, handsome, titled, blond with blue eyes, not much luck on the marriage mart to date. The description fit Berkeley perfectly. Damn his tall, handsome, blond-haired, blue-eyed hide.

Owen's gaze flashed back to Lavinia. She was also watching Alex as if her interest in Berkeley had piqued her curiosity as well. Owen closed his eyes briefly and forced himself to stride over to Lavinia.

"My lady." He bowed.

Lavinia's face turned to a mask of stone. She sighed. "My lord."

Her friends giggled. Owen ignored them.

"Happy to see me, are you?" he quipped.

She merely pursed her lips.

Behind her back, Owen could still see Alex and Berkeley talking. "I'd ask you to dance, but I have a feeling you'd say no."

"You're correct, my lord," Lavinia replied.

"Would you care for a rock?"

Lavinia gave him a look that clearly indicated she believed he might have lost his mind. "A rock?"

The other ladies giggled more.

"Never mind." Owen slid his hand into his pocket. "About the dance. Is there anything I can do to change your—?" Alex laughed at something Berkeley said, loud enough for Owen to hear, making him lose his train of thought. Then Berkeley offered Alex his arm and they headed back to the dance floor. *Two* dances with the same man in a row? Had Owen taught her *nothing*?

"What was that, my lord?" Lavinia's face registered her pique at Owen's sudden lack of full-blown attention.

"Excuse me a moment, Lady Lavinia." Owen didn't wait for an answer. Instead he stalked off to the dance floor, dodged the couples flying around him, and tapped Berkeley on the shoulder. "May I cut in?"

Berkeley, being Berkeley and the consummate gentleman, hesitated only a moment before turning his attention to Alex. "Do you mind, Lady Alexandra?"

Alex shook her head. "No. It's fine."

Berkeley gave Owen a sideways glance as he bowed to Alex and took his leave. Owen glared back. Then he spun Alex into his arms and resumed the dance.

"That was unexpected," Alex murmured once they'd found their pace. "Why did you do it?"

"The truth is I don't know why," Owen replied.

"My, but you truly know how to flatter a young lady, don't you?"

His lips quirked in a grin. "Why, Lady Alexandra, is that sarcasm?"

"Indeed," she replied, grinning back at him. "I saw you speaking to Lavinia."

"Yes, it was nearly as diverting as speaking to a garden snake."

Alex bit her lip to keep from laughing. "I'm sorry to hear that."

"I take that back. A garden snake is no doubt better company."

"Rejected you again, did she?"

"Frankly, I didn't even give her the chance to reject me again. I came to dance with you instead. You're infinitely better company."

Alex arched one dark brow. "I would take that as a compliment, my lord, if you hadn't just said Lavinia's company was less interesting than that of a garden snake."

"I enjoy dancing with you, Alex."

She blushed prettily and gazed over his shoulder. "Thank you . . . I think."

"I meant it as a compliment."

"Then thank you."

She was still looking over his shoulder. Damn it. Was she searching for Berkeley? "Did you enjoy your dance with the viscount?"

"Immensely."

"Then you were sorry to see me cut in?" Owen hated the grumbly quality of his voice.

"I didn't say that. I thought perhaps you might need to ask me something about Lavinia."

"You're right about one thing: I do want to speak with you, Alex. Alone."

CHAPTER TWENTY-TWO

"Will you come outside with me?" Owen asked.

Alex took a deep but shaky breath. She had spent the last hour talking to and dancing with the extremely courteous and kind Lord Berkeley. If ever two men were different, they were Lord Christian Berkeley and Lord Owen Monroe. Oh so different. Where Owen was brash and arrogant, Lord Berkeley was quiet and unassuming. Where Owen was always ready for a drink and a hand of cards, Lord Berkeley had announced his distaste for gambling, and while he'd had a glass of champagne, she barely saw him take two sips of it. Alex had thanked him so profusely for his help that the viscount had finally chuckled and said, "Think nothing of it. I'm always happy to help Lucy Hunt execute her impractical plots." It was a convenient thing that the man appeared to have a good sense of humor, at least. Although Alex already knew Lucy well enough to know that a certain gameness was a necessity if one wished to remain in her inner circle for any significant length of time.

Alex had tried to explain herself to Lord Berkeley. "I hope you don't think ill of me, attempting to gain Lord Owen's attention in this manner, it's just that—"

Lord Berkeley had held up a hand and shook his head. "No need to explain. We all do foolish things when we fancy someone. Remind me to tell you the story about how I once asked Claringdon to write love letters to Lucy for me."

Alex's mouth had formed a wide O. "You? Wrote love letters to Lucy Hunt?"

"No," Lord Berkeley replied, shaking his head and chuckling. "I asked her future *husband* to do it for me. Of course, I didn't know at the time that the two had an affinity for one another." He laughed again. "It was all rather outrageous upon reflection. But then again, Lucy is known for her outrageousness. It's what makes her so endearing."

Alex had studied the viscount carefully. He was tall and blond and broad-shouldered with crystal blue eyes and a ready smile. He was thoughtful, helpful, and a bit shy, which made him even more appealing. According to Lucy, he also had an unfortunate habit of stuttering when in the presence of a female whom he particularly fancied. He hadn't stuttered once in Alex's presence. Apparently, he was no more enamored of her than she was of him, Alex thought with a wry smile. Though she couldn't help but think that Lord Christian Berkeley would make some very lucky lady a fine husband one day.

"Will you come?" Owen repeated, snapping Alex from her thoughts.

She wanted to go with him, but she was no longer the ready little wallflower she'd been mere days ago. Thanks to Owen, she understood the rules of the game now. And she intended to play by them. She gave Owen her most practiced coquettish smile and turned to the side to blink at him over one shoulder. "Ah, but someone quite wise once told me never to go alone somewhere with a man who might try to take advantage of me."

Owen lifted a brow, giving her a skeptical look. "What if I promise to behave myself out there?"

She pressed the tip of her closed fan to her lips. "Where's the fun in that?"

Both his eyebrows shot up this time, and Alex couldn't help but feel a bit silly for her flirting. He'd taught her how, after all. He had to know what she was about.

"Come with me and find out," he replied in a tone that made Alex's knees turn to honey. He flashed that charming dimple when he said it. She swallowed, trying desperately to still the pounding of her heart.

"Very well," she said simply, walking past him on her way to the French doors that led to the balcony. She tried to ignore his rugged manly scent as she walked past.

Owen followed close behind her.

As soon as the door to the balcony closed after them, she turned to him. "So, what is it you wanted to say to me? Alone."

Owen shoved a hand in his pocket and took a few steps to be nearer to her. "Lord Berkeley?" He allowed the name to hang in the air as a question with no further elaboration.

Alex kept her eyes downcast so Owen couldn't read her thoughts. This "being demure" business was actually quite difficult. "I don't know what you mean."

"You said you enjoyed your dance with him immensely," Owen replied. "Is he the man you fancy?"

She couldn't do it. She couldn't bring herself to say the lie about her affections outright. Cass and Lucy had instructed her on this point. "Let him think you fancy

Berkeley. We've spoken to him. Christian will play the consummate suitor. He's the perfect choice." It had been nothing more than pure, perfect coincidence that Lord Berkeley just happened to possess the physical qualities she'd already mentioned to Owen.

Alex pressed her lips together. "You knew I had a fancy for someone. . . ."

There. That wasn't quite a lie, but it also wasn't telling the truth. Oh, God help her for being so awful.

A muscle in Owen's jaw ticked. Was he angry? "I had no idea it was Viscount Berkeley."

"You never asked. I never told you." More prevaricating. "What does it matter who it is?"

Owen slapped his hand against his thigh and paced away from her. "It doesn't. I simply—" He turned back sharply to face her. "Do you think it wise to spend time with him? While we're still trying to make Lavinia jealous?"

Alex could have been knocked flat with a pin. Was Owen Monroe actually indicating that he didn't want her to spend time with another man? "I didn't know you cared so much about making Lavinia jealous," she countered.

"I don't, but I—" He paced away again, scrubbing his hands through his hair. "I suppose your part of our plan worked if Berkeley is now paying you attention."

This was going to be the most difficult part. "Yes," Alex breathed. "Thank you for that." She fought the tears that unexpectedly popped to her eyes. If only Lucy and Cass hadn't been so adamant. "Make him think Berkeley is the only man for you," Lucy had said. "Tell him how much you've fancied him," Cass had added. Jane had merely looked up from her book and rolled her eyes a bit. "I want no part of this," she'd declared.

"Don't act so innocent, Janie," Lucy had said, her

hands on her hips. "You pretended to have a nonexistent chaperone once upon a time and were embroiled in a positive scandal of your own making."

"Yes," Jane had replied. "That's precisely how I know how much trouble it all leads to." She'd pushed up her spectacles and turned to Alex. "I wish you the best, Lady Alexandra, truly. But I cannot offer any advice. Besides, Lucy is the real plotter here. I hate to say it, but if you follow her advice, you have a very good chance of getting exactly what you want . . . eventually. Even I must admit that a bit of competition worked with me and Mrs. Langford, the war widow, when it came to Garrett."

Alex hadn't particularly liked how Jane had said "eventually," but she'd been heartened by the rest of the statement. And Lucy had been adamant that Alex *insist* that she was madly in love with Lord Berkeley.

Owen turned to Alex with a sharp slant to his voice, drawing her away from her thoughts once again. "So, that's it? You've got what you wanted."

Alex's heart tugged. She didn't have what she wanted at all. But she had to continue to play this game. "I still intend to help you with Lavinia," she assured him. "What else do you want to know about her?"

He shook his head. "I don't have any idea. It seems entirely hopeless."

"How did it go with her . . . tonight?"

"As badly as you'd expect. She doesn't seem to be impressed with the things you told me to mention. I think it's because they're coming from me. I could tell her everything she'd ever wanted to hear, and she'd reject it coming from me."

Alex stared at her slippers. She pushed one along the stone floor beneath her feet. "I'm sorry you're disappointed."

He groaned. "I need you, Alex. Tell me something, anything that will help to make her come around to the idea of marrying me. I doubt my trying to woo her is of any use anymore. She seems to have a heart of stone, but *something* has to melt it."

Mine is already melted.

Alex gulped. He wasn't jealous after all. At least not jealous enough to stop trying to court Lavinia. Oh God. What had Alex expected? Their parents were all counting on an engagement between Owen and Lavinia. In their world, one did what one's parents told one to do. That was how it worked. It would take more than one dance with another man to make Owen jealous enough to defy his father.

Alex paced over to the balustrade and stared out into the darkened gardens. "I don't know what else to say," she murmured. "Perhaps you should simply tell Lavinia the truth. That Mother and Father want you to marry each other. See what she says."

He strode over to her, and Alex looked up at him. The breeze ruffled his hair. "Thank you for your help, Alex." He turned back toward the door.

Alex's voice was soft and low. "You're quite welcome."

How had this conversation begun with Owen seeming to be jealous over Lord Berkeley and ended with him asking for additional ways to win Lavinia?

With one foot resting on the stone step that led back inside, Owen said, "Good luck with your viscount."

Alex watched him go and expelled her pent-up breath.

CHAPTER TWENTY-THREE

"Get up!"

Owen blinked against the harsh sunlight that was streaming through the window of his bedchamber. Though he'd come home quite alone, he'd gone on a bender last night. One of which he was not particularly proud, and now his head pounded like the devil and someone had kicked his mattress and yelled at him.

He blinked through his bleary haze some more, opening his eyes to see his father's rotund form standing above him.

"What time is it?" he asked through a cracked, dry throat.

"Well past noon, of course." His father always sounded judgmental.

"I was out till after four."

His father rolled his eyes. "That makes it all right?"

"No. That makes it exceedingly early. For me."

Owen struggled to his feet and pulled on his dressing robe. Then he sat on the edge of his bed, braced his palms on his parted knees, and contemplated his father through unfocused eyes. "What can I help you with?"

His father grabbed his lapels and began to pace in front of Owen. "I want to know how you're progressing. With Lady Lavinia."

"Ah, so the parents want a progress report, do they?"

His father hesitated briefly. "Yes. We do. All four of us."

"It's progressing as well as can be expected." Owen yawned and rubbed his fingers through his hair.

"Yet you were out till all hours instead of courting her?"

Owen rolled his head around on his neck. "On the contrary, I went to a ball to see her and then I went out till all hours." And he'd gone out till all hours to try to blot out the memory of Alex dancing with Viscount Berkeley.

His father grunted. "You're not witty, you know."

"I have reason to believe otherwise."

His father yanked at his lapels again and resumed his pacing. "Is she taking a liking to you? Showing interest?"

"That task has proved impossible. The girl is an icicle. I've decided I'm just going to tell her we're meant to marry. Reason with her."

"No!" His father's voice shook the rafters. "You must make her fall in love with you."

Owen rubbed his temples. "I'm telling you that's far easier said than done."

More lapel tugging ensued. "What's this? Lost your confidence, have you? Where's the lad who was so certain of himself not a fortnight ago?"

"He's been trying to pay court to a dragon," Owen muttered.

"I won't have you insulting the chit, Owen. Now, listen here—"

"If it's a match with the duke's family you want so dearly, Father, why can't I court Lady *Alexandra* Hobbs instead? She's Lady Lavinia's younger sister."

His father's eyes widened, and his face quickly turned a mottled shade of red. "Lady Alexandra—Why, that's preposterous! Is the girl even wearing long skirts yet? It's Lady *Lavinia* whom the duke wants you to marry, and it's Lady Lavinia you shall marry."

"I don't see why he's so set on it. She's a horror."

"You're not exactly the most brilliant catch yourself. You should be honored the duke will accept you, what with your tarnished reputation."

"Not to mention my ignominious matriculation at Harrow."

His father turned toward the door, completely ignoring Owen's remark. "The one thing I thought I could count on you to do, Owen, was charm a female."

That was it. His father had just thrown down the gauntlet. There was no way Owen wasn't going to scoop it right up.

"Fine. Don't worry. I have everything perfectly in control. I have . . . help."

His father's bushy eyebrows arched. "Help? What sort of help?"

"I've enlisted the aid of someone quite close to Lady Lavinia to give me the details on her likes and dislikes. I'll redouble my efforts to woo her in the span of a fortnight."

His father narrowed his eyes on him but looked a bit mollified. "Very well. See that you do, Owen. We're all counting on you. Don't fail me. For once."

* * *

The door to Brooks's swung open, and Owen was welcomed by a bowing footman. "My lord," the man intoned as Owen handed him his hat. Owen glanced around. The club was busy for a Wednesday afternoon.

"Have you seen the Duke of Claringdon? Or the Earl of Swifdon?" Owen asked.

"I believe they're in the blue drawing room, my lord," the footman answered.

Owen went directly there. He found Claringdon, Swifdon, Cavendish, and a man who looked exactly like . . . Cavendish. The four men were talking, laughing, and drinking brandy.

"Monroe, there you are," Swifdon said, standing to clap Owen on the back. He gestured to a seat next to them. "Join us."

"Good to see you, Claringdon." Owen slumped into a nearby leather chair. "I must say I'm a bit surprised to see you here again, Cavendish. Let alone *two* of you."

"Have you met my twin brother, Cade?" Cavendish flourished a hand in his brother's direction.

"I don't believe I have." Owen shook hands with the captain's twin.

"Always a pleasure to meet another blue blood," Cade replied. Owen noticed that the captain winced. He didn't know much about Rafferty Cavendish's twin, other than the fact that Cade had recently returned from years of being at sea. Apparently, until his return, Cavendish had believed Cade to be dead.

"The pleasure is mine," Owen said, settling back into his chair.

"How is your engagement proceeding?" Claringdon asked. He stopped a footman to order a brandy for Owen.

"As you all already told me, the lady is . . . difficult."

"I'm sorry to hear that," Swifdon said. "Can't you just tell her your parents want the match and be done with it?"

Owen sat back in his chair and rested his arm over his head. "I wish I could. It's more complicated than that."

"How?" Swifdon asked.

"First of all, the duke insists that his daughter fall in love with me."

Claringdon winced. "That's not easy."

"No it is not, and with this particular lady, it's even more difficult than usual. She has the personality of an angry she-cat."

"And?" Cavendish prodded.

"There's something else?" Swifdon asked.

"There's always something else," Cavendish said with a grin.

"What else?" Swifdon asked.

Owen took a deep breath. "In the course of trying to court Lady Lavinia, I've gotten to know her sister and I find I am much more interested in pursuing *her.*"

Cavendish's brows shot up. Claringdon nodded sagely, and Swifdon whistled.

"Good God. That does seem like a pickle," Swifdon said.

"Have you mentioned this to your father?" Claringdon asked.

"Yes. He insists it's Lady Lavinia or no one. He's threatening to cut off my allowance. Apparently, the duke is interested in marrying off his daughters one at a time."

Cade, who had been entirely silent up to this point, announced, "Well, that's easy enough." He took a hearty sip of his brandy.

Owen's head snapped to the side to face the man. "Easy? How?"

"Just find a chap to marry the first chit and run off with the second," Cade said with a roguish grin.

Swifdon and Claringdon laughed. Rafe shook his head and groaned. "The man's not like you, Cade. He has morals."

Cade tossed a hand in the air and went back to drinking his brandy. "Morals are overrated."

"Don't listen to him," Rafe said. "You cannot run off with the girl."

Owen rubbed the back of his neck. "At present, I'm not at all certain she even *wants* to run off with me."

Now Swifdon shook his head. "You might begin by telling her how you feel."

Owen shifted uncomfortably in his chair. Cade looked positively horrified.

"We're not all of us adept at writing love letters as you did with Cass," Rafe said with a laugh to Swifdon.

"You can always do what I did with Lucy," Claringdon announced.

Owen took another gulp of brandy. "What's that?"

"Get drunk, punch a tree, climb up into her window, and kiss her."

CHAPTER TWENTY-FOUR

There would be no more meetings, no more stolen moments in Cass's ballroom. Alex read the letter from Owen with a mixture of frustrated tears in her eyes and burgeoning anger in her heart.

You've done all you can for me, he wrote. *Thank you for your assistance. I will endeavor to do my best alone.*

He had been jealous seeing her with Berkeley; Alex knew he had been. She couldn't prove it, but she knew it deep down. Just as Cass and Lucy had assured her he would be. Then why wasn't it working? Why wasn't he coming to heel? Why wasn't he admitting that Alex was the one he had feelings for? Were his father's edict and Lavinia's dowry so important to him after all? Had Alex been wrong about him?

She posed these same questions to Cass and Lucy several hours later when she paid a call to the countess. The duchess happened to also be visiting her friend.

"Oh, dear, no, no. You're not seeing it clearly," Lucy said, stirring two lumps of sugar in her teacup.

Cass sat in front of the window, an easel in front of her, painting a vase of roses in soft watercolors. "Lucy's correct, dear," she replied. "Owen has a great deal of pride, and seeing you with Berkeley once is not enough for him to admit how very wrong he's been."

Alex shook her head. "I don't understand."

"He's been telling you all this time how he wants to marry your sister. Just think how it will look for him to suddenly declare his love for you. Besides, he's in something of a snare, having to defy Father and all that."

"So I shouldn't expect him to declare himself?" Alex asked.

Lucy took a sip of tea, made a funny face, and set it back down to administer even more sugar. "Of course he'll declare himself, but he obviously needs more inducement first."

Alex let her head fall into her hands. "More inducement? What do you suggest? That I begin flirting with every gentleman in the *ton*?"

Cass looked up from her painting and tapped the end of the brush against her cheek. "Now, that idea is not half bad."

"I agree," Lucy said, sipping her tea happily now. "I think only good can come from him having more competition."

"But this isn't how I wanted it to go at all." Alex groaned.

"Of course not, dear. It never goes the way we *want* it to go," Lucy continued. "But it always goes the way it was meant to."

Alex raised her head and blinked at the duchess. "What is that supposed to mean?"

"It means just what I said, dear," Lucy replied. "These things are complicated. They take time. Owen is a rakehell. Getting him to admit he's fallen for an innocent is not about to happen quickly. Keep doing exactly what you're doing. Lord Berkeley has agreed to continue to help you. He's a prize. In fact, if you weren't so set on Owen, I'd say you should turn your attentions to him."

Cass frowned at Lucy. "I'll thank you to leave my future sister-in-law alone."

Alex had to smile at their banter. "Lord Berkeley is quite nice, but . . ."

Lucy sighed. "I know. I know. You're madly in love with your rakehell."

Alex's cheeks heated. "I can't help it."

"Of course you can't, dear," Cass called. "Owen is quite a catch, too, and I've always known the right lady would make him into a doting husband."

Alex sighed. "Doting? Owen? I cannot imagine it."

"Once he commits to you, he'll dote on you. Take my word for it." Cass flourished her brush on the canvas once again.

Alex pressed her hands to her cheeks. "Very well. So you both think that I should continue to do what I'm doing—flirt with Lord Berkeley and the other gentlemen who've shown me attention, and completely ignore Owen?"

"Don't *completely* ignore him, dear," Lucy replied. "Throw him a glance or two and a friendly wave from time to time. It's far too obvious if you *completely* ignore him."

Alex groaned again. "This is driving me mad."

A wide grin spread across Lucy's gamine face. "It's driving him mad also, dear. That's the entire point."

CHAPTER TWENTY-FIVE

The Miffletons' ballroom was ablaze with the light of a thousand candles. Alex paced back and forth near the refreshment table. She wore a stunning fire-colored gown that she'd just recently purchased from Madame Bergeron, her mother's favorite modiste on Bond Street. The gown was so gorgeous that Lavinia had pouted when she saw Alex in the foyer before they made their way outside to the coach. Mother had had to assure Lavinia that she, too, looked ravishing in her own ice-blue gown. Thomas had gone back to school, and so Alex was alone with her parents and sister. Again.

She searched the ballroom, looking for any signs of her friends. Finally, she saw Lord Berkeley standing head and shoulders above most of the other gentlemen. Thank goodness. She'd been a bit worried that he wouldn't appear tonight, and where would it leave her?

Lord Berkeley spotted her, nodded, and made his way through the crush to her side. "My lady," he said with a bow.

"My lord," she replied, curtsying and sharing his smile.

"I have it on the best authority—namely from Lucy— that Owen Monroe has just entered the ballroom. Given that, may I have this dance?"

Alex nodded and placed her arm on his. "What would I do without you, my lord?"

They danced, and Berkeley, the dream that he was, ensured that he steered them to the far side of the room, where Owen was holding court with his sister and Lord Swifdon. Alex's gaze darted around the ballroom. Lavinia was nowhere to be seen at the moment.

Keeping Lucy's advice in mind, Alex glanced at Owen, who appeared to be glaring holes in Berkeley's jacket. A muscle in Owen's jaw ticked and he took a stiff drink from the brandy glass he clutched in his left hand.

She smiled at him politely but briefly, barely indicating she was aware of his presence before turning her attention back to Lord Berkeley and delivering her most dazzling smile. She laughed at something he hadn't said and batted her eyelashes at the viscount.

Lord Berkeley glanced over to Owen's group. "It's working," he said. "Keep doing what you're doing. I've little doubt Monroe wants to call me out right now."

Her hand on his shoulder shook a bit. "Do you truly think it's working?"

Lord Berkeley's smile was friendly and warm. "I *know* it's working. I think he's close to crushing that unfortunate brandy glass."

"Oh, I do hope that doesn't happen," Alex said, biting her lip.

"I'll give him about two more minutes before he cuts in again."

Butterflies scattered in Alex's belly. She waited and

waited, her anticipation growing with each turn on the floor. But Owen did not come. She danced with Berkeley one more time before finally admitting defeat and asking him to deposit her back at the refreshment table. "I cannot ask you to do more, my lord."

"He's a stubborn one, I'll give him that," Berkeley said as he escorted Alex across the room. "Perhaps it's best if you give him time to come and greet you."

Alex nodded but she didn't feel much hope. If Owen had wanted to cut in on their dance, he would have. He'd done it before, after all.

She found Jane Upton at the refreshment table, filling a plate with tea cakes.

"Tea cakes are the only things that make balls tenable in any way," Jane said, balancing her plate on the palm of her hand.

Alex was just about to reply with a laugh when a dark shadow appeared at her side.

"Do you truly think it wise for your reputation to dance with the same man twice in a row? *Again?*"

Alex jumped and whirled to the side. Owen stood there with his hands on his hips and his jaw tightly clenched. He was clearly angry. And he'd been drinking.

She straightened her shoulders and continued to pluck a tea cake from the serving platter. "You're the one who taught me these things," she whispered so they wouldn't be overheard. "Two dances are enough to keep him wanting more, but never a third. Isn't that what you said?"

Jane and her tea cakes suddenly disappeared.

"I was a fool," Owen barked.

Alex forced herself to count to three and remain calm. She'd had a great deal of practice remaining calm in the face of anger, after all. She lived in the same home as Lavinia. "You said it, I didn't."

"I need to talk to you. Meet me in the library in ten minutes."

It was a command, not a request. Alex briefly considered ignoring it, but in the end, she made her way to the library, ensuring that no one saw her steal off and that no one was behind her. She arrived after twenty minutes, though, not ten. Owen had taught her that, too. Never be on time for a rendezvous with a gentleman. He'll always wonder if you've changed your mind, and he'll have to work harder next time.

When she reached the appointed room, she slowly pushed open the door and took two tentative steps inside.

Owen was there, standing near the cluster of seating arrangements in the center of the room. He swung around to face her. His hair was a bit mussed. When he saw her, worry drained from his face.

"I didn't think you were coming," he said.

She opened her mouth to reply.

"Wait," he said. "I know. You're an apt student."

She wasn't about to admit it. "Why did you want to see me?"

"Actually, I want to see you again, tomorrow. At Cass's house." He strode closer to her.

"I don't understand. Why?"

"We need to talk."

"We can't talk now?"

"I still need your help . . . with Lavinia."

Alex's stomach clenched into a knot. "I thought your letter said you were done with that. That you would endeavor to do your best."

"I changed my mind," he snapped.

Alex turned away from him sharply and crossed her arms over her chest. "I don't know if I can help you anymore, Owen." *It's killing me.*

"Now that you've got your Lord Berkeley, you've forgotten me?"

"No, but—" She turned to meet his gaze. "Do you love Lavinia?"

"You know I don't."

"But you still intend to marry her?"

"Yes. It's all to work out the way it's meant to."

Now was the time, the time to end all of this, the time to tell him that she loved him. To tell him that she'd lied to him, made up nearly everything she'd told him about Lavinia. Now was the time to tell him that Lavinia was as awful as she appeared to be and he'd never be happy with her. That *she* was the one who liked all the things he liked. That *she* was the one who would appreciate him for who he was.

But she couldn't. She wanted him to want her and to choose her over Lavinia first. Not after she begged him. Not after she convinced him. And Lucy's words came back to haunt her: "Getting him to admit he's fallen for an innocent is not about to happen quickly."

Alex glanced down at her slippers and blinked away the tears in her eyes. "I cannot meet you tomorrow, Owen. I have other plans."

CHAPTER TWENTY-SIX

Owen hated himself. Detested himself, actually. He sat in his coach, having given his coachman instructions to wait down the street from the duke's town house until the duke's carriage emerged from the mews. Alex had said she couldn't meet him today because she had other plans. Plans? What plans? Was she meeting Lord Berkeley? And since when had Owen become such an overbearing broodish knave that he was going to follow her to wherever she was going? That was right. He detested himself.

But there he was, sitting on the velvet seat, glancing furtively out the window, waiting to see the duke's carriage pull around the end of the street. As soon as it pulled away, Owen rapped on the door separating himself from his own coachman. "Follow them," he commanded, feeling like a fool.

As the conveyance took off down the street, Owen considered the events of the last few days. His conscience had forced him to write Alex the note thanking her for her help and telling her he didn't need to see her anymore.

He'd gone so mad that he'd actually even considered Cade Cavendish's advice. He'd actually contemplated paying a chap to marry Lavinia so he could run off with Alex. He might have even done it if he thought such a chap existed, one whom that harridan would accept. He couldn't imagine anyone voluntarily choosing her, though. No, Owen was the gull who'd been stuck with her.

The coach bounced along the streets of Mayfair and then headed into the part of town where he went only when he was looking for a certain type of gaming hell, and even that was rare. He and his friends preferred the hells that catered to the aristocracy. He glanced out the window again. No mistaking it. There were in the rookeries. He had no way of knowing whether Alexandra was in the carriage ahead of them, but if she was, what in God's name was she doing going to the rookeries?

Several minutes later, they pulled to a stop along a dirty street filled with shoeless ragamuffins scurrying about. The sign on the door to the building where the duke's coach stopped was written in scratchy, badly drawn letters.

POOR HOUSE

"What the—?" Owen slinked low in his seat and watched from nearby as Alexandra and her maid emerged from the carriage with two baskets in their hands. Their coachman helped them down. Heedless of the muck in the road, Alex walked directly up to the front of the establishment. She balanced her basket on her hip, knocked twice on the large door, and waited until it swung open and a woman wearing a cap on her head and a poorly fitting linen robe ushered the two women inside.

Owen cursed under his breath. A lady unescorted in this part of town was courting trouble. Alex had her maid with her, but the small young woman would hardly be of much assistance if they were accosted by brigands or thieves or worse. Owen kicked open the door, leaped from his coach, and ran across the filthy road. He quickly made his way to the front of the poorhouse and knocked as forcefully as he could.

It took several minutes, but the same woman eventually answered the door.

"Yes?" the woman said. Upon closer inspection, her linen robe and cap were threadbare.

"I'm Lord Owen Monroe," he explained. "I'm here to—I saw Lady Alexandra Hobbs come in, and I wanted to ensure she is all right."

The woman eyed him skeptically. "Do you know her?"

"Yes, you could say she is my friend."

Something in Owen's demeanor must have convinced the woman because her face softened and she said, "I'm Miss Magdalene. And I believe you. Lady Alexandra is the soul of kindness. Wait here. I'll tell her you're here." She ushered him inside.

Owen paced about the clean but dingy foyer while Miss Magdalene disappeared into the bowels of the building. His hat in his hands, Owen paced some more and turned his hat over again and again.

Several long minutes passed before Alex and her maid appeared, carrying empty baskets. Alex strode into the foyer and stopped abruptly as soon as she saw Owen.

"What are you doing here?" she asked in an angry whisper.

Owen stopped pacing. His hat fell to his side in his hand. "I thought you were in danger."

Alex glanced about as if she wanted to ensure that Miss Magdalene didn't overhear. Her voice remained a heated whisper. "I'm in no danger. I come here twice a month. And that doesn't explain why you followed me here." She marched past him out the door back to her carriage, her maid close at her heels. The maid scurried up into the conveyance while Alex waited outside on the street and turned to Owen with the empty basket propped against one hip.

Owen straightened his shoulders. He felt like a complete arse. "I thought—You said you had plans, and I wanted to—"

Alex tapped her slipper along the dirty road. Her jaw was tight. "Know what I was doing?"

"Yes."

She glared at him. "That's a bit heavy-handed of you, don't you think?"

"Yes."

She tossed one hand in the air. "Do you have any explanation for yourself?"

Owen shoved his hat back on his head. "I thought you were going to meet Lord Berkeley or—"

She shook her head. "In the rookeries? Besides, what if I *had* been going to meet Lord Berkeley? Is it any of your concern?"

Owen waved a hand toward the poorhouse. "Damn it, Alex. What are you doing here at a place like this?"

She glanced around and kept her voice to a low hiss. "Not that it's any of your affair, but I drop off my embroidery and that of some of my friends twice a month. The people here sell it on the streets for a bit of money."

Owen was stunned. "Charity? You're here for charity?"

"Why else would I be here? I'd bring food, but Mother would notice and Cook would be scolded." Alex wrenched open the door to the coach. The coachman leaped from his spot in front and stood at the ready to help her into the vehicle.

"I'm leaving now," Alex announced. "You're making a spectacle."

Owen glanced around the street. It was true. A small crowd had formed and was watching them.

"Wait." His hand on her arm stopped her. He lowered his voice, too. "Does your mother know about this?"

Alex rolled her eyes. "Of course not. She'd never allow me to come here. Even though I bring Hannah."

"That's what I thought. It's dangerous here. Your mother would be right to worry."

Alex met his gaze. "I've found in life that there are some things that are more important than worry."

Owen searched her face. She never ceased to amaze him. "Does Lavinia give you her embroidery, too?"

Alex's lips turned up in a half-smile. "Are you jesting? Lavinia would toss her embroidery in the fire if she thought the people here would even so much as touch it, let alone sell it. I collect her discarded bits and bring them with me. She doesn't miss them."

Owen stared at Alex as if seeing her for the first time. "It means that much to you to come here? To defy your mother? To risk your safety?"

Alex shrugged. "Mother isn't always right about things. Neither is Father. I asked Mother's permission once to come here and she said no. She left me no choice but to sneak out of the house."

"You could send one of the footmen."

"That's cowardly. Besides, I've come to enjoy my outings here. Miss Magdalene is a dear."

Owen glanced back at the poorhouse. Miss Magdalene was standing in the open door, watching them, concern etched on her brow. Wonderful. Now the woman thought Alex needed protection from him.

He took a step away from Alex to ease Miss Magdalene's mind. "I never expected something like this of you, Alex."

This time Alex advanced on him. "What? Charity work? Doing something more useful in life than sipping tea and wasting my pin money on fripperies? Rest assured, that's how Lavinia prefers to spend her time. It's not how I prefer to use mine. I want to be useful, Owen, to someone, for someone. You have that opportunity, too; you simply choose to squander it."

He blinked at her. What in the devil was she talking about? It was on the tip of his tongue to ask what she meant, or to tell her that he sent some of his allowance to an orphanage, but he'd long ago given up trying to convince anyone to think kindly of him. He wasn't about to start now.

"You do realize most of these people are probably buying gin with the money they get from your embroidery, don't you?"

"You're an ass." She turned sharply around and allowed the coachman to help her into the carriage. Owen had a glimpse of her maid sitting inside the darkened interior.

The door to the coach slammed shut behind Alex, and the carriage pulled away, heading back toward Mayfair. Owen stood in the dirty street, watching it go.

CHAPTER TWENTY-SEVEN

Alex claimed a headache that night. She had good reason to. Mother was planning a dinner party. A dinner party that included Owen Monroe, and Alex simply didn't have the fortitude to see him again. Not after her interaction with him at the poorhouse. It had been deplorable of him, following her there, but at least it proved that he cared what she was doing, didn't it? Oh, the entire mess had gotten so convoluted, she didn't know what made sense anymore. But she wasn't about to allow him to follow her about and say rude things, no matter what Lucy and Cass said. He either needed to declare himself or leave her be.

To make matters worse, Alex had barely missed being discovered by Mother this afternoon. Apparently, the woman had come in search of her. One of the other maids, Hannah's friend, had insisted that Alex was taking a nap. If the maid hadn't been so adamant, Alex might well have been found out. As it was, Mother came back not long after Alex had returned from the poorhouse and insisted upon speaking with her. She'd barely had time to undress with Hannah's help, toss on a night rail, and climb beneath the covers before Mother came gliding into the room.

"Alexandra," Mother had said in a whisper loud enough to wake her had she truly been sleeping.

Thomas would have been proud of her acting skills. She'd rolled over, rubbed the pretend sleep from her eyes, and blinked at her mother. "Mother? Is that you?"

"Yes. I must speak with you."

"What about?" Alexandra sat up slowly and plumped the pillow behind her back.

Her mother took a seat on the edge of the mattress. "I wanted to speak to you about what you said the other day . . . about Lord Owen."

Dread filled Alex's chest. She'd been waiting for this conversation. Had been surprised, actually, that her mother had not addressed it before now. "Yes?" Her voice shook.

"I'm certain you'll agree that we're all hoping for a wonderful match for your sister."

Here it came, the why-Lavinia-should-be-put-first speech.

"I would love nothing more than for Lavinia to make a love match, Mama." That much was true.

"Yes, well, as to that, your father is quite convinced that Lord Owen Monroe is the best match for Lavinia."

Alex tugged the sheet up higher beneath her arms. "But, Mother, you know how Lavinia feels about it. She wants no part of him."

"I can't say I was too keen on your father when I first met him. His being a future duke was certainly tempting, but I found him to be a bit overbearing. He still is, if I'm being honest."

Alex rubbed her temples. Her mother was completely

inappropriate. "Lavinia has quite definite opinions, though, Mother."

"So does your father, and he's settled on Lord Owen for her. I hope I can count on you to keep this to yourself, but we've already begun working out the contract."

"Lavinia's not going to like that."

"I'm hoping she'll warm to him, given enough time," Mother said, patting Alex's hand.

"What do *you* think, Mother? Do you think Lavinia and Lord Owen are well suited?"

"Oh, my dear, being well suited has little to do with marriage. Your father wants Lavinia to fancy Lord Owen, but I told your father not to count upon it."

Alex balled the bedsheets in her fists. "So, you're here to tell me I shouldn't spend any time with him?"

Her mother patted her leg this time. "It's what's best for your sister. And what's best for Lavinia will leave us all in peace. I know she's not easy to get along with."

"That's putting it rather mildly."

"I've spoiled her, Alexandra. I know that. There's not a day that goes by that I don't blame myself for how she acts. But, regardless, the contract has been drawn up and Lord Owen is set to be Lavinia's husband."

"Even if I actually like him and enjoy his company and Lavinia obviously detests him?"

Another soft pat. "I'm sorry, Alexandra. I hope one day you'll understand." Her mother stood up and drifted toward the door.

Her mother left. As usual, Mother hadn't even noticed that Alex hadn't agreed to a thing. It was merely taken for granted that everyone in this household would do what was best for Lavinia. Alex ripped the pillow from behind her head and savagely threw it across the room.

* * *

Owen had been suffering Lady Lavinia's barbs and rudeness for the better part of two hours. He'd attempted to open a discourse with her on the writings of Mary Wollstonecraft, but far from being interested in the subject, Lavinia had made it abundantly clear that she had absolutely no desire to speak about the rights of women. "That's the sort of drivel Alexandra enjoys," she'd sneered. To make this odious dinner party worse, Owen had been looking forward to seeing Alex tonight, but apparently, she was abed with a headache. He didn't blame Alex. If he were her, he wouldn't want to suffer through this dinner party either. In fact, next time he might just claim a headache himself. Her words kept playing themselves over and over in his mind. "You have that opportunity, too; you simply choose to squander it," she'd said. Those words haunted him.

Meanwhile, the duke and duchess were making markedly feeble attempts at getting Lavinia to show Owen any favor. It was failing miserably. The only thing that made it bearable was the wine he'd ingested. But he hadn't had nearly enough. He was determined not to let his father down this time.

"So, Monroe," the duke's voice thundered across the table. "How do you feel about the toll road bill? I'm in favor of it myself."

Owen thought about it for a moment. If it were his father asking, he'd say he didn't give a toss about the toll road bill. But that wasn't true. He *pretended* he didn't give a toss about the toll road bill. The truth was he had thought about it. Had overheard some of the gentlemen at the club discussing it a time or two. He'd read all he could on the subject since encountering the farmer on the road the other day. And Owen was convinced that the toll road bill should be struck down. It called for an increase in the tax paid at the entrances to town. It was the reason why the farmer couldn't get his poor sick daughter to the doctor.

Owen had been haunted by the memory of that little girl he met on the road outside London. He actually went there earlier, after he'd left the rookeries, to the store-fronts near St. Paul's, looking for a doctor who might have catered to the sick girl. He hadn't found her, but he vowed to continue looking. All he could hope for for the time being was that the sovereign he'd given her father might have helped her plight.

Yes. Owen had studied the arguments for and against the toll road bill and the money that the Prince Regent hoped to make from the increase in the tax. And Owen indeed had an opinion on it. It made him sick to think that another little girl might one day be denied care in order to line Prinny's pockets. He opened his mouth to say as much to the duke but just as quickly closed it. God. What was happening to him? He wasn't an MP. He was a ne'er-do-well. A scoundrel. A profligate. Good only for drinking and carousing. Hadn't his father told him that often enough? "Don't fail me," his father had said. "For once." All his father thought he was good for was charming women, and he clearly was failing even at that.

Owen glanced over at Lady Lavinia, who rolled her eyes at the conversation. Clearly, she was as uninterested in tolls as she was in the rights of women. He focused again on the duke. "I haven't given it much thought, Your Grace."

Lavinia sneered at him and Owen recoiled. What the blazes did she want him to say? He considered pushing back his chair and leaving the room. In fact—he decided right then and there—that's *exactly* what he would do.

Temporarily, at least. He pushed his chair away from the dining table.

"Will you excuse me, Your Graces, Lady Lavinia?" He stood, grabbed his conveniently refilled wineglass, bowed, and dropped his napkin to his seat. "I find I need some air for a moment."

Lavinia's jaw dropped as if she couldn't possibly comprehend that anyone was leaving her esteemed presence, but the duke and the duchess nodded to him as he made his way out of the dining room. He turned down the corridor and headed toward the back of the house, where he knew the exit to the terrace was.

Using his free hand, Owen pushed open the doors to the balcony and stepped outside. He kicked the door closed behind him and downed the entire contents of his glass in one gulp. He balanced the glass haphazardly on the balustrade and strolled into the garden, scrubbing his hands into his hair. This was one of the longest, most disagreeable nights of his life. Made worse by the fact that Alex wasn't here.

Alex. Why couldn't he stop thinking about Alex? Blast it. He rubbed his hand over his scalp harder, as if he could wipe away the memory of her.

"What are you doing here?"

Alex's voice? Had he conjured her from his thoughts? He blinked and narrowed his eyes to squint into the darkness of a nearby hedge.

Alex materialized from the shadows. She was wearing a dressing gown and slippers and was twirling a violet between her fingers. Her hair was down, and the surge of lust that hit Owen squarely in the groin when he saw her nearly sent him to his knees.

"Alex?" he whispered, afraid she was only a figment

of his imagination and would disappear if he spoke too loudly.

"You shouldn't be here. Or I shouldn't be here. Either way, you shouldn't see me like this."

"I like seeing you like this." He gestured to her dressing gown.

She pulled it more tightly around her neck with one hand and blushed beautifully.

"How is your headache?" he asked, leaning against a nearby tree and contemplating her. The familiar scent of strawberries filled his nostrils and he wanted to reach out and pull her into his arms.

"How is your dinner?" She nodded toward the house.

"Excruciatingly boring," he replied with a grin.

The hint of a smile touched her lips. "That bad?"

"Worse."

She made to walk past him. "I should get inside before anyone sees us—"

"Wait." He reached out and grabbed her soft arm. "Earlier at the poorhouse, you said I had the same opportunity you have but I choose to squander it. What did you mean?"

She pulled her arm away and turned to face him, still clutching at the throat of her gown. "It doesn't matter."

"It matters very much . . . to me."

She sighed. "I only meant that you're a future earl. You're a member of the *ton*. A male. You have so much power and you don't even choose to use it. You could take a seat in the House of Commons now, and someday you'll be in the House of Lords. You could campaign for the rights of the poor, ask Parliament for money for the poorhouses. With your connections and your fame, Owen, you could do so much more than I do, giving them my bits of embroidery from time to time." Her eyes flashed dark fire at him.

He spoke slowly, deliberately. "Do you respect me, Alex?"

She swallowed and glanced away. "What do you mean?"

"You heard me. Do you respect me?"

"I don't know why you're asking or why you would care what I think."

"I'm asking for the same reason I care. Because it matters to me what you think of me."

She sucked in her breath. "Why?"

"I've been trying to discern that myself for days, but I do. What do you think of me, Alex? Do you think I'm a fop, or someone pretending to be someone I'm not so that I can line my pockets with your sister's dowry? Or a scoundrel? Out only to seek my own pleasure?"

Her eyes met his. Hers had tears swimming in their dark depths. "Is that what you think of yourself?"

"That's what I am."

"Not to me. Never to me. I know what happened at Eton, Owen. Cass told me."

"She had no right to—"

"I know who you are. I see who you are. You can't pretend with me."

Owen wanted to silence her. He pulled her into his arms and kissed her. It was rough, fierce, a bit punishing, but also hot and wet. He crushed her to him, and when her arms went up to thread around his neck, Owen groaned. That was all he needed. He swept her up, took two steps over to the giant oak tree hidden behind the hedge, and pressed her against it. He braced an arm behind her to keep the rough bark from her back, but no doubt it scratched her in a few places regardless. Apparently, she didn't care. She clung to him and Owen deepened the kiss, lips and tongue clashing with hers. She tasted like strawberries. Just as he knew she would. He couldn't get enough of her. His hands reached down to her hips, and he picked her up at the waist. Her legs wrapped around his outer thighs.

"Does it hurt?" he whispered, nodding toward the tree.

"I don't care," she moaned against his mouth.

She locked her ankles behind his hips and pulled him hard against her. His erection pressed against her most intimate spot. Despite the sweet ache in his groin and the unbearable lust riding him, Owen tried to force himself to pull away. Anyone could come around the hedge and see them then. She would be ruined. But all he could think of was Alex's mouth on his, his hips levered against her, his tongue plunging in her mouth over and over, and his cock pressing against the juncture in her thighs, taunting her, teasing her. Making him want her even more.

When the kiss was over, he let her drop to the soft grass. He set her down softly and pulled her back away from the tree. "Are you all right?"

Alex pressed her fingertips to her burning lips. "Wh-why?"

His breathing was labored. "I—"

"Why," she repeated, searching his face. "Tell me why you did that. I want to hear you say it."

He closed his eyes and pushed his face toward the sky. "Would you believe me if I told you that I did it to teach you how to properly kiss a man?"

"No," she breathed.

He opened his eyes again and stared into her soul. "Then I'll tell you the truth."

"Which is?" Her hand was shaking.

"I did it because I want you."

CHAPTER TWENTY-EIGHT

Alex rushed back into the house and up the servants' staircase the same way she'd come minutes earlier. Only this time she was completely changed. She'd sneaked outside to get a bit of air to clear her head. She'd had no idea she'd encounter Owen alone in the gardens and even less of an idea that he'd *kiss* her, of all things.

And good heavens—*what* a kiss it had been. More than a kiss. An entire assault to her senses. One she hadn't wanted to end. She pressed her fingertips to her burning lips. If only she could keep her mouth untouched forever with the feel of Owen's lips meeting hers, seared in her memory.

She inspected the back of her torn dressing robe and night rail in the looking glass as best she could. They weren't ripped badly, but they were still ruined. She'd have the devil of a time explaining it to Hannah. She tugged off both garments and pulled a fresh night rail from her wardrobe. She crumpled up the ripped ones and stuffed them into the back of the cabinet. She'd ask Hannah to cut them into bits for the poorhouse tomorrow. There was no possible way her mother would see them and not ask questions.

She climbed under the covers and took a deep breath, trying to still the pounding of her heart. Owen Monroe was a conundrum. He didn't believe in himself. He should, but he didn't. He'd asked her if she respected him. Of course she did, but she'd wanted him to admit why it *mattered* to him what she thought. She'd wanted him to admit that he cared about her, cared for her. And he had. "I want you," he'd said. He'd admitted it. He'd tasted like wine. He'd obviously been drinking, but she'd overheard her father say often enough that a sober man's thoughts were a drunken man's words. Had he been drunk when he kissed her? She was too inexperienced to tell for certain. But Owen did care for her. She was sure of that. And that's what she'd wanted to hear. Only it didn't matter, because he'd made it clear that he still intended to marry Lavinia.

Alex considered the kiss again. Their first kiss in Cass's ballroom when she hadn't stepped away, that had been pleasant, memorable even. But this one, this was the kind of kiss you remembered when you were a very old lady with a very poor memory. This kiss had been full of passion and longing and—when he'd pushed himself between her thighs! Oh yes, she'd be on her deathbed remembering that kiss.

Which presented the problem: How in heaven's name would she go about forgetting it now? Owen couldn't have been more clear yesterday when she'd asked him about Lavinia. He still had every intention of marrying her. He had even accepted her parents' dinner invitation tonight with the express purpose of continuing his suit. He would remain adamant until Lavinia herself agreed. How much more obvious did it have to be that he was planned for

Lavinia? Even her mother had said so. Everyone, it seemed, wanted the match, except Lavinia and Alex. But no longer. Alex intended to remove herself from the equation. It was madness and heartache to continue to hope for something that could not be. She was through with the whole awful, painful thing. She tossed herself onto her bed and viciously tugged the covers over her head. Anger filled her. If Owen Monroe was such a lackwit that he couldn't see what was so obvious . . . well, he deserved to spend the rest of his life with her sister.

Lavinia would be the only obstacle. Lavinia herself. Owen seemed to believe he could convince her. Or perhaps Mother and Father would change their minds and attempt to talk some sense into her. At any rate, the man was meant to be Alex's brother-in-law, and they'd already kissed, more than once. There could be no more of such things or it would make for exceedingly awkward family holidays in future.

This was it. No more.

CHAPTER TWENTY-NINE

Owen groaned and rolled over. The sunlight pouring through the window wasn't helping his pounding skull . . . not one bit. He rubbed his hand over his face slowly, then flexed his hands and feet. *Must check for all limbs after a night of extremely heavy drinking.* But wait. He hadn't drunk heavily last night. No. His headache was from *not* drinking much. He pushed himself up to a half-sitting position and rang for his valet to bring him a bottle of brandy. Good man, his valet. The chap could be counted on to perform a wide variety of tasks.

While he waited, Owen slowly contemplated the events of the night before. There had been dinner, wine, arguing, and . . . He groaned again. Kissing. He'd gone and kissed Alex. Well, at least he hadn't punched a tree. That was something, but what the hell had he been thinking? He thumped his palm against his forehead. That had been a bad idea. The valet returned with a tray that contained a brandy bottle and a glass.

Owen snatched up the bottle. "Thank you. That will be all."

If his valet was surprised by his employer's behavior, he did not so much as raise a brow in indication. Owen popped the stopper off the bottle, and raised it to his lips. Alex's voice rang in his head. "Not to me. Never to me," she'd said when he asked her if she thought him a scoundrel. "I see who you are. You can't pretend with me." Damn it. He eyed the bottle of brandy and called his man back. "Take this." He shoved the bottle into the man's arms.

The valet eyes rounded. "Yes, my lord." He turned to leave.

"My father hasn't been here, has he?"

"No, my lord," the valet replied.

Thank God.

"Good. Should he arrive, please tell him I am unavailable."

The valet bowed. "As you wish, my lord."

A lot of good such a pronouncement would do. His father was *always* told he was unavailable, and the older man never cared. Owen laid his head back against the pillow. What had he been thinking about?

Oh yes, last night. Dinner, kissing, wine. Not entirely in that order. He'd kissed Alex. Why? Because he'd wanted to.

She'd kissed him back. Why? Because she'd wanted to? He had no earthly idea. It was no use examining her reasoning, then. He must examine his own.

His father was correct about him. He was a scoundrel, the worst sort. Only such a scoundrel would kiss the younger sister of the lady he was supposed to be courting.

The worst part wasn't even that he'd *done* such a thing. No. The worst part was that he felt no guilt over it.

Perhaps it had been poorly done of him, but the truth was he'd wanted to kiss Alex last night, and more truth was he wanted to do it again.

Alex was everything he was not: fresh, young, innocent, idealistic, hopeful. Why in the world the girl had allowed him to kiss her, let alone kiss him back with such eagerness, he'd never know.

She was also everything her sister was not. Lavinia was shrewish, spiteful, hateful, and cold. When faced with the prospect of spending the rest of his life with *that* one, perhaps it wasn't such a mystery why Alex was more tempting.

But that still didn't grant him an excuse for kissing her. The only good thing about it was that he'd done so in private. There would not be a scandal. Alex's reputation was not in danger.

For a moment he wondered if that were true, but then he relaxed. If so much as a hint of a scandal were afoot, his father would already be here, upending the bed. No. Owen could rest assured on that count, and that was a relief.

Alex didn't deserve a scandal. All she'd ever done was try to help him. She didn't deserve his dirty reputation to smear off on her. He had to stay away from her. For *her* sake.

After last night, it was clear he possessed little self-control when it came to her. If he couldn't keep his hands or mouth off her, he could bloody well keep himself away from her entirely.

"You're a member of the *ton*. A male. You have so much power, and you don't even choose to use it," she'd said, staring up at him with those big beautiful brown eyes. So full of trust and hope and . . . something else he didn't want to contemplate.

Alex was right. He was a male member of the *ton*, but he could no more affect change than if he were a washerwoman. No one would take him seriously in Parliament. He was a known rakehell, a wastrel. He wasn't like Claringdon or Swifdon or even Upton or Cavendish. Owen didn't belong in the sacred halls of Westminster, giving speeches and attempting to sway his countrymen into voting the way he saw fit.

No. After his father died, Owen fully intended to be one of those members of the House of Lords who arrived seasonally for the sessions and missed more votes than not, due to social obligations. That was common enough, wasn't it? And no one was the less off for it. He'd leave the introduction of difficult bills like the one for the families of the soldiers to men who'd actually fought next to those who'd died. Owen hadn't stepped foot on foreign soil. He'd been carousing the clubs and taverns of London, not risking his life against Napoleon's forces.

Owen wished he hadn't sent the brandy away. He called for his valet again. Yes. His father was right about him. He was good for nothing but shaking off last night's drinking with today's drinks. And Alex—pure, sweet, innocent Alex—was wrong about him, too. So wrong. He wasn't a hero. He was an arse. Someone like him couldn't make a difference. But he *could* do one decent selfless thing. And he would. He would stay far away from Alexandra Hobbs.

CHAPTER THIRTY

Cass was hosting a ball this time, one that Alex seriously suspected was being held in honor of her flirtation with Lord Berkeley for Owen's sake. But Alex didn't feel like faux-flirting with Berkeley tonight, and she certainly didn't feel like making Owen jealous.

"You look positively glum, dear. Are you all right?" Cass asked after wrenching the last plate of tea cakes away from Jane Upton and placing them back on the refreshment table.

Jane harrumphed and said, "I'll just be in the library."

"Of course you will, dear," Cass replied, waving at Jane as she left.

"You should smile, Alex," Lucy said. "Owen has to believe you're having a wonderful time."

"I'm having a miserable time." Alex took a halfhearted sip of champagne from the flute that dangled from her fingers.

"Oh no. Why is that?" Cass asked. "Come and tell us."

The three women made their way over to the corner

to continue their discussion in private. As soon as they were situated, Alex took a deep breath. "Owen kissed me and told me he intends to marry Lavinia."

"What!" Cass's face drained of color. "Of all the detestable, wretched, unconscionable—"

"Wait." Lucy held up a hand. "We need more details, Cass." She turned to face Alex. "Did he kiss you and then immediately tell you he intends to marry Lavinia? And how was the kiss? Passionate or sisterly?"

"Passionate, definitely passionate," Alex replied, taking another sip of champagne. "And the truth is that first he told me he intends to marry Lavinia. Well, he told me that earlier in the day, actually, after he followed me to the rookeries, but—"

Cass's cheeks were bright pink. "Oh goodness, dear. It seems you've left out a great deal. What in heaven's name were you doing in the rookeries?"

"That's quite a long story. But I went there and Owen followed me and—"

"And he kissed you?" Lucy interjected. "In the rookeries? That doesn't seem terribly romantic to me."

"No. Not in the rookeries. In the rookeries he told me he intends to marry Lavinia because I asked what his intentions were. Then I left."

Cass's brow was furrowed. "So when did he kiss you?"

"Last night, in the gardens, at my father's house. I didn't come down to dinner. Instead, I went out for a bit of fresh air. Owen was there."

Cass pressed her hand against her reddening throat. "Let me see if I have the right of it. First my brother followed you to the rookeries and then he made his way into your father's gardens and kissed you? I had no idea Owen was such a sneak."

"He didn't sneak into the gardens. He was invited. To

dinner, at least. But he must have gone out for air the same time I did, and I saw him there, quite by accident, and—"

"*Then* he kissed you!" Lucy pointed a triumphant finger in the air.

"Yes." Alex nodded.

"Then it's perfectly fine," Lucy replied, fluttering her hand in the air.

Alex puffed air into her cheeks. "Perfectly fine? How is *that* perfectly fine?"

"Yes, how *is* that perfectly fine?" Cass echoed.

"Don't you see? He kissed her *after* he declared his intentions for Lavinia," Lucy explained with a sage nod.

"That appears to make him a complete rogue," Cass replied, her brow still furrowed.

"Not at all," Lucy continued. "He'd be a complete rogue if he kissed her and *then* declared his intentions for Lavinia."

Alex pressed her gloved hand against her cheek. "I'm afraid I have absolutely no idea what you mean."

Lucy sighed. "I mean that he made his declaration, which is all fine and well, but *then* he was unable to keep his hands off you, despite his best intentions. It's good. It's quite, quite good."

Cass tapped a finger against her cheek. "Ah, I see what you mean. You may have a point."

Alex turned to Cass. "She does? She has a point?"

"Yes," Cass replied. "He wants to keep his promise to Father, but he's clearly head over heels for you."

Alex downed the last of her champagne. Perhaps if she drank enough, these two would begin making sense. "It certainly doesn't feel that way to me. He hasn't sought me out once tonight, and the last time I looked, he was deeply engaged in conversation with Mrs. Clare."

"Mrs. Clare?" Cass scowled. "The widow?"

"Yes?" Alex replied. "Why?"

Cass rolled her eyes. "She's been chasing after him for years. Makes no attempts to hide it. She's a determined little baggage. I wouldn't have invited her, only my mother-in-law seems to enjoy her company. If I'd had any idea she'd throw herself at Owen tonight, I would have conveniently lost her invitation."

Lucy had been busily searching the crowd. "Seems she does have every intention of throwing herself at Owen tonight." Lucy pointed to the far corner of the room. Alex rose up on tiptoes and strained her neck to see Owen and Mrs. Clare laughing and talking. Mrs. Clare had her hand on Owen's sleeve and was standing far too close with far too much décolletage exposed.

Cass gasped. "Oh, Alex, dear. I'm so sorry. I'll go run her off."

"No!" Alex said before straightening her shoulders and speaking in a more modulated tone of voice. "No. Don't. Please. If Owen wants to spend his time with Mrs. Clare, I'm not about to stop him."

"I don't think he knows what he wants." Cass was shaking her head sadly. "Or at least he's not ready to admit it to himself. The idiot."

"I'll go get Berkeley," Lucy said to Alex. "You should dance."

"No, really," Alex said quietly. "I'm tired. Exceedingly so. I think I'll go off into the library with Jane and sit and rest for a bit."

Cass and Lucy both had sorrowful looks on their faces. Cass patted Alex's shoulder. "Are you certain?"

"Quite certain. In fact, it's the only thing I'm certain of at the moment." She turned away from her new friends and headed toward the library.

*   *   *

The good thing about devoted readers like Jane Upton was, they knew how to be quiet. Alex spent the better part of the next hour silently sitting in the library with Jane, who was happily engaged reading a book. And that was just the way Alex preferred it. Chaperoned quiet was the perfect balm at the moment for her bruised soul. Finally, the clock on the mantelpiece chimed midnight and Alex sighed, stood up, and yawned.

"I should go back to the party now, Jane," she said. "No doubt Mother will be looking for me. She rarely likes to stay at any gathering past midnight unless Lavinia is particularly enjoying herself, and Lavinia is never particularly enjoying herself."

"I understand entirely," Jane said, glancing up from her book. "If you see my husband—Oh, never mind. I was going to say if you see Garrett, tell him he can fetch me in the library, but it just occurred to me that he already knows." Jane smiled, adjusted her spectacles, and returned her attention to her book.

Alex made her way out of the library and down the corridor. As she passed the foyer, she heard a woman's tinkling laughter and Owen's voice. "You don't know how bad I can be."

Alex froze. Her hands began shaking. She didn't want to take another step, but she forced herself to continue walking. The sooner she passed the foyer, the better, and there was no other way to return to the ballroom, not that she knew of, at least. She briefly considered rushing back to hide in the library with Jane, but she discarded that cowardly notion just as quickly. No. She would walk past him with her head held high.

And that's just what she did.

Alex tried not to look. Truly she did. At first the couple

standing far too close to one another in the foyer were little more than a shadow and a blur, but when Alex came into sight, the woman gasped, Alex looked, and Owen's head snapped up to face her. He took a guilty step away from Mrs. Clare.

"Alex," he said in a calm, clear voice.

Alex nodded to him, trying to force her feet to keep moving, but she was rooted to the spot. "My lord," she uttered. "What are you doing?" Her heart thumped so hard in her chest that it hurt.

He turned and the gorgeous blond widow turned, too, and narrowed her silvery eyes on Alex.

"You shouldn't be here, Alex. You shouldn't be seeing this." His words rang out like shots that cracked against the marble pillars of the foyer.

"Seeing this," she echoed, lifting her chin and subtly straightening her shoulders. She was fighting to not let him affect her. "You didn't answer. What is 'this'?"

The widow pulled her shrug more tightly around her shoulders. "What adults do, sweet. Now, run along and play with the other *children*."

Alex's head snapped to the side as if she'd been slapped. But she forced herself to raise her chin again, and she met Owen's gaze with unshed tears in her eyes. "Is that what I am to you, Owen? A child."

The widow laughed a deep sultry laugh and opened her mouth to say some other—no doubt equally biting— thing, but Owen raised his hand in a signal that stopped her. His voice was low and harsh. "Go back to your party, Alex."

CHAPTER THIRTY-ONE

Owen made it all the way into the widow's bedchamber before he realized he wouldn't spend the night with her. Or, more precisely, he *couldn't* spend the night with her. Helena was gorgeous, lush, and curvaceous. Her arms wrapped around his neck and her lips attached to his, but he felt nothing. Hollow. All he could picture was Alex's sweet face when he'd said, "Go back to your party." She'd lifted her magnificent chin and faced him head-on. He could tell she'd been struggling to keep from crying. Damn it. Damn him. He was nothing more than a scoundrel. He wasn't good for Alex. He wasn't good for anyone.

Owen swallowed hard and pulled the widow's arms away from his neck. Her face immediately screwed into a practiced pout. "What's wrong, darling?"

"I have to go." He stepped away from her.

"Go?" She laughed a throaty laugh. "You *must* be joking."

"No. I'm not. I find I'm—ahem—indisposed this evening."

"Indisposed? What the hell does that mean?" Her brows were two furious blond slants above her gray eyes.

He turned toward the door.

"If you leave here tonight, Monroe, you won't be offered another opportunity."

He paused only briefly. The hint of a smile touched his lips. "I understand." And then he was gone, down the stairs, across the marble floor of her impeccable foyer, and out the front door to his coach, which was still waiting. The coachman had clearly settled in to take a long nap; his hat had been covering his face and he'd been slumped to the side of the conveyance.

Owen rapped once on the side of the coach. "Home," he barked.

The coachman jumped so quickly and so high that his hat flew into the air and he fumbled to catch it. The poor man looked beyond shocked to see him. "Yes, my lord. Right away, my lord," he choked, righting his hat atop his head and speedily gathering the reins in his hands.

The conveyance took off down the street moments later with Owen inside cursing furiously at himself.

CHAPTER THIRTY-TWO

Four brandies were really not so many when one stopped to contemplate the matter. Owen held brandy number five beneath his nose and contemplated it through only partially bleary eyes.

"Monroe, are you going to stare at it or drink it?" Cavendish asked from beside him. They were at Brooks's, having just finished a hand of cards that Owen had lost. Ever since, he had been intent on blaming his excessive drinking.

"I'm going to drink it, of course," he said, bowing his head toward the glass. "But since when am I more inebriated than you are, Captain? Or should I say, Viscount?"

"Call me whatever you'd like. I no longer find my pleasure at the bottom of a brandy glass. Daphne is more than enough to amuse me these days."

Owen snorted and rolled his eyes. "You people who fancy yourselves in love make me quite ill."

"I think it's the brandy making you ill, not me," Cavendish replied.

"I thought you detested the clubs," Owen pointed out. "And yet, I've seen you here each time I've come."

"Now that I'm a proper viscount, I need to get used to them, don't I? And it's the only place my brother doesn't like to go."

"He did seem a bit unimpressed the last time he was here. Do you plan on hiding from him forever?"

"I'm not hiding from him, I'm merely—"

"Avoiding him?"

"Yes, exactly. Much easier that way. Wherever Cade goes, trouble has a tendency to follow. And I want no trouble, especially before my wedding."

"I understand," Owen replied.

"Let's play one more hand," Cavendish said. "Then I promised Daphne I'd meet her at the Haverfords' ball. Until the wedding, we're limited to how much we can see each other."

Owen snorted. "The Haverfords' ball. Damn bunch of innocents, there."

"Yes." Cavendish eyed him over the tops of his cards. "No doubt Lady Alexandra will be there."

Owen glared at Cavendish. "Do you think I care?"

Cavendish grinned. "Yes, actually. I think you do."

"Well, I don't."

"So you don't want to accompany me there, then?"

Owen tossed the cards on the table. "Damn you, Cavendish, call your coach."

Half an hour later, Cavendish's carriage pulled up to the front of the Haverfords' town house. Owen didn't even bother with the receiving line. Taking his leave of Cavendish, who quickly located Daphne Swift, Owen bypassed the throngs of people and elbowed his way into the massive crowd. Voices called to him from all around.

"Good to see you, Monroe."

"Surprised you're here."

"Have a newfound taste for *ton* balls, eh, Monroe?"

He ignored all the banter and kept making his way through the throngs. Thankfully, he stood head and shoulders taller than most of the other partygoers. He scanned the room, looking for another tall man, Lord Berkeley. Wherever Berkeley was, Alex would be. Unfortunately, Owen spotted his sister first. Cass was standing in a small group that consisted of Lucy Hunt, Jane Upton, Berkeley, and . . . Alex. Yes. Alex was there, wearing a blue gown with silver ribbons and long white gloves. She looked as prim and pretty as a violet. He squared his shoulders and took off toward the little group with no idea what he would say once he got there.

"Alex, dance with me."

Apparently, that's what he would say once he got there, because those forceful words came out of his mouth as soon as he reached the group.

All four ladies' mouths flew open, and Berkeley turned toward him, assuming a protective stance in front of Alex.

"Owen, what are you doing here?" Cass asked, finding her voice first.

Owen ignored Cass and glared at Berkeley. "Stand down, Viscount. I don't want to meet you outside and beat you to a bloody pulp, but I will if I must."

Berkeley narrowed his eyes on him. "I'd like to see you try."

"Wait!" Alex stamped her foot, and the entire party turned toward her.

"What, dear?" Lucy Hunt asked Alex, blinking at her inquisitively.

"I want to know *why,*" Alex replied.

"Why what?" Jane Upton asked, pushing up her spectacles.

Alex's eyes never left Owen's. "Why?" she asked. "Why do you want to dance with me?"

Because I can't stop thinking about you? Because I try to drink enough to erase you from my memory but there's not enough brandy in the kingdom?

"Because I want to talk to you," he replied simply.

"Owen, have you been drinking?" Cass ventured, her brow furrowed with obvious concern.

His eyes didn't leave Alex's face as he answered his sister. "Yes. Far too much," he admitted.

Berkeley stepped forward. "In that case, I must ask you to leave."

Owen turned on the viscount with a snarl. "It'll be the last thing you ever ask, you son of a—"

"Wait!" Alex's voice stopped Owen's diatribe again. "Why do you want to talk to me?"

Because you're the only person who understands me. Because I miss you when you're not with me.

He cleared his throat and glanced around at the disapproving faces of the others. "I have something to say to you."

Actually, he had no idea what he would say to her, but if he could get her alone, away from Cass and her friends and Berkeley, damn him, Owen would say . . . something. Blast. He was an ass. A drunken ass. Perhaps he'd just say that.

"You didn't have much to say to me last night," Alex continued. "What's changed?"

Nothing.

Everything.

"Owen, if you have something to say to Alexandra, I think it's best said here," Cass informed him. His sister was merely concerned for Alex, but he didn't happen to appreciate it at the moment.

He took a step toward Alex. "Dance with me or come out to the gardens for a walk with me. Hear me out, at least."

"Owen, I—" Cass made to move in front of Alex, but Alex stepped forward more quickly.

"I'll go with you," Alex said simply. She turned on her heel and strode toward the French doors that led to the terrace. She turned back to her friends. "If I'm not back in ten minutes, please come look for me."

"Done," Berkeley said, eyeing Owen up and down with distaste.

The doors shut behind Alex and she marched across the terrace, down the stone steps, and onto the garden path. She didn't stop to look behind her to see if Owen had followed, and she certainly didn't give a fig if the entire assembly of the Haverfords' ball saw her stalk off into the gardens with the town's biggest rake on her heels.

She was angry, incensed at Owen for bursting into the ball, causing a scene, and acting like a demanding jackass. But she was even angrier at herself for being so overwhelmed by curiosity at what he wanted to say to her that she couldn't even tell him to go to hell. It would have been so satisfying to tell him to go to hell. But after she'd spent the first half of last night crying into her pillow, thinking about him spending the night with the widow Mrs. Clare and the second half of the night punching her pillow and pretending it was his treacherously handsome face, she still couldn't find it in herself to *not* wonder what he possibly had left to say to her.

She took three steps onto the gravel path before she twirled so fast that her skirts swished against her ankles and the fat curl Hannah had left to dangle out the back of her coiffure flew over her shoulder to bounce along her décolletage.

Owen was there, only a few steps behind her, looking both handsome and appropriately chagrined, a lethal combination for her heart. She summoned the memory of crying into her pillow, crossed her arms over her chest, and glared at him.

"Well?" She tapped her slipper against the gravel.

"Walk with me," he said in a domineering voice as he came to stand next to her. He offered her his arm, and Alex had to struggle to remember herself punching the pillow as she slid her hand over his muscled forearm. He smelled like soap and leather and—oh, this wasn't helpful. As soon as her hand was settled, he turned down the more secluded of the two garden paths that was lit with candles and pulled her along beside him. Alex struggled to keep her breathing straight.

"Berkeley's coming for me in ten minutes," she reminded him.

"How could I forget?" He gave her a tight smile.

"What do you want to say?"

He stopped abruptly and turned to face her. "I wanted to begin with an apology . . . for last night."

"What you did last night is absolutely none of my concern." She turned her head away sharply.

"I didn't do anything last night," he said softly. "I left Mrs. Clare at her home. Alone."

Alex clenched her jaw. "Is that supposed to matter to me?"

He stepped away from her, and her hand dropped from his sleeve. He moved toward the hedge and then turned back to face her. "Damn it, Alex. I don't know what you want from me. All I know is that I cannot stop thinking about you."

"No, Owen. I don't know what *you* want from *me*. I've always thought so much of you, but not anymore."

He stepped toward her and searched her face. "Always thought so much of me? What do you mean?"

"You don't even remember, do you?" Tears streamed down both Alex's cheeks.

Owen ripped a handkerchief from the inside pocket of his coat and offered it to her. "Remember what?"

"That night. The ball at Father's country house. Three years ago. You came outside. Some young men were making sport of Will the stable boy, and Thomas was there," she sobbed.

Owen's eyes narrowed as if he were trying to recall. He scrubbed a hand across his forehead. "Three years ago? At your father's country house?" he echoed. "Blast it, Alex, I can barely remember what I did last week, let alone three years ago."

"You saved them from those awful men. You were so kind and thoughtful, and you spoke to me afterwards. Up in the window." She pressed the handkerchief to her swollen eyes. "Father always said a man's actions speak louder than his words. I believed that . . . about you."

She could tell the moment Owen remembered. He raised his head and searched her face again, but his features had softened. "That was you?"

"Yes." She nodded, blotting at her tears with his handkerchief. "That was me."

"What did I say?" he asked.

"You asked me not to tell anyone what you did. You said it would ruin your blackened reputation."

He smiled at that.

"And you said someone as lovely and spirited as I was shouldn't be cooped up in a bedchamber with such a delightful party going on," she continued.

His throat worked as he swallowed. "I offered to dance with you."

"Yes. And I knew then that you couldn't ever marry anyone else but me. I was devastated when I overheard Mother and Father talking about how you intended to marry Lavinia. I thought I had many more years to make you notice me."

He moved closer and lifted her chin with his thumb. "It was not my choice to become betrothed to Lavinia," he said quietly.

"I know that, just as I know you and Lavinia wouldn't suit. Lavinia wants a refined gentleman, someone who will write her poetry and do her bidding."

He snorted. "So the poetry part was true, at least?"

"Yes, that part was true."

"Any of the rest of it?" he asked.

"No." She shook her head and pulled away from him, plucking at the leaves of the hedge.

"The horses?" he asked.

"Lavinia adores them."

"The gambling?"

"She detests it."

"The cursing?"

"Also not a favorite of hers."

"I suppose I don't even have to ask about the rock."

Alex's shoulders lifted and settled. "She much prefers flowers."

"Damn it, Alex. Why did you do all this? Why did you go to so much trouble?"

She turned back to him. The tears continued to flow

down her cheeks, and the hand that held the handkerchief fell uselessly to her side. "Because I love you, Owen. Don't you see? I've loved you since that night three years ago. You've always had a reputation for being a scoundrel, but that night I saw you for what you truly were—a gentleman. A kind, sweet gentleman."

His face grew hard. "I'm nothing of the sort. You're only seeing me the way you wish I were. The truth is that I gamble, I curse, I treat women with nary a thought. I'm nowhere near good enough for you, Alex. Or your sister, for that matter. For God's sake, I've been using you to try to court Lavinia, whom I don't love, just to line my own pockets. Don't you understand? I'm a scoundrel just like everyone says. Just like my father says."

Alex turned toward him, her feet braced apart, her jaw tightly clenched. "No. You're not. You're *not* a scoundrel, Owen Monroe. I've seen you do things. I've seen you be kind, loving, thoughtful. I don't care what your father says about you. I don't care what anyone else says either. I know the truth. And you *are* what I think you are. I think *you* just don't know it yet."

He clenched his jaw. "That doesn't make any sense."

"I know that a good, decent man lurks beneath your rakehell exterior. You're not useless. You're not a scoundrel. You're not a rogue. Or at least I used to think you weren't. Now I don't think I know you. Now I wonder why I ever thought I loved you."

"Alex, I—"

She pressed the handkerchief hard against her eyes, promising herself she would not allow so much as one more tear to drop. She breathed in deeply from both nostrils and pushed up her chin. "I must go. I promised the next dance to Lord Berkeley."

"Berkeley can go to the devil," Owen growled.

"What was that?" Boots scuffled against gravel, and Lord Berkeley himself materialized from the shadows.

"Lord Berkeley, you came?" Alex cried.

Lord Berkeley's hands were on his hips, and his jaw was clenched, too. "I do hope Monroe hasn't upset you."

Alex took one more deep breath and shook her head. "No, he—"

Owen took a running leap, pulled back his fist, and punched Berkeley dead in the face.

CHAPTER THIRTY-THREE

Owen fell to the ground solidly on top of the viscount. The two men struggled, rolling in the grass and gravel, and damned if Berkeley didn't give as good a punch as he'd got. Owen was certain his jaw was never going to be the same again. He managed to land another blow to the viscount's temple, and Owen sustained one on the chin that he was convinced chipped a tooth. They went on that way for several minutes before Claringdon came sprinting up and broke them apart. Or at least Owen thought the large blurry shadow that pulled him away was Claringdon. Apparently, Lucy, who'd accompanied Berkeley into the gardens, had summoned the duke. Swifdon was steps behind them, however, and Owen was only glad Claringdon had made it there first. He would have hated to throw a punch at his brother-in-law. But even as Claringdon hauled him up, Owen lunged at Berkeley again, and Claringdon and Swifdon both had to hold him back this time.

The good viscount seemed to be done fighting, and

while he was breathing heavily and glaring at Owen through narrowed eyes, Berkeley was already brushing grass and dirt from his evening clothes. Alex rushed over to Berkeley and dabbed at his bloody lip with a fresh handkerchief she'd produced from her reticule.

"Are you all right, Lord Berkeley?" she asked in a sympathetic voice that made Owen lunge for the viscount again.

"For God's sake, Monroe, get ahold of yourself," Claringdon ordered in a voice that Owen was certain many a soldier had heard on the battlefield.

But it was Cass's worried voice that finally broke through his mindless rage. "Owen, what's come over you? I've never known you to be so violent," his sister said in a shaky, unhappy murmur.

Owen tested his jaw and shrugged. "First time for everything?"

Cass shook her head at him disapprovingly. "You must go home now. Before anyone else from the party comes out and sees this."

Owen glanced around. His sister was right. Thankfully, the only people currently in the garden were his sister and their friends. If anyone else happened along, questions would be raised, and no doubt a scandal would be well on its way to boiling. A scandal that might ruin Alex's reputation, and that was the last thing he wanted to do.

"Sober up, Monroe," Claringdon warned under his breath.

Owen wrenched himself away from the duke's hold. "I'll go," he growled, tugging at his cravat and straightening his waistcoat.

Cass produced a handkerchief from her reticule and

she dabbed at a spot where blood dripped from Owen's eyebrow. He spat some blood on the ground.

"I suggest you go out the garden gate," Swifdon said. "I'll go through the house and have your coach brought round."

"I came with Cavendish," Owen replied, his eyes still fixed on Alex. Alex barely glanced at him as she saw to Berkeley's wound. But when she did briefly meet his gaze, the look in her eyes was accusatory and unforgiving. She and Berkeley and the others soon returned to the house. Claringdon stayed to escort Owen off the property, no doubt.

Owen dabbed at his bloodied brow with Cass's handkerchief. Damn it. He wasn't the type to get into a common brawl. And he especially wasn't the type to fight a man at a formal event. But the way Berkeley had appeared, so smug and confident, Owen couldn't stand the thought of Alex being with him, going off with him, leaving Owen alone. He couldn't stand the thought of her dancing with him.

He tested his jaw. Blast. That must have been how Alex felt last night when he'd gone off with Helena Clare. And she'd said she loved him. Alex loved him. Loved him enough to help him and to lie to him about her sister's likes and dislikes. He spat another mouthful of blood.

"Watch where you're aiming," Claringdon said, sidestepping away from him. The duke was half dragging Owen along the garden path toward the gate that led to the front of the property.

"I can't help it. It feels like the inside of my cheek is ripped open."

"No more than you deserved, taking a swing at Berkeley like that. The chap did nothing to deserve it. And did no one ever tell you that jealousy is *not* an attractive quality? But not to worry, I'll have my coach take you home."

Owen merely growled and simmered. Claringdon was right . . . unfortunately. Jealously wasn't attractive, and Berkeley didn't deserve it. In fact, Berkeley wasn't even the man whom Alex had been in love with this entire time. It was . . . him. It was *him*. It had always been him. And he'd gone and acted like a complete fool. Punching Berkeley had been just another in a long string of stupid things Owen had done of late. It was time to end the streak.

CHAPTER THIRTY-FOUR

"If anything, I'd say it worked *too* well," Lucy Hunt announced the next morning as the ladies strolled through the duke and duchess's gardens. Lucy was wearing a spring green day dress with daisies laced through her hair. Cass wore a lavender silk gown and a lovely strand of pearls. And Jane Upton wore a gorgeous shade of ice-blue with a stunning silver necklace that matched her ever-present spectacles. As for Alex, she was wearing a light gray gown and no jewelry. Her ensemble matched her mood. The four women walked two by two along the pretty winding garden path among the bright yellow mums.

"Far too well." Cass sighed, shaking her head.

"Yes," Lucy agreed. "We only wanted Owen to get jealous, not cause poor Lord Berkeley to bleed."

"Is it any wonder blood was let, Lucy?" Jane asked, stopping to smell a rose in a vine that lined the stone wall of the house. "Your plotting was involved."

Lucy, who was walking ahead of Jane with Cass,

paused along the mulched walkway and put her hand on her hip. She turned to face Jane. "I take offense to that, Janie. To date there has been no bloodletting during any of my so-called plots."

Jane arched a brow. "What did you tell me Owen said last night? First time for everything?"

Cass turned to Alex. "I'm sorry, Alex. We certainly didn't mean for anyone to get hurt. Though I daresay Owen got as good as he gave. When I visited him last night, he said he thought his jaw was broken."

"I doubt it," Jane announced. "If it had truly been broken, he couldn't have spoken. It's most likely no more than a bad bruise."

"Well, that's a relief," Cass replied before turning her attention back to Alex. "Are you very upset, dear?"

Alex took a deep breath. The truth was she didn't know how she felt after yesterday's debacle with Owen. Upset? Angry? Embarrassed? Tired? A bit of them all, if she was honest.

"I'll be fine," she answered as they continued their stroll. That was all she could say for sure. She *would* be fine. It was true that her silly childish dream had died along with Owen's rejection of her and his outlandish behavior, but she also wasn't a child anymore, and didn't all childish dreams die sometime? She used to believe in fairies and elves, too. Was this so much different? Perhaps her parents had the right of it. They were older and wiser, after all. They'd lived longer, seen more of human behavior. If her parents believed that marriage was more successful when based on family trees and money and land changing hands, who was she to gainsay them? Besides, Owen Monroe had proved himself to be exactly what he'd tried to tell her he was from the outset: a scoundrel, a rogue, a . . . jackass.

"I'm only sorry I dragged poor Lord Berkeley into the fray," Alex added, stooping to inhale the fresh scent of huckleberry.

"That was our fault, dear," Cass hurried to assure her.

"I still say it worked," Lucy declared, plucking a pink rose from another vine and twirling it between her fingers.

Jane shook her head. "Lucy, you've never learned how to admit when you're wrong."

"Who's wrong?" Lucy pressed the rose to her nostrils. "It seems to me that Owen is jealous, and that is exactly what we wanted."

"He and Lord Berkeley nearly ripped each other to shreds," Jane replied.

Lucy wiggled her shoulders. "There's nothing wrong with a bit of male drama. They accuse us of it often enough."

Jane rolled her eyes. "I cannot believe you just said that, Lucy."

"You're looking at this all wrong," Lucy continued. "Berkeley handled himself easily, and I'm certain he doesn't mind a bit of bloodshed in the name of helping our friend here secure a proposal from the man of her dreams."

"No!" The word shot from Alex's mouth with more force than she'd meant it to.

"No?" Lucy's face fell.

"No," Alex repeated with less vehemence, but this time she shook her head. "I don't want a proposal from Owen. I never should have wanted one. I never should have accepted your help, and I'm quite through with Owen Monroe." She reached out and touched Cass's sleeve. "Though I hope I haven't offended you, Countess."

"Oh, Alex, how could I be angry with you for your

decision? I cannot possibly defend Owen's behavior. He's acted like a complete reprobate."

"No. No. No. Alex, don't you see? You can't stop now. We're nearly through the rough part," Lucy pleaded.

"The rough part?" Alex repeated. "If this is the rough part, I don't want to keep going."

"It is always darkest just before the dawn," Lucy quoted.

"Thank you for all your help to date, Your Grace, but I'll say it again: I am completely through with Owen Monroe."

CHAPTER THIRTY-FIVE

Owen was still abed when the loud thumping on the door to his rooms began. The events of last night came thundering back through his skull in excruciating detail. It was official. He was a useless ass. But he wasn't about to listen to his father rail at him today of all days. He was not in the mood. Holding his aching head in his hands, he called to his valet. "I'm *not* in!"

"Of course not, my lord," the valet replied, clicking his heels together and bowing.

A few minutes later, after a loud exchange at the front of the apartment, the door to Owen's bedchamber cracked open, and Julian Swift stood under the arched entryway, his feet braced apart and a decidedly unhappy look on his face.

"Still abed?" Swifdon asked in a slightly mocking voice.

Owen groaned and let the pillow drop atop his face. "Where else would I be after last night?"

"I don't know. I thought perhaps you'd be at Lady

Alexandra's father's house, begging for her forgiveness for the scene you caused last night."

"Alex doesn't want to see me," he mumbled from under the pillow.

Swifdon's voice was tinged with a bit of irony this time. "I never said she did."

"If you've come to make me feel guilty, let me save you the trouble and tell you that I couldn't possibly feel more guilt."

"Good. You *should* feel guilty. But that's not why I'm here."

Owen pulled the pillow away from his face and eyed the earl warily. "Then why *are* you here?"

Swifdon yanked the chair away from the writing table. "I'm here because someone needs to talk some sense into you, and apparently your father's not particularly good at the task, so as your brother-in-law, I'm taking it upon myself. You're welcome, by the by."

Owen continued to watch him warily out of his blurry eyes. He stuffed the pillow underneath his head and hoisted himself up. "Very well. What is it you wish to say to me?"

Swifdon swiveled the chair around and straddled it. He braced both arms along its back. "I wish to tell you that it's high time you stopped acting like a child and started acting like a man."

Owen looked twice. Blast. Had his brother-in-law truly just said that?

"I didn't realize that I was acting like a child. Thank you for that."

"What else do you call someone who's allowing his father to dictate his marital plans? I certainly didn't allow my father to pick for me—neither did Claringdon or Cavendish, for that matter."

Owen groaned and rubbed his aching skull. "I hate to point out the obvious, but you all conveniently have fathers who are dead."

"They may be dead, but you can rest assured that had any of them been living, they wouldn't have chosen for us."

Owen closed his eyes and considered Swifdon's words for a moment. The truth of the earl's words hit him like Berkeley's punch to the jaw last night. By God, the man was right. Why *was* he allowing his father to dictate to him? He'd spent his entire life being a disappointment to the man. He hadn't questioned being a disappointment to him in his choice of a bride. But instead of picking someone of whom his father disapproved, he'd merely been failing miserably at attempting to woo the unsavory lady of his father's choice.

Alex's words came back to haunt him as well: "Mother isn't always right about things. Neither is Father," she'd said the day Owen followed her to the poorhouse. Even at eighteen years old, she knew better than he did.

"You're agreeing with me, aren't you?" Swifdon asked, shaking Owen from his thoughts.

"I have to admit your words make a great deal of sense. I regret what I did last night, but Alex lied to me, too. She lied to me about her sister, and I suspect she was actively attempting to make me jealous with Berkeley."

"From what I've heard from Cassie and Lucy, I think that's exactly what she was doing, though not without some *advice* from her friends."

Owen groaned. "I should have guessed as much."

"I can't say I disagree with you there, Monroe. We are speaking of the same young women who invented a non-existent person and then invited a great many people to a house party in her honor."

"We are indeed." Owen pressed his arm to his forehead. "Speaking of advice, what else did you want to say to me?"

Swifdon sighed and shifted his folded arms along the back of the chair. "The next bit is hard-won advice from my own life, but I think it will help you."

"Help me?"

"Yes. And I think you desperately need a bit of help at present."

Owen pressed his fingertips to his throbbing temples. "Very well, Your Lordship. What is it?"

"You know your sister and I traded letters for years while I was gone to war."

"Yes, everyone knows that."

"We fell in love through those letters. Only we didn't quite realize it yet. Not until I returned home."

Owen nodded. "Cass spent all those years afraid for your life."

"I know, and I regret that she had to be worried for so long. But when I returned, she made a choice, the choice to pretend she was someone she was not. She had reasons for her choice, and of course, Lucy Hunt was involved, but regardless, Cass's choice nearly cost us our future."

Owen groaned. "Is this where you're going to tell me that I shouldn't allow Alex's lies to cost me our future?"

Swifdon nodded solemnly. "If you want a future with her, yes. If I had allowed Cassie's mistake to cost us each other, it would have been the biggest regret of my life."

"And you think I'm making the biggest mistake of mine?"

"Marrying a woman you don't love, who doesn't love you? Yes. Regardless of your future with Alex, that would be a mistake, don't you think?"

Owen expelled his breath. "Damn it, Swifdon. Why do you always have to be so wise?"

Swifdon chuckled. "It's the way of us old, settled, married men, don't you know? Now, I suggest you start making the right decisions for yourself, and if you agree that one of those decisions is a future with Alexandra, then a great deal of groveling may be in order. You need to do something momentous to make it up to her."

"Momentous?"

"Yes. Something romantic and unforgettable. You'll no doubt need help planning it."

"How am I supposed to do that?"

"I'm not certain," Swifdon replied, standing and pushing the chair back under the writing desk. "But might I suggest you begin with Upton. Seems to me, I recall the chap owes you a favor."

CHAPTER THIRTY-SIX

Garrett Upton did indeed owe Owen a favor. Last autumn during the house party in which Cass and Julian had fallen in love, Upton had bet Owen against a hand of cards that if he won, Owen had to keep his mouth shut and watch his sister pretend to be the fictitious Patience Bunbury for the remainder of the party. Upton, that sharp, had won, and Owen had kept his word despite the myriad misgivings he'd had about the entire ordeal. Cass and her friends were often cooking up plots, and a great deal of trouble had ensued before it all finally ended in Cass and Julian's betrothal. Regardless, after agreeing to play along with all that, Upton was in Owen's debt, the blasted hand of cards be damned.

"Monroe," Upton said the minute the future earl saw Owen walk through the doors at Brooks's. "Haven't seen you in days. I heard a rumor that you were escorting young ladies about to balls lately. Tell me that's not true."

"I'm afraid I cannot," Owen replied.

Upton arched a brow. "It's true?"

"Entirely."

"That's surprising."

"No doubt. But then, that's why I've come. I require your help, Upton. Yours and your wife's."

Upton eyed him warily. "I don't like the sound of that."

Owen grinned at him. "I'd bet on it against a hand of cards, but something tells me you'd win."

"Something tells me you're right. Have a seat."

Owen settled into a chair next to Upton and leaned toward him to ensure they would not be overheard. "Here's what I want you to do."

CHAPTER THIRTY-SEVEN

Now that he had Upton in place, Owen had only a few more things to take care of before he could execute the remainder of his plan. First, he took his coach back to Seven Dials and paid a visit to Miss Magdalene. That fine woman was weeping tears of joy when he left. He'd provided her with a bank draft in the amount of his full monthly allowance. Next, he paid a call to Lord Hopbridge, the man who was opposing the toll road bill in Parliament. He informed the man in no uncertain terms that he had Owen's full support and that he would begin lobbying his friends in Parliament right away. In so doing, he began his campaign for a seat in the House of Commons. Lord Hopbridge agreed to meet with him again so they might discuss it in more detail. Finally, Owen decided to go teach young men at the orphanage how to properly tie their neckcloths.

He woke up early. A novelty. He was busy all day. No devil of a head. By the end of the day, he felt a singularly unique feeling, one he'd never felt before. Owen felt . . .

useful. Useful and productive, as if he were actually accomplishing something, doing something good with his time, with his life. And he had Alex to thank for it. What he realized now was that Alex had been right about him all along. She'd always been right about him. She saw him for something he didn't even see in himself. She made him want to be a better man. And he realized that with her love and support, he *could* be a better man. Alex had been the one to point out to him the opportunity he had to do good, the unique position he was in to make a difference. And she was right. It was up to him—not his past, or his reputation, or even his father. No, it was *Owen's* choice how he spent his time and whether tomorrow was the same as yesterday. He couldn't wait to tell Alex, to thank her for what she'd done for him. Would she be proud of him? The idea struck him quite unexpectedly. He'd never wanted anyone to be proud of him before, not like this. But as he rode in his coach back toward Mayfair, he realized that he wanted not only for Alex to be proud of him—he wanted her to admire him, too. But first he had to become a man worth admiring. He knocked on the small door that separated him from the coachman.

"Yes, my lord?" the servant called.

"Take me to the Duke of Huntley's town house."

A quarter of an hour later, Owen was standing at attention in the duke's study, his hands clasped behind his back, his chin lifted, his booted feet braced apart, while the esteemed man behind the desk narrowed his eyes on him.

"Your mind is made up?" the duke boomed.

"Yes." Owen nodded briskly. "Entirely. Not only do Lavinia and I not suit, but I have every reason to believe that she is vehemently opposed to my courtship of her."

Owen braced himself for a thunderous rebuke. He was surprised when the duke merely pushed back in his overly large leather chair, tossed his quill to the desktop, and sighed. "Damn it, Monroe. I hate to say it, but I fear you're right."

Owen exhaled the breath he didn't even realize he'd been holding. "I can't tell you how pleased I am to hear you say that, Your Grace."

The duke tugged at his beard. "Lavinia's mother and I had hoped she'd see reason, but we've done all we can, hosted a ball, invited you to a dinner party, and heaven knows we've been touting your qualities around here for weeks. Apparently, all to no avail."

"I know you wanted your daughter to make a love match, Your Grace, but I'm sorry to say it cannot be with me."

The duke tapped the quill against his sand pot. "If only she'd take a fancy to *someone*. Someone eligible."

Owen bowed once. "I sincerely hope she does, Your Grace." The duke had no idea how much Owen truly meant those words. Without knowing Alex's heart yet, he wasn't prepared to ask her father for her hand, but he'd be back as soon as he knew. "You still insist upon your eldest marrying first?" he couldn't keep himself from asking.

The duke's eyebrows shot up. "You've no idea the squalling that would ensue within the walls of this home if Alexandra were to announce a betrothal before her sister."

"Sometimes a squall isn't the worst thing that can happen." And with those cryptic words, Owen bowed to the duke. "Thank you for your time, Your Grace, and your understanding."

Owen was nearly to the door when the duke's words

stopped him. "I've always believed you're a good man, Monroe. I do hope you find the right lady one day."

"Thank you, Your Grace. I think I've already found her. And she is magnificent." He paused. "I only hope she'll have me."

The duke inclined his head. "She'd be foolish not to."

Owen pulled open the door and stepped into the corridor. Lady Lavinia, in a quagmire of golden skirts, nearly fell atop him. Owen pulled the door closed behind him and bit the inside of his cheek to keep from smiling. Apparently, Alex wasn't the only one in this household with a penchant for eavesdropping.

The lady scrambled to right herself and pressed one pale hand against her throat.

"My lady," Owen said. "Are you all right?"

She straightened to her full height and patted her coiffure. "Yes, quite."

He wasn't certain how much of the conversation she'd overheard, but he thought it best to be forthright. "You might as well know that I've informed your father that we don't suit. He agrees with me. You'll no longer have to suffer my company."

Her lips thinned to a narrow line. "Is that so?"

"Yes. I assume you're happy with the news. I apologize if I've offended you with my presence. It's as you once told me—our parents were much more interested in the match than either of us." He began to chuckle, but stopped when he saw the sour look on her face. Whatever she thought of the news, she was *not* laughing. "I'm sorry if I've hurt you in any way, Lady Lavinia," he decided to add to be safe. No use poking a cobra.

"You haven't, my lord. I assure you." Her smile was predatory.

He inclined his head to her. "Well, then, good day, my

lady—and all the best to you. I'm certain to see you again sometime." *Seeing as how I hope to soon be your brother-in-law.* But he could put up even with Lavinia upon occasion if it meant having Alex forever.

He began to stride away, but Lavinia's words stopped him. "I heard you say you've already found the right lady."

Ah, so she *had* been eavesdropping and obviously felt no shame over it. He grinned. He couldn't help but grin whenever he thought about Alex. "That's correct."

"Is it Alexandra?" Lavinia asked, her eyes narrowing to slits.

Owen tugged at his sleeve. He supposed it was safe enough to admit it to her. "Yes, my lady. It is indeed."

"I see," she replied, turning away.

For a split second, Owen thought he saw a flash of pure anger in her eyes. He should soften his words. "I do hope you find a man worthy of you, Lady Lavinia." *Or at least willing to put up with you.*

She seemed to be looking through him, her eyes unfocused. She was barely paying attention. "I just may have, my lord."

Well, that was a surprising bit of news. But certainly a welcome bit. Owen wanted to shout. Excellent! If Lavinia were engaged, he and Alex would be free to wed.

"I wish you luck, then," he replied.

"I don't need luck," she spit, her voice cold enough to freeze water. "I always get what I want."

Owen left the house and jogged down the stairs moments later, shaking his head. The good luck he'd offered her was for whichever unfortunate chap Lady Lavinia had set her sights on. Owen didn't envy the poor bastard. He whistled as he flipped his hat atop his head and headed for his coach. He was nearly ready to speak with Alex.

But first he had to have a talk with one more person.

CHAPTER THIRTY-EIGHT

This time it was Owen who barged into his father's bed-chamber. The old man had been taking a nap . . . in the middle of the afternoon. Imagine that.

"Wake up, Father. I have to speak with you. It's urgent."

His father sat up and sputtered and coughed while Owen strolled over to the window and yanked open the curtains. Sunlight poured through the ornately decorated room with its red velvet upholstery and dark carved wooden furnishing. His father held his arm in front of his eyes to block the light.

"Owen, for God's sake. What do you think you're about?"

"I'm sorry. Did I wake you? That's awfully bother-some, isn't it?" Owen braced his feet apart and folded his arms over his chest.

"I was merely resting my eyes for a bit. I haven't been feeling well. My gout is acting up and—oh bother, I can-not believe Shakespierre allowed you in."

"Ah, but I failed to tell Shakespierre I was looking for you," Owen replied, referring to his father's butler. "I believe he thinks I'm visiting with Mother in one of the drawing rooms."

"By God, I'll have his head when I—"

"Don't worry, Father. I'll be brief. I merely came here to inform you that I wouldn't marry Lady Lavinia Hobbs if she were the last lady in London. In fact, I intend to marry Lady Alexandra Hobbs, if she'll have me. I am in love with her and am planning to do everything in my power to make myself worthy of her, including a bid for the House of Commons in order to promote legislation that addresses the issues I care about, some charity work, and giving away all my material possessions if I must."

His father's eyes were wide gray orbs. "Wh-wh-what are you saying? What about your allowance? Your inheritance?"

"Oh yes, about that. I don't give a toss about it and have already donated this month's allowance to a poorhouse in Seven Dials. Lady Alexandra was gracious enough to point out their dire need."

His father's sleeping cap was askew. He looked old and tired. For a moment Owen was worried for him, almost pitied him. Here was a man who'd used his status, money, and authority to order people about and bully them into doing his bidding his entire life. His servants were frightened of him, and his wife never dared to confront him. Owen silently vowed he'd never act that way. He and Alex—if she'd have him—would have a loving, equal partnership filled with happiness and respect.

"You'd give up your inheritance so easily?" his father sputtered, trying to clutch at lapels that were not there.

"I needn't remind you that the estate is entailed to me upon your death, but yes, I give it up for the remainder of your life without a second thought. Alex means that much to me."

His father's jowls shook. "I do believe you've lost your mind."

"I have, Father. I lost my mind the moment she entered my life. And I've never felt better about a decision. Good day." He nodded, bowed, turned around, and walked directly out the door.

CHAPTER THIRTY-NINE

Bath was always a good idea. Or so Lucy said more than a dozen times on their way there. Alex had agreed to accompany Jane, Garrett, Lucy, and Cass on a trip to the hill town where Garrett owned a house. Lucy, Cass, and Alex rode in one coach. Jane and Garrett rode in a second. The servants and trunks came along in a third.

At first it had sounded like a splendid idea. The chance to get out of London and her mother's prying eyes held a special appeal. The chance to distance herself from Owen held even more. She might be traveling with his sister, but *he* wouldn't be there. But with every turn of the carriage wheel, Alex couldn't help but wonder if she'd return to find him engaged to Lavinia. And the prospect twisted her heart.

She shook her head. No. She refused to think such thoughts. She'd foolishly believed she fell in love with the man as a starry-eyed fifteen-year-old, and once she'd gotten to know the real person behind his debonair façade, she saw him for what he truly was.

"Did you hear that Lady Sarah Highgate is betrothed to the Marquess of Branford?" Lucy asked, interrupting Alex's thoughts.

"That was to be expected," Cass chimed in. "She was the belle of the Season and he the most sought-after bachelor. Well, Owen's sought after, of course, but not quite a marquess," she said, giving Alex a sympathetic smile.

"I wish Lady Sarah well," Alex said simply. "And I'd much prefer not to speak about Owen, if it's quite all right with you, Lady Swifdon."

Lucy and Cass exchanged uneasy glances.

Lucy was the first to speak again. "Yes, well, Garrett and Jane are having a ball tomorrow night." She clapped her hands. "And you'll get to meet Aunt Mary."

"Garrett's mother," Cass interjected.

"Oh, a ball? I didn't realize there would be a ball." Alex struggled to keep a smile pinned to her face, but a ball sounded positively awful at the moment. She'd wanted a holiday, not more of the endless social rounds. "I look forward to meeting Mr. Upton's mother." At least that much was true.

Late that afternoon, their carriage pulled up to the lovely stone town house on the crescent, and the friends alighted. Aunt Mary came hurrying down the stairs, distributing kisses to all and exclaiming first over Alex's beauty, then how tired she must be, and finally how famished.

Their small party partook of bread, cheese, and fruit while the trunks were unloaded from the coaches. They shared news from London with Aunt Mary, including Lady Sarah Highgate's engagement.

How is your brother, Lord Owen?" Aunt Mary finally asked after no one had mentioned him. Perhaps it was a bit conspicuous.

"Oh, he's . . . well," Cass replied, reaching over and patting Alex's hand.

Aunt Mary glanced back and forth between the two of them.

Alex looked away, out the window. She refused to think about Owen, let alone speak of him again. She'd told him she loved him, and he'd punched her friend. The man was an ass.

"I hate to be a bother, Mrs. Upton," she said to Garrett's mother, "but I'm exceedingly tired and—"

Aunt Mary held up a hand. "Say no more, my dear."

In short order, Alex was escorted to a bedchamber and instructed by the solicitous Aunt Mary to take a nap. "We'll have a quiet evening at home tonight to rest from your trip," Aunt Mary said as she left Alex at her bedchamber door. "The ball will be tomorrow evening."

Alex forced a smile to her lips.

There she was in a gown of royal blue, looking heartbreakingly beautiful, her face a mask of ice. He'd taught her too well. She was laughing, dancing, and flirting with her string of admirers, touching one man lightly on the shoulder with her fan, hiding her gorgeous smile behind her gloved hand, her tinkling laughter filling the space, clutching at his heart. Her eyes were sparkling and full of intrigue and promise. Owen's gut clenched. He had made her into this, this dazzling young lady, this sought-after prize every man wanted to win. He'd made her into this, and he'd also made her hate him.

They'd planned this, he and Upton. Upton would dance with her and bring her to the far half of the room on the other side of a trellis that had been set up just for the occasion. Owen would be waiting there, and Upton would hand her off to him. She couldn't possibly object in the midst of a dance in the middle of a crowded ball-room, could she? He would soon find out.

As Owen waited, he realized he was holding his breath. His foot was tapping, too. He was—by God, he was nervous. He'd never been nervous a day in his life. Upton came around the trellis just then and twirled Alex in his direction. When Upton stopped and spun her out of his arms, Owen caught her. The look on her face when she glanced up and realized he was there was a mixture of both surprise and anger. But dare he hope—was it only wishful thinking?—that for a split second between those two other emotions was a flash of . . . happiness? Relief?

Alex didn't take up dancing with him, however. Instead, she stopped, gasped, and stepped back. "What are you doing here?" She glared at Upton for his betrayal.

Upton cleared his throat and clasped his hands behind his back. "I'll just leave you two to talk." He rushed off before Alex had a chance to object.

Alex lifted her skirts and turned away from Owen. "I'm going back to the—"

"Wait," he called, his nerves making his voice harsher than he'd meant it to be.

She stopped, her face in profile. "Why?"

"Alex, I—"

She turned and advanced on him. "What are you doing here?"

"I have a confession to make. I asked Upton to get you here."

"Pardon?"

"I wanted to see you, away from London."

"Garrett planned this?"

"With help from his wife and her friends."

Anger blurred Alex's vision. "Those awful sneaks!"

"Please don't blame them. Upton owed me a favor. I called it in."

She stalked away from him, under the trellis, and crossed her arms over her chest. "Very well. You've got me here. What do you want to say to me?"

"I want to ask you to give me another chance. I want to apologize for my behavior that night—with Mrs. Clare. I want to—"

"Give you another chance for what? We didn't have a first chance. There's nothing to try again."

"I don't think you believe that any more than I do."

Alex flourished a hand in the air. "I was fifteen when I fancied myself in love with you. I'd been shut up in my bedchamber most of my life, listening to strains of waltzes and dreaming about my life when I turned eighteen. I was a fool. Things don't work out the way they do in fairy tales, and the first handsome gentleman to arrive under your windowsill is not meant to be your future husband."

"But he could be."

Alex stopped. Swallowed. Clenched her teeth. "I gave you my heart, Owen. But I no longer believe I can trust you. Please do as I say when I ask you to leave me be."

CHAPTER FORTY

Alex spent the next two hours deftly trying to ignore Owen's presence. What had her new friends been thinking, inviting him here? Cass might be his sister, but they all knew how Alex felt about him at the moment. They liked to be up to mischief, but she'd had no idea they would trick her this way. She needed to be alone. She considered the library but thought better of it. Despite being the lady of the house, Jane Upton would no doubt be perched on the sofa in there. Instead, Alex made her way outside onto the terrace and into the gardens. She hadn't made it two steps down the garden path before the door opened behind her.

"Wait," a man's voice called.

For an excruciating moment, she thought it was Owen. But it wasn't. She'd apparently made it clear that she wanted nothing more to do with him tonight, perhaps ever. No. The man holding open the door to follow her was Lord Berkeley. The viscount released the door and strolled toward her.

Alex stopped and smiled at him. "My lord?"

"I wanted to say . . . good-bye." Lord Berkeley bowed to her. "I came to see my cousin who lives here in Bath and thought I'd stop by Upton's party tonight as well."

"I'm glad you did."

"I'm glad, too. Glad for the opportunity to say good-bye to you. I'm leaving for my property in the North tonight."

Alex tugged at the string to her reticule. "I do hope to see you again sometime soon."

"I'm afraid not. I don't plan to return to London for the better part of a year."

"I'm sorry to hear that." She reached out and squeezed his hand. "Thank you so much, for everything, my lord."

"I wish you well with your pursuit of Monroe. I only hope I've not done more harm than good there."

Alex didn't want to talk about Owen. "Thank you. I can only hope for you to find your true love someday."

Lord Berkeley bowed at the waist. "It was my pleasure, Lady Alexandra. I, too, hope to find my true love one day. I've had the devil's own luck so far." He smiled at her. "I've decided to give up for the time being and retreat to my Scottish hunting lodge, where I won't have to think about debutantes and dancing and being charming for a bit. I'm greatly looking forward to time away from London and all its social obligations."

Alex laughed. "I don't blame you." At the moment, she, too, wanted to get away from London and all its social obligations. Hence, the trip to Bath. Society, it seemed, had followed her here. "But you're always charming, my lord. I don't doubt for a minute you'll find someone quite special. It doesn't matter where you may be residing."

He grinned at her and bowed again. "Until we meet

again." He turned away to go back inside, but Alex stopped him.

Confound it. She couldn't stop herself from asking. "Lord Berkeley?"

"Yes?"

"Did you know Owen would be in attendance here tonight?"

Lord Berkeley shook his head. "I didn't. And something tells me the time for trying to make him jealous is over."

She glanced away. "Long over."

"For what it's worth, he apologized for punching me."

The hint of a smile touched her lips. "Did you accept his apology?"

"Yes." He stepped closer again. "I'll let you in on a secret: The man may be a bit of a hothead from time to time, but I think he's a decent chap, deep down. And for what it's worth, I think he truly loves you."

CHAPTER FORTY-ONE

After Lord Berkley left her in the gardens, Alex didn't have much enthusiasm left to stay at the party. She was unhappy with her friends for tricking her, she was angry with Owen for appearing without warning, and she was sad to say good-bye to the one good friend she treasured, Lord Berkeley. Despite his insistence that Owen loved her, she couldn't be certain of that at all. The man had never said as much and she had no other reason to believe it, other than her remnant of wishful thinking. Besides, Lord Berkeley was the type who has obviously wanted to make her feel better. Alex lifted her skirts and turned toward the door. It was time to go to bed. She would just go back inside, find Jane, her hostess, and say good night.

Alex was slowly walking up the terrace steps when the door opened and Lucy Hunt came hurtling out. Lucy plunked her hands on her hips. "Don't tell me you're retiring already." The duchess sounded displeased.

Alex nodded. "Yes, I'm quite tired, and I—" Why was

she explaining herself to Lucy Hunt, at any rate? She was angry with the woman. "Your Grace, I beg your pardon, but I'm not particularly pleased with you at the moment and I wish to go to bed, so if you'll just—"

"You mean you want to hide from Owen," Lucy said.

Alex scowled at her. "No. Certainly not. I—"

Lucy wrapped her arm through Alex's and led her back down the steps and into the gardens. "You're angry with me for orchestrating this event and inviting Owen, but if you'd only see it's for your own good, you'd be ever so much happier sooner." Lucy released her arm and smiled at Alex. "And yes, you are hiding from Owen. Don't try to deny it. I was in a great deal of denial and confusion at this very house not long ago. I know denial when I see it."

Alex narrowed her eyes on the duchess. "What do you mean?"

"Derek punched a tree, then climbed one—a different tree, that is—this one right here, actually." She flourished her hand in front of the huge oak that rested in the center of the lawn. "Look up there. That large branch nearly meets the window of that bedchamber. I happened to be staying there at the time, and, well, Derek climbed right up."

Alex supposed she should be shocked at that bit of news, but from what she knew of the duchess, it sounded in keeping with her exploits. "That's my bedchamber," Alex whispered.

"Oh, *that's* interesting," Lucy said, a sly smile on her face.

"But you didn't finish what you were saying. Derek climbing up the tree confused you?"

"No. The tree climbing didn't confuse me half so much as the fact that after I allowed him into my bedchamber to see to his bloody fist and ensure such an esteemed war hero didn't fall to his death, he kissed me."

"And *that* confused you?"

"Entirely." Lucy nodded and lowered her voice. "Though the truth is that had I known then what I know now, I wouldn't have allowed him to leave my bedchamber with only a kiss."

Alex gasped and clamped her hand over her mouth.

"I'm so sorry, dear. Have I shocked you? I didn't mean to. Cass always says my mouth works faster than my brain sometimes."

Alex shook her head. "I'm certain you were quite in love with His Grace, and planning to marry, but Owen and I—"

"Oh no, no, no. I wasn't settled on him at all. That's what I'm trying to tell you. When Derek kissed me that night, it was the beginning of a great deal of confusion. You see, I thought he was going to become betrothed to Cass, and I would never betray my closest friend."

Alex gasped again. She couldn't help herself. "Cass? But she and Lord Swifdon—"

"Julian. Yes, I know. Oh, it's a *very* long story, dear. Long and complicated, but suffice it to say that everyone knew that Derek and I were a better match. Everyone *except* the two of us, of course."

"So you're saying that Owen and I—"

"Are obviously a perfect match. We agreed to invite him here so that you would have the opportunity to talk and see the truth yourself. Owen was quite adamant that he see you and have the chance to speak with you alone. But you've been quite stubborn and refused to listen to him. I came out here to say I think you should give him the opportunity to tell you how he feels."

Alex sniffed. "You don't know everything he's done, and—"

"I may not know all the details," Lucy agreed. "But I've known Owen since I was a child, and he's a good man. A very good man."

"I know, you told me, the story about Eton and—"

"It's not just that, dear. It's many things he's done over the years. The way he treats Cass. The way he speaks softly to his horses. The respect he's always shown his mother. Take my word for it. He may have acted like an ass of late, but we all do stupid things at times. Let him tell you how he feels."

Alex sighed. "Owen's not the sort to tell a lady how he feels."

"Perhaps not in the past, dear, but give him a chance. These men of ours, they do surprise us from time to time."

Alex pressed the back of her hand to her forehead. This night was becoming more exhausting and more confusing, not less so. "So what are you saying? Owen should punch a tree, kiss me, and confuse me?"

"Not at all. I'm simply saying that you should hear him out." Lucy turned away briefly and then peeked back over her shoulder with a sly smile. "And, if he just so happens to climb up to your bedchamber, don't let him leave."

CHAPTER FORTY-TWO

Alex couldn't sleep. She tossed and turned and flipped her pillow over at least a dozen times. It was too hot in her bedchamber. That was the problem. She climbed out of bed and made her way over to the window in the dark. Feeling her way around, she pushed open the casement. A rustling sound in the tree caught her attention. She peered and blinked out into the inky night sky. The light from the moon illuminated enough to see the outline of a man swinging from the large branch nearby. Alex's heart nearly stopped. It couldn't possibly be . . .

She rubbed her eyes and looked again. Yes. There was Owen . . . scaling the tree. She opened the window farther and nearly screamed as he swung himself inside. He landed in an ignominious heap on the floor just inside the window. He'd ripped his shirt, and there was a smudge of dirt on his cheek.

Alex clamped a hand over her mouth to keep from screaming and waking the household. "Owen," she whispered fiercely. "What in God's name are you doing? You could have been killed!"

Owen groaned, pushed himself to his feet, and brushed leaves from his hair. "Yes, I know that now. But I spoke to Lucy earlier, and she indicated that you may have had a change of heart from what you said to me earlier in the ballroom. And damn me, but I decided to take Claringdon's advice."

Alex hurried over to the bedside table and lit a candle. She returned to where Owen was standing, holding the stick aloft. "Claringdon's advice?"

"Yes," Owen replied. "Claringdon suggested I get drunk, punch a tree, climb into your window, and kiss you."

She eyed him distrustfully. "Are you drunk?"

"No. I haven't been drunk in days, actually."

"Are you mad?"

"Not that I'm aware, but there's every possibility. I've ruined a damn fine shirt, and my coat is resting on a hedge down there somewhere. I admit I fear for its safety. Though I have yet to punch a tree, so the odds seem to be in my favor. But I did climb one. Apparently, Claringdon's in much better physical shape than I am because I nearly killed myself doing it. Perhaps it's easier when you're drunk. I can't be certain."

Alex stared at him with her mouth open. "You have gone mad."

"Look, Alex, please listen to me." He turned to her and addressed her fervently, pulling her hand into his. "Hear me out—and then if you want me to leave, I'll go, immediately. You have my word."

"Very well," she said. "I'll hear you out."

Owen squeezed her hand. "When I was teaching you

how to be a coquette, how to flirt and dance and bat your eyelashes, I was doing everything wrong. The reason you're special is because you're honest and forthright and refreshing."

Alex held her breath. Had he just said she was special?

"You don't play games," he continued. "You don't pretend to be someone you're not. And that's what I love about you. Among many other things."

Tears stung her eyes. She swallowed past the lump in her throat. "Did you say 'love'?"

"I did. I do. I can only hope that you will—" He dropped to one knee. "Lady Alexandra Hobbs, please tell me you'll consider doing me the honor of becoming my bride."

"You want to marry me, Owen?" The tears fell from her eyes.

"Yes, of course." He fumbled in his coat pocket for a handkerchief and pressed it into her hand. "Please don't cry, darling. Please."

She dabbed at her tears. "I can't believe you're here, saying this. I can't believe you traveled to Bath, and climbed a tree, and—"

"I not only traveled to Bath and climbed a tree, but I also gave all my money to the poorhouse, am planning a run for the House of Commons, and have begun volunteering at an orphanage."

"Pardon?"

"That's what I'm trying to tell you, Alex. You've made me a better man. From the day I first met you, you have. I've stopped drinking, I can't remember the last time I gambled, and my life has purpose now."

She quickly pushed the candlestick onto a nearby table and grabbed both his hands and squeezed. "Oh, Owen. I'm so happy for you. Truly, I am. I always knew you could find your way."

"Do me a favor, love?"

"Anything." She clutched his hand to her heart.

"Answer my question." He grinned at her. "You never said. Will you marry me?"

"Yes. Yes, I'll marry you." She nodded, brushing away fresh tears.

He pulled her into his arms, and his mouth captured hers.

Alex's head fell back and her eyes closed. "Take me to bed," she whispered.

His hands trembled. "Are you certain?"

"Entirely." She stared deeply into his eyes.

Apparently, that was all Owen needed to hear. He swung her into his arms and carried her to the bed. He laid her there so gently. The only light was from the one candle that she'd left burning across the room. He fell atop her and kissed her ravenously, and Alex wrapped her arms around his neck and pressed against his erection, which was poking at her most intimate spot through her gown. He ripped off her night rail and then stopped to remove his boots and cravat and shirt and breeches. They were all gone in short order.

"Are you certain, Alex?" he breathed again. She'd pulled the bedsheets up to her neck, but they didn't stop her from looking her fill at his magnificent body. She'd once thought he looked like Adonis. More so when he was naked. His shoulders were wide and strong, his forearms muscled, his chest taut and lightly haired, and his abdomen flat. His hips were angular and his manhood stood out, in stark relief, reaching for her. He was huge. She wanted to touch him. Now.

"I'm certain," she whispered, licking her lips.

There was a flash of relief across his face and then he smiled—and that dimple was her final undoing.

"Don't hide from me, Alex. Let me see you."

Alex hesitated but allowed him to pull the sheet away to uncover her nakedness.

"You're perfect," he breathed, his hands skimming over her belly and hips and breasts. He cupped her breasts and squeezed lightly. "Exactly as I imagined you would be."

"You imagined me . . . naked?"

He snorted. "More often than I should have, I'm sure. What about me? Did you ever imagine me, like this?" He glanced down at his body.

"I couldn't imagine," she replied, biting her lip. "But I did hope I'd get to see."

He chuckled at that and then kissed her again, deeply, his jaw jutting out. She ran her fingertips across its rough surface. Oh, this man was gorgeous and he was hers. Or at least he was going to be hers tonight.

"I only hope I don't disappoint you," she whispered in his ear.

He stopped, pulled back, and cupped her face in his hands. "Alex. You could never disappoint me. But I want to make it good for you."

"What are you going to—?"

But he had already begun to move downward, and his mouth quickly found her right nipple. She gasped and nearly lunged off the bed. His wide hands on her shoulders pressed her back down. Then he moved a hand under her backside and pushed up. Her back arched and her breast strained into his mouth. She groaned and her fingers tangled in his hair. His mouth was doing things to her breast she'd never imagined possible. His teeth nipped at her. His tongue rubbed roughly against the sensitive peak. She arched her back farther, wanting his mouth to never stop.

"Owen," she groaned. His other hand moved from her

back to her other nipple, and he twisted it and rubbed it. She arched into his mouth and hand. He sucked her while she held his head, desperately hoping he didn't move away, didn't stop. Stabs of pleasure shot from her breasts to the secret spot between her thighs, and she clamped her legs together so the pressure building there wouldn't be so unbearable.

"I'm going to make you come, Alex. Do you know what that means?" His hot wet mouth circled her breast. His words were warm puffs of air against her tortured nipple.

She shook her head frantically against the pillow. "No." But whatever it was, she desperately wanted to find out.

He kept his hand on her nipple, squeezing, pulling, nipping, rubbing, while his mouth moved lower to the juncture of her thighs. "Spread your legs," he commanded, his breath a hot brand on her soft skin.

"Yes," she breathed. His hand pushed against the inside of her knee, spreading her open to him. His other hand remained on her nipple. Then his scorching tongue descended into the apex between her legs—and Alex forgot to breathe.

"Owen!" she cried softly as he licked her deeply. His tongue played with her, brushing the nub that was pulsing, throbbing, responding to the thrills still shooting down from her breast. He brought up his other hand from her knee and pulled her hand to her breast. "Touch yourself," he whispered.

She tentatively squeezed the soft mound and then her fingertip glanced over her nipple and she gasped. She flicked her thumb over the sensitive spot just as he'd done moments earlier, just as he was still doing to her other breast. "Oh, Owen, I—"

But she didn't know how to finish the sentence.

Pleasure streaked down her abdomen, white-hot pulses of pure lust shooting from both breasts, fulfilled by the hot deep strokes from his lush tongue. He sucked her there, too, and her hips nearly came off the bed, the feeling was so intense. She whimpered. He brought his hand down and slowly pushed one finger inside her. Alex's head fell to the side and she groaned. "Owen."

"Just feel it, Alex, feel it. Let go."

His mouth between her thighs, his thumb stroking her nipple, and then his finger pressing inside her, pulling out, pressing again—the combination was too much for her. Both her hands moved down to tangle in his thick hair, and he licked her again, again, again, pushing against the spot inside her that made her cry out and shatter. She clamped her thighs against his head as shudders—uncontrollable, delicious shudders—rocked her entire body.

Owen moved up between her legs and gazed down at her. He had a self-satisfied smirk on his face. He stroked her side, her arm, her shoulder, while Alex slowly floated back to earth.

"I can't believe—I had no idea—I am simply—"

"I adore making you speechless." He leaned down and kissed her deeply, and Alex tasted her salty sweetness on his tongue. It was probably wrong, but it felt so sensuous. She shuddered again.

"Yes, speechless," she conceded. "That's what I am."

"Good." His eyes hooded and he leaned down and kissed her once more. "Alex, I want you," he whispered into her mouth.

"You have me," she whispered back.

"I mean I want to be inside you." He kissed her again, and liquid heat pooled between her thighs.

"Yes," she breathed.

* * *

"Touch me," Owen commanded. He pulled her hand down between his legs and wrapped her fingers around his cock. Sweet Jesus. The feel of her hand on him was torture. He closed his eyes and groaned. He moved her hand up and down, showing her exactly how he liked to be touched.

"Is this right?" she asked in a shy voice.

"Oh, love, it's so right." He closed his eyes and pressed his forehead to hers, hard.

He increased the tempo, wanting to plunge inside her but not wanting to frighten her or hurt her. His hips rocked to the rhythm set by her torturous hand. He thrust into her palm again, again, again. His hand moved between her legs to ensure she was ready for him; he slid one finger inside her. "You're so hot, so wet. Do you want me, love?"

"Yes." Her eyes were tightly closed but she nodded and she still had the hint of a satisfied smile on her gorgeous face.

"I want to make you fly," he whispered into her ear, his tongue dipping inside the sensitive shell. She bucked beneath him and he pushed his hands to her hips, holding them to the mattress to steady her, readying her for him.

"Let go," he commanded, and Alex's hand fell away from his cock. He twined his fingers through hers and pushed her hand high above her head against the mattress, pinning her beneath him. "I've dreamed of this for so long," he breathed, pressing himself into the wet heat of her. "I've dreamed—" His words were lost in his own groan as he pushed inside her. Her eyes flew open from shock, and he knew the second he'd breached her maidenhead.

She clenched her jaw, and a small wince appeared on

her fine features. He kissed her nose, her eyelids, her cheekbones, her forehead. "Did I hurt you? Are you all right?"

She shifted beneath him. "I think so."

He didn't want to laugh, but the scowl on her face was adorable. He kissed the tip of her nose. "I love you," he murmured, pulling out slowly and pushing back inside. "I love you," he repeated each time he pulled out and pressed home.

Soon Alex's head was flitting from side to side on the pillow. Sweat lined her brow. Owen's hips pumped into her again and again, and he had to bite the inside of his cheek to keep from coming too soon. He wanted to make it good for her again. He lowered his hand between them and circled the tiny nub of her pleasure. Her eyes flew open and widened. "I didn't know we could—"

"We can do anything." He nipped at her shoulder. His forehead was slick with sweat, and he groaned against the desire to rock into her one last time and lose himself in her. "I want you so much, Alex. Come for me, love. Come for me." Her hips were rocking, too, of their own accord, matching the rhythm of his hand. Her breath was coming in fitful little spurts and her hand moved up to stroke her own breast, just as he'd taught her.

"That's right, touch yourself, come for me, Alex." He moved his head down and sucked her nipple and bit it lightly. She arched off the bed, her thighs squeezing him tightly, his name on her lips.

Owen moved his head back up and kissed her deeply. His tongue plunged into her mouth and owned her. He cradled her face in his hands as his hips pressed into her once, twice, a third time, before he let himself go completely, his orgasm shaking him so badly, he cried out against her mouth and collapsed atop her gorgeous sweat-sheened body.

Moments later, Owen rolled over and pulled her atop him. Her magnificent hair was down around her shoulders, and he leaned up and pulled her neck down so she would meet his mouth. He kissed her again, long and slowly.

"I'll never get tired of kissing you," she said when he pulled away, pushing her hair behind her ear.

"I hope you never do. And I'll never get tired of making love to you."

She pressed herself to his chest and snuggled her head under his chin. "I hope not, Owen. I know you're a rake, but—"

He pushed himself up on one elbow and took her chin in his hand. "No. Listen to me. I mean it. I will never give you cause to believe I've been unfaithful. I've sowed all my wild oats, and I'm quite through with it. What we did here tonight was a first for me, too. We made love. I'm entirely committed to you, Alex. I love you."

Alex sighed and laid her hand against his heart. "I love you, too, Owen." She ducked her head and blushed beautifully. "Now, do you think we could do that again?"

CHAPTER FORTY-THREE

Alex couldn't stop smiling. She smiled at the coachman who drove her back to London. She smiled at the footman who opened the door for her once she and Hannah arrived on her father's doorstep, and she smiled as she fell asleep that night, knowing that Owen loved her and intended to ask for her hand. In marriage. *Marriage.* She was going to *marry* Owen Monroe. And Mother and Father couldn't possibly object. Not even with Lavinia unmarried. Not after what she and Owen had done.

Late the next morning, Alex was startled awake by a sharp rap on her door.

"Come in," she called, and was surprised to see Lavinia stroll in. Her sister was wearing a lemon-colored gown with matching ribbons in her hair. She carried part of a newspaper in her hand. It had to be the Society pages. That was the only part of the paper her sister ever showed any interest in.

"Good morning, Lavinia," Alex called, stretching her arms high above her head. Even her sister's sour disposition couldn't spoil her mood today. "What time is it?"

"It's nearly eleven," Lavinia said in her usual pinched voice. "How was your trip to Bath?"

Still smiling, Alex sat up straight and fluffed the pillows behind her. She was ready to launch into every delicious detail with her sister. Who cared that she and Lavinia had never been close? Today she wanted to shout her happy news across the rooftops of London. Why, she'd discuss it with a fence pole if she thought it would listen. "Oh, Lavinia. The most wonderful thing has happened. You'll never guess."

Lavinia's mouth spread into a tight smile. "I have some wonderful news of my own."

Alex paused. "You do?" Years of experience had taught Alex that Lavinia intended to tell her story first, but Alex was tired of Lavinia always coming first. "That's wonderful, but let me tell you—"

"I'm engaged!" Lavinia blurted out.

Alex gasped, her own news temporarily forgotten in her shock. "You are? Oh, Lavinia, how absolutely perfect." Alex's smile widened. Things could not have worked out any better. If Lavinia was also engaged, that would immediately put an end to her mother's only objection to her own engagement. "I'm so happy for you. Who is your bridegroom?"

Lavinia smoothed her hand over the paper. "Why, it's Lord Owen Monroe, of course."

Alex's breath caught in her throat. She tried to speak, but no words would come out. She *must* have heard her sister incorrectly. "Lord Owen Monroe?" she finally managed to croak.

"Yes. That's right." Lavinia's face was blank with only the hint of a curl at her lips. "It was quite sudden, really."

Alex struggled to pull air in and out of her rapidly deflating lungs. Her sister was lying. Lying or wrong or mad. One of the three, for certain.

"See?" Lavinia tossed the paper onto the bed. "Here is our engagement announcement."

Alex grabbed the paper and scanned the page. It didn't take long to find it. Lavinia was right. There it was, clearly printed for all of London to see. The engagement of Lord Owen Monroe to Lady Lavinia Hobbs.

Lavinia made her way over toward the window and stared out.

"There must be some mistake," Alex murmured. "This can't be—"

"Lord Owen paid a call yesterday afternoon," Lavinia said, contemplating her fingernails. "He said he had to know where my affections lie."

"He was here? Yesterday?" Alex hated the smallness of her own voice.

"Yes. He said he was prepared to ask another young lady to marry him. But he couldn't make the commitment to do so until he knew for certain there was no hope whatsoever with me. He explained to me that our parents wished it. Apparently, he decided his father's wishes and his allowance meant more to him than he'd originally realized."

Tears—hot, fat, ugly, awful, shameful tears—stung Alex's eyes. She savagely wiped them away "He said that?" Her voice cracked.

"Yes," Lavinia replied, still gazing out the window. "Of course, it was a surprise to me that I'd accept him. You know how I've felt about him in the past."

Alex could only nod, even though she knew her sister couldn't see her. "Yes," she managed.

"But the truth is, I've had a change of heart lately. You and Mother were so adamant about his being suitable, and he seemed so intent upon wanting me, well, I can hardly blame the poor man." She laughed an affected laugh. "At any rate. I decided you're right. He's handsome. He's eligible. I cannot remain a maiden forever. He must have been eager to announce the news because he went straight to the papers, apparently." Her sister took a breath. "Of course, I remember you saying you might try your luck with him, but I assume you decided your affections lie elsewhere, given *your* good news."

Alex wiped away the latest set of tears as her sister turned fully around.

"We're planning a spring wedding," Lavinia finished.

"A spring wedding?" Alex echoed.

"Yes, I've always wanted a spring wedding."

"So have I," Alex barely whispered.

Lavinia returned to the bed and shrugged and sighed. "Well, enough about me. What is your good news, Alexandra? Are you engaged? Perhaps to Lord Berkeley?"

"No! No. It's . . . it's nothing so grand as your news."

"I see. Well, I do hope you'll help me plan the wedding. I know we've never been close, but I'd truly like to change that." She reached over and patted Alex on the hand.

"Of . . . of course." Alex watched, dumbfounded, as her sister turned and flounced to the door.

"I thought you'd be happier for me, Alexandra," Lavinia said with a bit of a pout on her lips. "This is wonderful news for you, too, you know? It means that now you're free to become engaged as well."

"Yes," Alex whispered brokenly.

Her sister opened the door and flitted away while Alex vowed never to shed another tear for Owen Monroe.

CHAPTER FORTY-FOUR

Owen wanted to punch his fist through the wall of the coach. His mind had transformed into a haze of angry red mist. After seeing that farce of an engagement announcement in the *Times* this morning, he'd gone to the Duke of Huntley's residence to both demand an explanation and ask for Alex's hand in marriage. The duke seemed to be entirely ignorant of how the announcement had made it into the paper, but he refused to allow his eldest daughter to be embarrassed by a retracted announcement. Lavinia, it seemed, had had a change of heart and was willing to accept him now. The duke had told Owen in no uncertain terms that Alex would *not* be his. Owen could marry Lavinia or no one.

Owen knew exactly who had sent the announcement to the paper. Lavinia was just the sort of devil to do such a thing. He'd underestimated her and made a grievous mistake when he'd told her he loved Alex. None of that mattered, however. He need only talk to Alex. He had no idea what her reaction to the announcement in the paper was. She was probably angry too. But they'd figure something out. Damn it. They'd strike out for Gretna Green tonight, if that was what she wanted. Her father had refused to send the butler to fetch Alex. Owen had waited outside for hours, hoping to catch a glimpse of her. He'd finally bribed one of the footmen to discover from her maid where she was planning to go tonight. He'd learned that she was attending the Bennetts' affair, and that's exactly where he was headed.

His coach had barely come to a rolling stop in front of the Bennetts' town house when Owen leaped out and headed toward the house with ground-devouring strides. Apparently, he was making a habit of plowing through crowds without observing the social niceties in search of Alex.

After scouring the house for the better part of half an hour, he found her, sitting forlornly near a potted palm along the sidelines of the dancing. He made his way over to her quickly.

"Alex, there you are," he said breathlessly. "There's something I have to tell you."

She looked up at him as if she'd seen a ghost. Pure horror registered on her face. Had she been crying? She held up a hand. "No, wait."

Judging from her swollen eyes, perhaps she'd already heard. He took a deep breath. "You're not going to like it, but I've been to see your father and—"

"Yes. I know." She kept her jaw tightly clamped. She wouldn't look at him. What was wrong?

Owen scrubbed a hand through his hair. "He told you?"

Alex stared off into the crowd, still refusing to look at him. "It's quite the news at my house. Did you think I wouldn't find out?"

"I want you to know, this doesn't change anything, I still plan to—"

"No!" She snapped her head toward him and met his gaze. "I don't want to hear it. It's over. Let's part ways with a bit of dignity."

He searched her face, incredulous. "Alex, no. I—I told your father that—"

"Save your breath. I told Father I wouldn't accept your suit if you were the last man on earth. It's perfectly fine. It's all to work out the way it's meant to, isn't it? You told me that once, Owen, do you remember?"

He glanced about to ensure they were not being overheard. "Yes, but what about Bath? What about—?"

She tugged viciously at the string to her reticule. "Oh, that. I only did *that* on a dare from Lucy Hunt."

His face crumpled into a mask of disbelief. "What are you saying?"

Her voice was a harsh, low whisper. "I wanted to see what it would be like, my first time with a rake. Thank you for your experience, my lord. It was quite enlightening."

He snapped his head to the side as if he'd been slapped. "You don't mean that, Alex."

"Yes, I do, and I mean this, too: Marry Lavinia, Owen. You deserve each other." Alex stood and hurried away.

CHAPTER FORTY-FIVE

If the Duke of Huntley's butler was at all surprised to see three well-dressed young married ladies of varying aristocratic lineage knocking on the front door that afternoon, he betrayed his surprise by neither word nor deed. In fact, Alexandra had to wonder at the poor servant's shock when the three ladies introduced themselves as the Duchess of Claringdon, the Countess of Swifdon, and Mrs. Garrett Upton. But the butler must have recovered himself soon after they announced they were here to see Lady Alexandra Hobbs and not Lady Lavinia, who was indisposed at any rate, as she was upstairs having fittings with her modiste, Madame Bergeron. Lady Alexandra, however, was quite free to receive company and was sitting in the drawing room, working on her embroidery, when the three esteemed ladies marched into the room. They came in looking like a set of well-heeled fairy godmothers in smart gowns and kid gloves, their bonnets having been removed at the door. Alex glanced up from her embroidery, looked twice, and watched in awe as they fanned out around her, took seats, and deftly asked the butler for tea.

"I assume you received my note, Cass," Alex said, letting her embroidery fall to her lap.

"I did indeed, and I was entirely horrified," Cass replied.

Alex furrowed her brow. "I do hope you're not here to attempt to convince me to forgive Owen, because I simply cannot—"

"We're not here to convince you of anything, Alex. But you must listen to us," Cass said quietly.

"We've done some investigating," Jane announced. She did not have a book in her hand. This had to be serious.

Lucy nodded. "Yes, even Jane got involved this time."

Jane shrugged. "I cannot abide injustice. It's a particular vexation of mine. And I do have a bit of experience when it comes to sleuthing about."

"Investigating? Injustice? Sleuthing? But what has this to do with me?" Alex turned her head in a wide arc to meet each of their gazes.

"Something about the story you sent to Cass didn't quite make sense, dear," Lucy said. "So I summoned your sister's maid."

Alex blinked. "Martha?"

"Yes, a lovely woman. I asked her to tell me what she knew, and she did. I don't know what it is about me, but people always seem to tell me the truth. It's as if I'm a vicar or something."

"Oh, I wouldn't go *that* far." Jane rolled her eyes.

"Regardless," Lucy sniffed, "Martha was quite a source of information. I learned long ago—if you want to know a lady's secrets, start with her maid. They know everything, don't they?"

The two other ladies nodded.

"Martha told me the entire sordid story," Lucy continued.

Alex frowned. "What sordid story?"

"Why, the fact that your dear sister placed a false engagement announcement in the *Times* and then lied to you about accepting Owen's suit."

Alex's eyebrows shot up. "False engagement announcement?"

"Seems she overheard Owen when he came to speak with your father. Owen informed the duke that he would no longer be paying court to Lavinia. He mentioned that he wanted to offer for your hand instead and would be back to do so as soon as he'd secured your agreement. Only he didn't mention your name specifically. But apparently, Lavinia guessed."

Alex scowled. "I don't understand."

Jane nudged her spectacles. "Your sister overheard it all and became positively green with jealousy."

Alex expelled her breath. "But she never even wanted him."

"It appears she changed her mind the moment it became clear that he not only no longer wanted her but wanted *you* instead," Lucy continued.

"Which is positively horrid!" Cass declared loyally.

"*Egad,* she's worse than Mrs. Langford, the woman who tried to steal Garrett from me. But at least Mrs. Langford wasn't my own *sister*!" Jane exclaimed.

"I cannot believe she's my sister," Alex said brokenly.

"Believe it, dear. I have the story straight from Martha," Lucy said. "Lavinia even had Martha deliver the announcement to the *Times,* the beast. Of course, the poor girl had no idea what it was at the time. She was quite distressed when she later found out what she'd done.

She likes you quite a lot, Alex. She says you've always treated her with much more kindness than Lavinia has."

Alex pressed a hand to her cheek. "That's not difficult to do." Her heart ached for poor Martha, forced to carry out her sister's awful plot. But her overwhelming feeling was disgust. Disgust and anger at Lavinia. "I can't believe she did this. Even for Lavinia, it's so low."

"She's quite vile," Lucy continued. "Apparently, she told Martha the entire tale as if she'd find it amusing. Your sister has much to learn about female friendships. Martha, poor dear, was afraid for her position, of course, but I assured her that should she be released from your sister's employ, I've no doubt I can locate a suitable position for her in my household."

Alex stood and paced across the room. She pressed a hand to her middle. "I feel sick."

"I would, too," Cass offered sympathetically. "I'm so sorry we had to tell you this."

Alex made her way over to the window and braced her other hand against the pane. She stared outside in silence for several long moments. Finally, she turned back to her friends. "You know, I once told Owen he didn't believe in himself. But I haven't believed in myself either. I've allowed my sister to dictate everything to me my entire life. It always seemed normal to me. Mother was so adamant about Lavinia's feelings and Lavinia's desires. I was always an afterthought. I never even had friends, because Mother wanted me to be at Lavinia's beck and call."

"Not having friends is so sad, dear," Lucy said. "I hope you'll consider the three of us your friends from now on."

"And Daphne, too," Cass added. "You've yet to meet her but I just know the two of you will get on famously."

"I will," Alex said, wiping tears from her eyes. "I do.

I'm absolutely privileged to call you all my friends. And as for kowtowing to Lavinia, I'm absolutely sick of it. I refuse to do it one moment longer. Not after this. I knew she was mean and selfish, but I never believed she'd stoop to this. I think that's partially why I believed her. I just couldn't imagine she'd do . . . *this*. I just—" Alex paced away again, biting her fingernail. "I only wish I knew what to do . . . about Owen."

Jane marched over and patted Alex on the shoulder. "It's become so complicated, you need all of us to work it out. That's what friends do. We help each other. We'll think of some way for you to get Owen back."

"But I was so awful to him. I refused him. I told him I wouldn't accept his suit if he were the last man on earth."

Cass winced. "Not a particularly fine moment, but one that I've no doubt can be corrected."

Alex looked up at her with more tears in her eyes. "Do you truly think so?"

"Absolutely," Lucy replied, her different-color eyes sparkling. "But you're going to have to be bold!"

CHAPTER FORTY-SIX

"Bold" was the same as "daring," and Alex had learned to love to be daring. If any day called for some daring, it was today. And Alex knew just how she'd go about it. Lavinia was still having her fitting when Alex marched upstairs in search of her. Lavinia was in the room next to her bedchamber that had been converted into a large wardrobe expressly for her use. Madame Bergeron and her trusty assistant were busily fussing over her while Lavinia held out her arms and surveyed herself in the looking glass. New gowns were one of the few things that made Lavinia happy. She was certain to be in a less foul mood. Alex smiled to herself. She would be sure to change that.

When Alex strolled into the room, Lavinia looked up. Her eyes betrayed a bit of nervousness. Good.

"New gowns?" Alex asked, pasting a pleasant but decidedly fake smile on her face.

Lavinia glanced back down to the beige lace gown she was wearing. "Yes, I need a few."

"God forbid you wear anything more than once," Alex muttered.

Lavinia's sharp voice stabbed through the air. "What was that?"

"Why, of course you'd need new gowns, what with your impending *marriage*." She turned her attention to the Frenchwomen. "Did you happen to see the announcement of Lady Lavinia's upcoming marriage in the paper?"

Madame Bergeron's hand flew to her throat. "*Oui*. But of course, and we would be honored to design you zee most beautiful wedding gown in all zee kingdom," she said to Lavinia. "Why, it shall rival Princess Charlotte's. It shall—"

"It's not *entirely* official yet." Lavinia's voice cut through the room again, ice dripping from her tone.

Alex eyed her warily. Her sister was growing more annoyed and angry by the moment. Good.

"Not official yet?" Alex allowed her eyebrows to shoot up. "Surely it's official if it's been announced in the paper."

Lavinia clapped her hands, her mouth shaped into an unpleasant pout. "Please excuse us, madame, mademoiselle."

The modiste and her assistant exchanged wide-eyed glances. "Of course, my lady." The two Frenchwomen hurried out of the room, closing the door behind them.

Alex strolled closer to her sister and crossed her arms over her chest. "I'm sorry. I didn't realize it wasn't 'entirely official,' or I wouldn't have mentioned it in front of them."

Lavinia's eyes flared. "I didn't mean that. I meant—"

"No. You know what is 'entirely official,' Lavinia?"

Her sister blinked at her.

"It's entirely official that you are a viper. A snake in expensive clothing."

Lavinia's mouth fell open. Her face turned red. "How dare you?" she thundered.

For the first time in her life, Alex turned fully toward her sister and matched her raised voice. "No! How dare *you*! How dare you lie to me? How dare you do it just to be mean? Just because you're pure evil. Owen never wanted you. And he certainly never asked you to marry him. And why did you do it? Because you fell in love with him? Couldn't live without him? No! You did it because you found out he wanted *me,* and you couldn't stand that. You're so selfish and awful that you simply couldn't bear to know he wanted me and not you. You're spiteful and you're hideous and you deserve nothing less than to spend your life alone."

Lavinia's eyes took on a wild look, and her face contorted with rage. "You've never appreciated me, you awful little brat."

"I can appreciate how hideous you are, believe me. But what I cannot for the life of me understand is *why.* Why would you lie to me when you knew you'd be found out eventually? You knew you weren't going to marry Owen. How did you expect to keep up the charade?"

Lavinia stuck her nose in the air and took a deep breath. "He *will* marry me. Father will see to it."

Alex backed away. Her sister couldn't possibly be that delusional, could she? "No. He's already told Father he won't marry you. You're insane."

With a loud snarl, Lavinia gathered the skirts of the gown she wore in her hands and ripped at them. The unfinished pieces came apart, and she flung them across the room in Alex's direction. "I am not! He *has* to marry me. Father is a duke. And I want it. I always get what I want!" She was screeching at the top of her lungs, and Alex backed away slowly. Lavinia had a feral look in her eyes, and she stamped her foot, spittle flying from her lips.

The door flew open, and their mother came hurrying in. "Lavinia, please!"

Both girls spun around to face the duchess.

"Tell her, Mother!" Lavinia screamed. "Tell her Lord Owen is going to marry *me*."

Mother shook her head. "No, Lavinia. It's not true. I've always worried that I indulged you too much, that I gave in to your every whim to your detriment, but I've been blind to how truly awful you've become."

"Mother!" Lavinia clenched her fists in her hair and screamed loud enough that the King's horses in the royal mews must have heard it. "I don't care what you say. I *will* marry Lord Owen." She flung herself to the floor and kicked and screamed, rolling around on the remnants of fabric that had been discarded during her fittings. "I will. I will. I will!"

Her mother calmly walked over to her eldest daughter and eyed her carefully. "Get up. You're making a complete fool of yourself. I've indulged your temper for far too long because I felt such guilt over your nearly dying when you were a child, but I refuse to indulge you for one minute longer. I've done you no favors. No one can stand to be in the same room with you."

Lavinia stopped screaming and rolled over to look up at her mother. Her hair was in disarray, and her face was blotchy and red. "I cannot believe you're taking the side of that little mouse, Alexandra."

Mother sighed. "It's high time I took Alexandra's side. She's been forced to suffer your tantrums for years. Not only am I taking her side, but your father and I have already agreed that she's free to marry Lord Owen regardless of *your* marital prospects. I daresay Alexandra shouldn't have to suffer and wait for someone to actually *choose* to marry you. With your spoiled disposition, no doubt she'd be waiting till death."

A wide smile covered Alex's face.

Mother turned to Alex. "I'm sorry, Alexandra. Can you ever forgive me?"

Alex reached out and squeezed her mother's hand. "Thank you for doing the right thing."

Her mother searched her face. "You do want to marry Lord Owen, don't you?"

Alex beamed. "Very, very much."

Lavinia jumped up and ran screeching from the room, a broken, mad doll.

CHAPTER FORTY-SEVEN

Owen had been sitting in Cass's empty ballroom for the better part of a quarter hour when he decided he'd had enough. He stood, adjusted his cravat, and took off toward the door to find his sister and inquire as to what the devil she'd been thinking, asking him to meet her here and then failing to appear.

He'd made it halfway across the wide expanse of parquet before the door to the ballroom opened and Alex came rushing through it. She was dressed in a gown of white, with her hair piled atop her head, and a daisy stuck fetchingly in the knot. She was clutching a leather-bound journal, and her cheeks had a bit of color to them. When she glanced up at Owen, she blushed gorgeously.

"Alex?" Owen breathed. "What are you doing here?"

Alex swallowed and bobbed a curtsy. "I must admit, I've learned that having friends is good for some things. Quite good for certain things. Like luring your intended bridegroom to his sister's deserted ballroom."

"Intended bridegroom? What the devil—?"

Her words came out in a rush. "I asked Cass to invite you here, because I wanted to talk to you. I wanted to apologize." She glanced down at her white slippers.

Owen clenched his jaw. "Funny. The last time I spoke with you, I was under the distinct impression that you detested me."

"I know. I—I was wrong. Quite wrong. You see, Lavinia told me that you'd offered for her. After we . . ."

He opened his mouth to speak, but Alex stopped him. "I know I should never have believed such a lie, but she can be quite convincing and I *never* thought she would lie about something like *that* and—Oh, Owen, it's always been difficult for me to believe that someone like you would choose someone like me and—I'm sorry." Breathless, she stopped and searched his face.

He furrowed his brow. "Someone like me? What do you mean?"

Alex shrugged. "You're so dashing and handsome and well dressed and well everything. I'm not willowy or ethereal, I spill soup on my gowns, and my slippers are often scuffed and I . . . I just couldn't believe you'd want me. But I remembered what you said about my being different—and that being why you loved me. I realized that I've spent my whole life trying to be like Lavinia. And . . . oh . . ."

He took a step toward her and put a hand on her shoulder. "Slow down. What are you trying to say?"

"I told you once that I wrote a list when I was fifteen. I wrote it the night I saw you under my window, actually."

He watched her cautiously. "The list of the things you hoped to accomplish in life?"

"Yes." She tipped down her chin and looked at the leather-bound journal she was clutching to her chest. "A list that included four things. I told you two of them. You asked me what the others were."

Owen stepped back. "What were the others, love?"

Alex bit her lip. "I remember them . . . mostly . . . but . . ." She tentatively offered him the journal. "I'm a bit frightened to look, to be honest."

"Frightening things are always better when you get them over with," Owen replied with a lopsided smile.

"Oh, are they?" She smiled back.

"Yes. Here, do you want me to read it for you?"

Alex closed her eyes and handed him the diary. She nodded. "Yes, please. The list is on the first page." Then she promptly covered her face with her hands.

Owen opened the book and cleared his throat. " 'Become brave and daring like Thomas,' " he read.

Alex peeked out from behind her fingertips. "That one's not so bad."

" 'Become beautiful, willowy, and poised like Lavinia,' " Owen read with a scowl. "Now, that one was entirely unnecessary."

"I quite agree," Alex replied, pulling her hands away from her face and plucking at her skirts instead. "I'm never going to be like Lavinia in either looks or temperament, and that is perfectly acceptable."

Owen stepped toward her again and pushed up her chin with the thumb of his free hand. "It's not only acceptable. It's preferable, Alex."

"Go on," she prompted, nodding toward the journal again.

He reopened the book and scanned the page. " 'Have a come-out during which an exceedingly eligible gentleman asks me to dance, thereby making the affair a smashing success.' " Owen glanced up at her, and his face softened. "I'm sorry that didn't happen for you."

"But it did! Just a few months after my *actual* come-out," Alex replied with a laugh.

"I wish I'd been at the first one."

"Read the last one," Alex prodded.

Owen turned his attention back to the journal. " 'Marry my true love. Must be handsome, dashing, witty, kind, true, and honorable.' " He cleared his throat. "Seems you've crossed out 'name to be determined later.' "

"Yes," she replied, and pressed her lips together. "I did that after I saw Adonis beneath my window that night."

Their eyes met.

"Keep reading," she prompted.

Owen bent his head toward the journal once more. "Lord Owen Monroe." His voice cracked. He snapped the book shut and pulled her into his arms and kissed her, then hugged her fiercely.

When he pulled away, tears were shining in Alex's eyes. "I told you I've loved you since I was fifteen."

He grinned at her. "Are you saying you love me now?"

"Yes, and I can only hope you still love me."

Owen kissed her again, and when he finally pulled his mouth from hers, Alex was staring deeply into his eyes. She traced the outline of his jaw with her fingertip. "I love you, Lord Owen Monroe."

"And I love you, Lady Alexandra Hobbs," he whispered.

Alex cleared her throat and stepped back. "I must admit, hearing that list again makes me a bit sad."

Owen reached out and pulled her hand into his. "Why, my love?"

"Because it's so clear to me how desperately I wanted to be someone else. I think I've wanted that my whole life. My brother and sister always seemed so much more than I was."

He squeezed her hand. "On the contrary, dear Alex, you're one who is concerned about charities and children and doing good things that make a difference in the world. You've always been perfect, just the way you are."

"Owen, promise me we'll always be happy. Promise me we'll always be in love. I tend to worry that—"

"Ah, ah, ah." He swung her arm with his. "Someone quite wise once told me that in life, some things are more important than worry."

Alexandra smiled at him. "That someone was quite wise, indeed."

"Yes." He squeezed her fingers again. "She was."

A mischievous look sparkled in Alex's eyes. "I have one final lesson for you, my lord. That's why I asked you to meet me here, in the ballroom."

He laughed out loud, and the sound echoed across the large empty room. "I see. What is it?"

"Your final lesson."

He arched a brow. "What's that?"

"How to be a good husband, of course."

His face turned serious. "I'm not certain I know how, Alex. But I promise you, I will spend the rest of my days trying."

"You'll learn. We'll learn. Together. That's the lesson, for both of us. We simply must do the best we can and help each other."

He handed her the journal and then picked her up and twirled her in his arms. "Yes, my love. I agree."

When he set her back down, Alex said, "Mother and Father have already told me they approve of the match and I need no longer wait for Lavinia to marry first."

Owen slid a hand into his pocket. "That's excellent because my father came to visit me yesterday and informed me that he respected the hell out of me for standing up to him. I have his blessing and approval. Apparently, your father spoke with him as well and told him he approved of our match."

Alex's eyes widened. "So you won't lose your allowance by choosing me?"

"No, but if I did, rest assured, I'd still choose you a thousand times."

"I'd choose you, too, Owen."

He pulled her back into his arms and kissed the top of her head. "So, how do we begin?"

Tears welled in Alex's eyes. "I do believe you may begin by formally asking me to marry you now."

"By all means." Owen fell to one knee and took her free hand in his. "Lady Alexandra Hobbs, I think you're the most perfect lady in the entire kingdom. You're beautiful, intelligent, witty, and kind. I don't pretend to deserve you, but I would be thankful for you for the rest of my life if you would do me the honor of becoming my bride. Will you marry me?"

Alex leaned down and stroked his cheek, her fingers pausing at his dimple. "Yes, my lord. I've been waiting for three years to say yes to you."

The door to the ballroom opened then, and Cass and Julian strolled in arm in arm. Alex glanced up guiltily from Owen, who was still on his knee.

"How is the newly engaged couple?" Cass called. "I'm not assuming too much by seeing you on bended knee, am I, Owen? I mean, I do hope that's what you're about . . . the business of a proposal."

Owen leaped to his feet and pulled Alex close to him, his arm around her waist. "Yes, that's exactly what I was about—and thankfully, the lady has agreed to become my wife regardless of being interrupted by my overly curious sister."

Cass and Julian made their way over to them, and Cass elbowed her brother in the ribs. "Why, I'd hardly be doing my duty as a chaperone if I allowed you two to stay in here all afternoon alone together. Besides, I want to talk about the wedding." Cass nearly clapped her hands. "I'm so excited. We have two weddings to plan. First Daphne's, then yours."

Before Alex could answer, the door to the ballroom cracked against the far wall and Lucy Hunt came rushing through it, pulling off her bonnet. "There you are. I've been searching the house for you. Oh, dears, you'll never guess. I just came from Lady Hargrove's tea, where I heard the *most* shocking news."

"What is it?" Alex and Cass asked simultaneously.

Lucy came hurtling over to stand next to them, plucking off her gloves and then pressing a hand against her coiffure to tame her dark curls. "It seems Lady Sarah Highgate has run off!"

"Run off?" Alex gasped. "She and Lord Branford have gone to Gretna Green?"

"No! Apparently, she's run off *without* Lord Branford. From what I gathered, she's quite alone."

"Alone?" Alex replied. "I don't understand. Whyever would she run off?"

Lucy shook her head. "No one is quite certain, but they suspect she's headed north."

"We have some news of our own," Owen said to Lucy. "Though perhaps not quite as shocking."

Lucy blinked at the two of them before a wide smile spread across her face. "You're engaged, aren't you?" She clapped her hands together and spun around in a circle. "Thank goodness the two of you finally came to your senses. That 'climbing the tree' business helped, didn't it?"

"Yes," Alex replied, blushing.

"Good heavens, whyever did you allow me to prattle on about Society gossip when we have a wedding to plan? When will the happy occasion be?" Lucy asked, obviously warming to her subject.

"I was thinking next spring would be nice," Alex replied.

Owen winced. "Have a care, darling. I don't think I can wait that long."

Alex smiled at him. "Yes, you can. You're no longer the impatient aristocrat. Spoiled and getting whatever he wants whenever he wants it."

Owen grinned unrepentantly. "I'm not?"

"No," Alex replied. "Don't you know? You're no longer the untamed earl. I've tamed you quite soundly."

"That you have, darling." He pulled her hand to his lips and kissed it.

Thank you for reading *The Untamed Earl*.
I hope you enjoyed Alex and Owen's story
as much as I enjoyed writing it.

I'd love to keep in touch.

- Visit my website for information about upcoming books, excerpts, and to sign up for my email newsletter: www.ValerieBowmanBooks.com.
- Join me on Facebook: http://Facebook.com/ValerieBowmanAuthor.
- Follow me on Twitter at @ValerieGBowman, https://twitter.com/ValerieGBowman.
- Reviews help other readers find books. I appreciate all reviews whether positive or negative. Thank you so much for considering it!

Coming soon...

Look for the next novel in the delectable
Playful Brides series by
Valerie Bowman

The Legendary Lord

Available in November 2016
from St. Martin's Paperbacks